Carnival Desires

Also by Mark Lindquist:

Sad Movies

Carnival Desires

Mark Lindquist

For Chip and Kathleen,
And good things in the future
for those we know.

June 19th 1990
[signature]

THE ATLANTIC MONTHLY PRESS
NEW YORK
•

Published simultaneously in Canada
Printed in the United States of America
First edition

Library of Congress Cataloging-in-Publication Data

Lindquist, Mark, 1959–
  Carnival desires : a novel / by Mark Lindquist.
  ISBN 0-87113-360-1
  I. Title.
PS3562.I51165C3   1990   813'.54–dc20   89-29427

The Atlantic Monthly Press
19 Union Square West
New York, NY 10003

First printing

for friends

I

"Classic rock, 97.1 KLSX. Now, new from U2—"

Libby turns off the radio as she drives into the cemetery. Signs read:

SPEED LIMIT 5 MPH

NO PETS ALLOWED

She turns past a small chapel and at the end of the line of parked cars she stops. Her shoes sink slightly into the earth as she cuts across the flat field of crosses and headstones. She shivers, then quickens her steps. The smell of the winter morning air reminds her of something she's not sure of.

"All the rivers run into the sea, yet the sea is not full." The minister is reading from the Bible and has on sunglasses and to Libby, looking through her own sunglasses, he seems shadowy and unsettling. "Unto the place from whence the rivers come, thither they return again. . . ."

She joins a tight group of people on the edge of the gathering. Her friends also have on sunglasses and quietly acknowledge her. Everyone is wearing black.

"You alone," Willie asks, looking past her.

"What?"

"Where's Bick?"

"I don't know."

"Why not?"

Merri, Willie's girlfriend, elbows him in the ribs. "Shh." She's wearing a black hat with a veil. "What happened," she whispers to Libby, "are you OK?"

"I'm fine," Libby says. "It just took me about an hour to decide which of six black dresses to wear. I don't know."

Merri nods.

"What did I miss?"

"Just this."

"I have seen all the work under the sun," the minister is continuing loudly and fiercely, "and behold, all is vanity and vexation of spirit."

Willie leans toward Libby. "Do you know if this is where Marilyn Monroe is buried?" he whispers.

"No. I don't know."

She becomes aware of the low noise of traffic beyond the trees.

Bick joins the group, edging up just to the right of Libby. His usual blue blazer and white shirt with tie are disheveled and she suspects he didn't sleep last night. He gives her a barely perceptible smile, then nods to Oscar. Oscar seems to be getting into the eulogy. Some of the bereaved are starting to stare their way. Maybe because of the late arrivals or maybe because Willie and Merri are semicelebrities or maybe, Libby suddenly realizes, because their group is smoking like a brush fire. She raises her fingers to her lips in a V and Willie offers her a Marlboro. Bick lights it for her. She had sex with Bick the night before last and after she has a good long taste of the cigarette she looks up and smiles at him.

He's looking off in the distance.

"I gave my heart to know wisdom, and to know folly. I perceived also that this also is vexation of spirit!" The shaking Bible catches Libby's eyes. "For in much wisdom is much grief and he that increaseth knowledge increaseth sorrow!"

"Duh," Mona mutters.

The minister pauses and clears his throat. Tim's mother, seated, is staring at the closed black and gold casket. Next to the casket is a big bouquet of white gladioli and Libby suddenly connects the smell in the air to water from vases of dying flowers.

"Tim's spirit was vexed," the minister says in a calmer voice. "Perhaps all our spirits are vexed. Much of what we see around us seems hopelessly senseless. But we must find strength in the senseless."

Bick is watching Joy, Tim's on-and-off girlfriend. Joy looks like a zombie. Libby wishes she had gotten to know Tim. Naturally, he seems more interesting now that he's killed himself.

"If we have that strength, that strength to live and love, then maybe nothing—including Tim's forsaking of God's greatest gift on Christmas Eve—is as senseless as it seems. It is up to us to find strength and create reason and that

strength and reason come from love and that is why family and friends are gathered together here today." He lowers his voice. "There was a time when suicides could not be buried beside natural deaths. This was some time back." He scans his audience. "A time many of you are too young to remember. A time when a cemetery was considered a holy place and suicide an unholy act. A time before we lost our sense of the sacred and the profane."

The minister seems to lose himself for a moment and Libby is suddenly cold again and shivers.

"Furthermore," he resumes, his voice rising, "it was feared that the unquiet souls of suicides would haunt the cemetery and all who came to pay their respects. I ask, *shouldn't* we be haunted by Tim's soul?"

Somewhere nearby a car honks.

"Shouldn't we be haunted by what is as compared with what could have been?"

This is Libby's first funeral as an adult. Her awareness of the minister's performance as theater only heightens her appreciation. She wonders for a moment if she's missing something by not being a churchgoer. She looks to Bick for his reaction.

He's still staring off in the distance.

Libby follows his gaze. The grass seems too intensely green to be real, as though spray-painted, but she reminds herself it is real and under the crosses and headstones and inside the mausoleums are dead people, including, possibly, Marilyn Monroe. She wonders what her friends are thinking about Tim.

"There's something gained in living and loving each moment and . . ."

Mona begins coughing.

Libby thinks forward to her New Year's Eve party and tries to remember which vodka everyone drinks these days.

At the post-funeral party, held in Tim's mother's backyard in the Valley, Joy is standing alone near the diving board. She blankly watches the yellow sun spots bouncing on the pool's surface until a voice breaks in—"I loved him so much," some young girl is saying between sobs. "I was with him just a few nights before and we were so happy. God, he was such a beautiful person. I miss him soooo much. . . ." Joy recognizes the young actress and her false emotion sickens Joy so much she feels dizzy. With a last shred of energy she whispers, "Don't talk about love, you didn't even know him. You dumb cunt."

The girl instantly stops sobbing.

Joy starts to cry. Her friends surround her with overlapping phrases of comfort—"it's OK, it's all right, we understand"—and even if the words are sometimes incomprehensible, the sound is sweet and soothing. Joy's tears start to subside, but then she thinks maybe the actress *meant* it, maybe the actress was having the first genuine emotion of her life and Joy spoiled the moment by lashing out. This makes Joy cry harder. Her tears start to subside again, but then she thinks, *No, probably the actress isn't capable of genuine emotion and never will be.* Joy cries still harder. Her friends are confused, but she can't explain and cries until she can't anymore.

"I didn't mean to be mean," Joy finally says.

"The bitch left," Mona says, "before I could ask to see her liposuction scars."

Joy smiles.

"She's uninvited from our New Year's party," Libby adds.

A hand-held camera chases a cord around a corner and down a hall and through a barely open door to a telephone beside a bathtub. A skinny pale girl with bobbed black hair is lying in the tub with eyes closed, feminine form seeming to sway under clean water.

Bick is watching this on the VCR while he listens to the stereo and talks on the phone. "If I had her, I'd be happy," he says.

"If we make this deal, I'll be happy," Lee responds from his car phone.

The girl's eyes open impossibly slightly. The camera pulls back as her dripping hand gropes for the Princess phone and a wildly phallic faucet pokes into the frame just above her head. Bick reaches for his pack of unfiltered Camels. He can't tell what she says when she puts the phone to her mouth since the sound is off.

"Listen," Lee says, "you should—"

"What was this rated," Bick asks, lighting a cigarette.

"PG."

"Damn."

"You should—"

"Wait."

She hangs up the phone and there's an awkward cut to a made-up girl in basic white bra and white panties sitting at a vanity-dresser mirror in a nice high-school-girl's room stroking on lipstick. It takes a moment to realize it's her.

Bick hears Lee hit his brakes and swear.

She blots her bright red lipstick with a Kleenex, creating a perfect kiss, then carelessly tosses the Kleenex into the wastebasket.

Bick's call waiting blips. He ignores it.

She smiles mischievously at herself in the mirror. Bick marvels sadly at how her innocent shine has been lost in the transformation.

"Bick?"

He wonders what happened to this Kleenex. Did a crew member save it and have her autograph it? Will it be auctioned off someday?

She picks up a square glass bottle of gold liquid and flicks it upside down for just a moment and then pulls the cap off and touches it to both sides of the neck behind the ear and rubs it in her scant cleavage, putting Bick in mind of a sacrament.

"Bick?"

She slices the glass cap across her wrist before putting it back on the bottle.

"Bick? Bick! What are you doing?"

"This is a fine scene."

"What? What's happening?"

Lee is constantly panicked and about nothing of any consequence as far as Bick is concerned.

"She's about to spray her Aqua-Net."

"*What?* What does that, what are—" Lee sputters.

"Wait."

Bick's call waiting blips again. He ignores it.

The camera comes in close on the cloud of hair spray and the scene dissolves to a backlit boot kick-starting a motorcycle as dry-ice machines spread billows of smoke across a dark wet street.

"OK," Bick says.

"What song is that in the background?"

"'Radar Love.'"

"I don't remember that. . . ." Lee sounds confused.

"Golden Earring. *Moontan* album. Mid-seventies."

"I mean I don't remember it from the movie."

"It's not in the movie. It's on my stereo."

"You're listening to the stereo while you watch the movie?"

Since that has been established, Bick sees no need to say anything.

"You're listening to *Golden Earring?* Why aren't you listening to the movie?"

"The dialogue was unbelievably bad."

"Her voice is sexy as hell."

"I know, but I couldn't stand the pain of watching this innocent girl suffer through that dialogue."

"I warned you it's a bad movie."

"I thought you meant bad as in uncommercial and uncompromising. I didn't realize you meant as in shitty."

"I've got better taste than you give me credit for."

"No you don't."

Lee laughs. "OK," he says. "But you like her?"

"I don't know her."

"You like what you see."

"Yes."

"And you thought the script had promise."

"Yes."

Bick had reluctantly read the script Lee sent him, *Till Death Do Us Part,* a high-school love story about two orphans who meet and have an obsessive sexual relationship and then discover they're brother and sister. To Bick's surprise it was good, unfocused but real with true emotions, and so he read the whole script but didn't see how it could be rewritten.

"You'll do it?" Lee says.

"No."

"You don't have to give me a decision right now."

"I just did."

"Bick, you can name your price on this one. You're the best gun for the job. You're wanted badly."

Bick is not flattered. Lee kisses ass indiscriminately. They worked together once before when Bick rewrote the script for the first movie Lee produced, which was a few years ago, just before Lee turned thirty. Bick found Lee superficial but smart in a limited way. The movie was a hit and stupid people began calling Lee a genius and Lee was smart enough not to believe them.

"That studio wants to hang me," Bick reminds Lee.

"Yeah, but *she* wants you so they want you."

This gives Bick pause. "Have the original writer do it," he finally says.

"I can't. He's crazy."

"So?"

"And he's in jail."

"What?"

"I didn't tell you this yet?"

"No."

"I guess I was saving it."

Lee laughs nervously. Bick waits because this is how they work: Lee lies or leaves out key details and Bick eventually has to silently intimidate him into telling the truth.

"Well," Lee says, "I found the script through a nobody agent and snuck it to Jon and things happened really quickly. The studio decided to buy before any of us realized the original writer was in jail."

"For what?"

"Well," Lee again laughs nervously. "Murder. Second degree though."

Bick can tell when Lee's not lying. "Who did he kill?"

"Uh—"

"Someone rewriting another one of his scripts?"

"No," Lee answers seriously, "his girlfriend. The girl in the script. The girl he modeled the female lead after."

"I'm glad I'm retiring."

"Retiring? What?"

"It's time. I'm almost thirty."

"You're *twenty-eight!*"

"Yes."

Lee forces a laugh, "OK," he says, "we'll talk seriously later. Are you still watching the movie?"

"Yeah," Bick says, "the guy on the motorcycle is picking her up."

"He does a pretty good young Marlon Brando."

"Yeah."

"He's gay. The actor that is, not the character."

"She's whispering something in his ear. Now she's kissing him on the lips. Cut to a close shot."

A second later comes the cut.

"She's a brilliant kisser," Bick says.

"Sixty-million worth."

"What?"

"The movie made almost sixty million."

"Nobody I know saw it."

"Teen market. She's a license to print money. When you're finished watching this movie, you'll be sold."

"I'm retired."

"If you're not going to do it, then why did you read the script and why are you watching this movie?"

"I like to know what I'm missing, so I don't miss it."

"I'm going into my garage," Lee says, "we're losing our connection. See you at Libby's. Will Oscar be there?"

"Probably."

"We're a movie waiting to happen," Lee says just before the connection turns to static.

She suddenly slaps the young rebel. Bick flinches.

He watches the rest of the movie, fast-forwarding through scenes without her. Watching her makes him lonely.

"How do you like my hat," Merri asks Willie. She is standing in their bedroom in front of a long mirror, naked. She is thin and not tan. The hat is peach colored and oblong.

"It's a cool hat," Willie says.

He's lying in bed smoking a cigarette. She knows he's not looking at the hat. He's staring out the window into the backyard, which has a swing set and a hammock and is separated from a golf course by a stained wooden fence. Golf balls occasionally soar into the yard and bounce against the house, but otherwise it's a perfectly good backyard in a suburban neighborhood. Merri, who could easily afford to move almost anywhere, is comfortable renting here. She decorated herself, going for the feel of a Maine summer house. Merri grew up in New York City and her parents didn't have a summer house in Maine or anywhere else.

Willie keeps an apartment in New York, but he's never there. He's either off working in a movie or he's in LA staying with her.

"What do you think," she asks, twirling, her long blond hair brushing across her breasts. "Feel free to flatter me."

"You have a beautiful lack of a tan."

Merri examines herself. "You think I should take that part with the nude scene?"

"If you don't mind murdering your parents first."

She turns towards him. "Don't you think twenty-nine is a little old to worry about parents?"

"No."

"You don't worry about yours."

"Mine are crazy." Willie leans his head so he can see himself in the mirror. "Looking good."

"I think you should start working out," she says. "Join the Sports Connection."

Willie laughs. "I'm not that vain."

"Yes you are," she says, turning back to the mirror, adjusting her position so she can see his reflection beside her own. "You're just lazier than you are vain."

"I'm not lazy."

"OK, you're undisciplined."

"Don't say it like it's not a virtue."

"You need a regimented exercise program."

"How about the Peter Fonda workout?"

"It's *Jane* Fonda."

"No, the *Peter* Fonda workout. You get up around noon and smoke a joint and then go beg your sister for money."

Merri giggles, a giggle interviewers routinely describe as Goldie Hawn–like. Willie calls it Merri Shelton–like. The dumbest things Willie does, the weirdest things, *any*thing, can make her happy, can make her laugh.

"You're developing a restaurant body," she says sternly when she quits giggling.

He goes "ho, ho, ho," and pats his stomach.

"If you don't get control now," she says, "you're going to grow up into the Pillsbury dough boy."

"I'm lean," he says, pulling his stomach back in.

"You're lean plus you have a belly. Like Joey Ramone."

"Joey Ramone is very cool."

"He's disgusting looking."

"I'm better looking than Joey Ramone."

"You need to flatten that belly."

"I'll do more drugs."

She gives him a dirty look. Merri does not do drugs. She will occasionally drink but not the way Willie drinks.

"We shouldn't go tonight unless you're sure you can behave."

"I'll behave."

Merri wants to believe him—he has kept clean since Tim's death. She tosses the peach hat and picks up a brown beret. "How about this," she asks, not wanting to provoke another argument.

"Goes well with what you're wearing."

"I think I like hats again," Merri says. "The funeral was the first time I'd worn one since I was a little girl. . . ." She catches Willie's reaction in the mir-

ror. He was closer to Tim. He crushes out his cigarette. "You sure you want to go to this," she asks.

"Hey," he says, bounding out of bed, "absolutely. I need the exercise. And Libby's your best friend, we have to go."

"Maybe it'll be fun. It'll probably be fun."

Willie walks into the bathroom, stripping off clothes as he goes.

Merri turns again in the mirror. Her body seems to her well shaped and firm and healthy. She doesn't consider her appraisal vain, but professional. Her looks are good enough she can play a part that calls for someone physically attractive, but not so good she is limited to parts that call for serious beauty.

"Ahhhhhhhhh!" Willie screams.

Merri bolts to the bathroom and swings open the door. Willie is standing in the shower, whistling.

"Hi," he says.

"What happened!?"

"Nothing. I just wanted you to join me."

Merri giggles, then suddenly stops. Though he can always make her laugh, he also scares her. A life of what he calls accelerated experience has aged him but has also allowed him to maintain his immaturity. He started working regularly as an actor at the age of twelve, dropped out of ninth grade, was a drunk by seventeen, a junkie at eighteen, cleaned up at nineteen, back to insanity at twenty-one and at twenty-five he's somewhere between clean and insane, commanding a million and a half per picture plus a half dozen Ding Dongs daily in his trailer.

He sometimes looks and acts like a grown-up, but Merri knows he doesn't feel like one. Every night they go out she prays he won't push past the edge of socially acceptable debauchery. And tonight has all the makings of an emotional speedball.

"Are you coming in or not," he asks.

She opens the stall door and steps into the steam. "You sure you want to go to this party," she asks.

"What are you doing in here nude?"

She giggles again. "It'll be a good party," she says, grabbing the bar of soap, scrubbing. "I want it to be a good year."

Mona picks one of Joy's black blazers off the canvas-covered couch and puts it on over her black turtleneck. "Let's get out of here," she yells.

"Quit bitching at me," Joy yells back from the bedroom they share.

"I'm sorry, but it's been a fucking hour. You don't own enough outfits to take this long."

Joy comes out of the bedroom. She is wearing black tights, a black shirt, a black skirt, a black blazer. "How's this look," she asks.

"Really dreadful."

"You're wearing the same thing," Joy points out.

"I know."

Joy turns back into the bedroom.

Mona goes into the kitchen, stepping around the roach motels. On the refrigerator door under a magnet shaped like a tit is her degree from the NYU cinema department. Under other tits are overdue bills and postcard fliers for various clubs and art openings.

She pulls a soda out of the refrigerator and sits on the counter and opens the *L.A. Weekly.* Mona used to drink Pepsi, but she despises the advertisements with such venom that she now drinks generic colas. They're bad for her ulcer, but she doesn't mind. She figures you should treat an ulcer like anything else that's bothering you: joke about it or ignore it.

A boyfriend once suggested the reason for her success as a student and her

ambition and her ulcer was a need to prove herself to the fucked-up family that caused her ulcer in the first place. When she told her therapist this, he agreed. She dumped them both. Mona takes pride in her intelligence. She's not witty and charming by nature but can be so when it serves her purpose.

Joy enters the kitchen. She is wearing black tights, a black skirt, a black shirt, a black blazer. "Well," she asks.

"You're wearing the same thing."

"Different tights."

"That was a ten-minute decision?"

"Don't be a bitch, OK?" Joy leaves the kitchen and Mona turns a page in the *Weekly.*

Joy was Mona's best friend in college. Mona had been the first in their class to realize Woody Allen's *Zelig* was stolen from a "Brady Bunch" episode. Joy thought this was something and so she worked as the art director on the first and last student movie Mona directed. Mona learned enough about directing first time out to know she wanted to produce. Joy then did the art direction on the two student films Mona produced. Since they graduated last summer, Joy has worked only once, as an assistant art director on a movie her father produced and directed. She doesn't know what she really wants to do, but her father sends her checks monthly and she could afford to live in an apartment without roaches and unemployed neighbors. Mona can't. Mona has only worked in low-paying production-assistant jobs since graduation. Joy doesn't mind living here because she grew up with money and knows it will be there when she needs it and slumming is only sport, an adventure in deprivation.

Joy returns wearing black tights, a black shirt, a black skirt, a black blazer.

"Beauteous," Mona says.

"Thank you," Joy says.

"You're in 'L.A. Dee Da' again," Mona tells her and hands the *Weekly* over.

Joy reads, "Libby Bridgham's crowd came to smoke insolently among themselves at the social event of the season, Tim Nixon's funeral." She frowns. "Tim worked as a doorman at the after-hours club twentysomething. He is survived by on-and-off girlfriend Joy Christiansen, who is rumored to be trying to reconnect with Tim on the astral plane." Her voice becomes incredulous. "A certain young actor was heard moaning, 'who's going to put me on the guest list now?'" She looks up. "Who would say that? Nobody we know would say that."

Mona wants to answer something like, *Making the "L.A. Dee Da" column is the most depressing thing about Tim's suicide,* but instead says in an exceptionally bored voice, "A lot of people we know probably said that." She hops off the counter. "Let's go."

"You're wearing one of my jackets."

"How can you tell?"

Joy opens the refrigerator. "Why isn't there anything in here besides your fucking colas?"

"Because neither of us know how to shop for groceries."

"Shit." She sighs. "Should we?"

"No, we're failures as women."

"No, we're failures as people," Joy says, "but Libby will have food at the party." She closes the refrigerator. "What's this?" She pulls one of the fliers from under a tit magnet. "'Paris before the Depression, Berlin before the War, San Francisco before the Hippies, LA before the ozone layer burns through.'"

"A reading at Café Largo," Mona explains. "Bad poetry for a bad world. Susie, Angie, Modi, Josh and Jeff, plus a few token celebrities. Same night as the fund-raiser there."

Joy scans the overlapping invites, "Mr. Toad's Wild Ride," "Botswana," "Enter the Dragon," "Impressionism Rides Again—Six Contemporary Artists," and sees the flier for a fund-raiser.

"'Art against AIDS'?"

"Yeah. Bet on AIDS."

Joy laughs and turns off the light. "I can't believe somebody would say that," she says as they head out.

"What?"

"About the guest list."

"You wish you couldn't."

In the front room Joy turns off the thrift-store lamp that stands next to a vase of gladioli with edges turning dry and dark.

"You want to take one of those," Mona asks.

"One of what?"

"A flower."

"They're gladioli."

"Whatever. You want one?"

"For what?"

"To wear."

"Are you?"

"Not if you are."

"Oh. Well, go ahead."

"No," Mona says, picking up a gladiola and snapping off the stem. "Here." She slips it into Joy's blazer breast pocket.

Before Oscar is a Steenbeck, an eerily steel-blue table with spinning reels. On one reel is the picture and on the two other reels is sound—one with dialogue, another with music. The room is cold and dark and mostly metal gray. Oscar feels at home.

Six out of seven days in the past few months he's been driving to the studio, arriving anywhere from 8:00 A.M. to 12:00 noon, depending on the night before. He checks in at his office with its two glass walls and takes messages from his secretary and sits down for a few minutes to drink coffee and maybe return phone calls. Then he hurries across a parking lot to this old building, where he can be alone with his movie.

He's watching the frames flash by on the small screen, the images coming in exactly the order, the rhythm, the intensity he desires. He has made the world he's watching, but it's not as good as the one he had in mind.

"Fuck me, John," he says.

He calls the Steenbeck John for John Steinbeck. He has never read John Steinbeck. He's hardly read any fiction since he was required to read Flaubert's *Sentimental Education,* which he thought was impressive for its sustained tedium. He's been calling the machine John since the day he was talking to Bick on the phone and Bick asked him what he was doing. "Hanging out with Steenbeck."

"Yeah, I've been hanging out with Hemingway," Bick said. "He wants to fight Steinbeck."

Oscar accepted this as a throwaway.

"Which book," Bick asked.

"What?" Oscar said.

"Which book are you reading?"

"What are you talking about?"

"Which Steinbeck book are you reading?"

Then Oscar laughed. "I'm not *reading,* I've been editing my movie. On a *Steen*beck. It's the *make,* you ignoramus."

Oscar and Bick both love telling this story as an amusing illustration of the other's limited point of view.

On the Steenbeck the climactic scene fades out. Oscar rewinds and plays it again: he and she see each other, move together, embrace, kiss. Then in reverse: kiss, embrace, move apart, look away. He feels nothing for these two and emotional involvement, he believes, is everything.

"John, what's wrong with this fucking movie?"

Oscar's first feature was a low-budget independent about high school that became a hit and he has tried to make his second feature, a moderately budg-eted studio release about high school, more sophisticated and artful. It's pretty much empty. Still, he thinks there's hope. He just doesn't know what to do. Repressed fears and doubts start making noises and Oscar tries not to listen. If he were to doubt the possibility of saving his movie, the avalanche in his psy-che would roll: bad movie, bad career, bad choices, bad life. Kill yourself.

He knows to tighten his focus on a fixable problem. *Stay on track,* he tells himself, *keep the head up.* "The thing between him and her doesn't work," he says. It occurs to him that this may be partially due to the lack of hers in his own life—maybe he's forgotten what it's like.

He runs his hands through the crew cut, which he had done recently because he didn't have time to worry about his hair. Then he rubs his eyes and massages his temples. Then he tries to work the tension out of his jaw by press-ing his cheeks together. This always just makes him feel like a fish. Sighing, he shuts down the Steenbeck. It's time to go to the party and pretend to have a life.

$\mathbf{B}$ick merges onto the freeway. Rain is coming down hard and the road under his wheels feels like a shallow stream, lanes spilling into each other. The speedometer needle jumps with his quick shifts. He speeds because the car is an old BMW 3.0 csi coupe that has been worked into a convertible and he feels like he should drive fast to justify the fifty-five hundred dollars a year he pays for insurance and because the top is down and he has to maintain an airfoil above his head for shelter.

Seems like he has spent most of his life in LA driving. During the day in traffic it's hell. At night, though, the roads open up and the signs and the billboards and the lights reflect on his hood in falling spilling halos of color and the stereo plays loudly and it's as close as he gets to peace.

He loves his car. The romance started when he came to this town where cars speak louder than words. He had just inherited the car from an uncle who died from a heart attack on his sportfishing yacht. He felt guilty because the joy the car gave him was far more intense than the grief from his uncle's death. He was getting over it when the BMW, once an obscure and cool car, rose to symbolize all things evil and stupid in the material world and the guilt came back to stay.

He knows it is wrong to love an object. Often he reminds himself a car can't keep him warm in bed.

Still, he loves his car.

The top is down and the heater and the radio are on. He doesn't feel like

getting to the party until it's too crowded and noisy for talk, so he decides just to drive.

On the right shoulder a couple black guys lean spread-eagled over the trunk of a big old white Cadillac while one cop stands behind them and another pokes a flashlight around, the beam shining in the drizzle. *Grim New Year's Eve,* Bick thinks as he checks to make sure he has a joint in his blazer side pocket next to his flask.

"Here's one for all of you who believe the music," the deejay says and segues into "It Never Rains in Southern California."

Amused for about two seconds, Bick pops in a cassette. He takes a half-inch hit off his flask and enjoys the Jim Beam throat burn and then tosses the flask onto the passenger seat. He taps the stick shift to the beat of "Radar Love."

When the song plays out, he pushes the rewind button. Passing a pickup truck with a bumper sticker that says COVER ME HONEY—I'M CHANGING LANES! Bick catches himself checking out the other driver, making sure he hasn't drawn a gun. This doesn't seem paranoid to him. He briefly glimpses a low stucco building near a freeway off ramp. Once it was an after-hours club, a dark furnitureless space with faceless scenesters and trash cans of Lucky beer and loud glam rock played by a deejay who sold not too badly cut grams, the kind of space, Willie observed one wired night, where they shoot snuff movies. *Good times.* Still, Bick hopes to spend none of next year at places like this.

The tape deck clicks and the song starts again.

Bick's inclination toward obsession, *controlled* obsession, seems to be intensifying. He came to LA in 1980, the year Ronald Reagan was elected—this he finds significant, at least when he's drunk. What originally attracted him to LA was its emptiness, its evil and superficiality, its cancerous absence of values. In time, however, this lost charm.

He has heard the city compared to an amusement park—a merry-go-round here, a Ferris wheel there, a roller coaster underneath the sky ride, chances to win prizes for your sweetheart everywhere, the lights and colors full of fun and wonder, an easy place to get lost. Bick isn't big on analogies, but this one works for him.

Most of the things he wanted when he was younger he has had. After one book of short stories he fell into screen writing and has since made his living writing. He has seen his words become images on the screen at the Cinerama Dome. He has earned the respect and envy of his peers. He has been on a blanket in the desert under a rising sun having sex with a wildly desirable actress he had wanted for years. He has wondered why he ever wanted any of these things.

His latest obsession is the pursuit of a normal life even though he's not sure yet what this means. The song plays out and he rewinds it again.

L ibby's pacing the bleached hardwood floors of the living room, barefoot, with a glass of Scotch, no ice. The Rolling Stones are on the stereo, "Sucking in the Seventies." Silver stars hang from the tall wood-beamed ceilings, shiny helium balloons rub against the walls, the bar is stocked and ready. She paces into the bathroom. The tub is full of ice and champagne. She pops a blue Valium.

Her doctor suggested a switch to Xanax, but she didn't want to take an antidepressant. She told the doctor she wasn't depressed, just so happy it makes her nervous. She stuffs the prescription bottle into the front pocket of her faded Levi's so it won't be stolen. After her last bash she was missing bottles of Valium, codeine Tylenol, and Robitussin. She knew it was a mistake to invite agents.

The doorbell rings and she's startled. She rehearses her smile in the oval mirror, then turns to answer the door. She hopes it's Merri and Willie, or Mona and Joy, or maybe Bick or Oscar.

Libby met Merri when they were both working as voter-registration volunteers. When Libby moved to LA a few years ago to become an actress after dropping out of Southern Methodist University, her mother advised her to become involved with the community. Merri was charming, like many of the people Libby was meeting here and, unlike many of the others, seemed a good

person. They became friends and Libby came to know Bick and Willie and then Joy and Mona and Oscar as well.

Libby opens the door and smiles.

It's two total strangers.

Bick drives past the seven-figure houses that are stuffed into the hill only a scream apart from each other. He would like to own a house himself, but not here. He wants land. What he pictures is a big wooden house alone on a long bluff above a stormy beach in the San Juan Islands north of Seattle, a house with mildly warped hardwood floors and at least two giant fireplaces—including one in his study—and plenty of bedrooms for visiting friends.

Coming up to a strip of the street lined with parked cars, Bick slows. He recognizes many of the vehicles. Behind a jeep on a muddy slope he finds space. He pushes in the cigarette lighter, puts his flask in his blazer, puts up the top, then lights a cigarette.

He turns on the alarm as he walks away from the car toward the social noise. The rain has lessened to just a sweet eucalyptus wetness in the air. He has that preparty excitement, that belief in a night's warm promise, belief in the possibility of making contact, as he and his friends sometimes say. He can't seem to shake this no matter how many times he's been disappointed. *Give up hope,* he tells himself, *and all you have left is irony* and *that's* depressing. About a hundred feet away he can make out the music—Led Zeppelin. He's relieved to know he's not the only adult who's regressing to high-school-era music, though it worries him the party has become nostalgic this early.

For a moment he remembers nights in the Northwest parked by the lake, kissing like it was important. If he'd known then what his life would be now? He would have joined a cult in Oregon.

The music stops as he steps up on the porch. He walks in and nobody else is in the foyer. No music, no people, just the vague milling noises of a mass somewhere close. "Fifty-nine, fifty-eight," someone starts. *"Fifty-seven, fifty-six,"* a crowd joins the count. Bick enters the main room. Two or three dozen people are gathered together under bright mini-mo movie lights and shiny balloons and hanging stars. Some are even wearing party hats. Another two or three dozen are outside the sliding glass doors on the patio by the glowing blue pool, backed by the miles and miles of shimmering orangy and blue and white city lights, chanting en masse. Leading the count from the diving board is Clock Girl, named for her appearances at parties and clubs with a six-inch white-faced clock hanging on a chain around her neck. This is the first time Bick has seen this unusual fashion accessory put to practical use. *"Forty-nine, forty-eight . . ."* He recognizes people but doesn't immediately see his friends or anyone he wants to talk with.

"Bick!" Libby air-kisses him. "You're late, lover."

"Love me anyway."

"I do, I do," she says quickly. "There's gallons of champagne in the bathtub and I hid a glass for you in the medicine cabinet." She kisses him again on the cheek. "Must go play hostess."

Bick watches her work back into the crowd. He likes her in old Levi's. He considers for a moment that she probably wore them for him and he's flattered, but then thinks probably not.

"Bick!" A young drunk girl surprises him with a kiss on the lips.

"October," he says. "How are you?"

"Fabulous."

He had sex with October once a few months ago and doesn't know why he didn't call her again. On cold nights he sometimes wishes he had. Instead, they became friends through Libby.

"You need champagne," October says, festive as hell. "It's in the bathroom."

"Actually, I've been drinking bourbon."

"Of course you have."

He follows her black net stockings and purple garters down the hall past a poster that lists big-name drug deaths, from Lenny Bruce to Len Bias, beneath the battle cry LET THE GOOD TIMES ROLL.

"Where have you been lately," she asks over her shoulder.

"Working."

"You finish that rewrite for Disney?"

"Yeah."

"Any good?"

"No."

In the bathroom Bick finds a glass in the medicine cabinet next to the Excedrin P.M.

"How'd you know that was there?"

"Seek and ye shall find."

"Are you like Libby's boyfriend now?"

"No, not really." He pulls a bottle of champagne out of the tub and quickly pops it and fills both their glasses.

"Yum," she says.

"Nineteen, eighteen . . ."

They hurry back into the main room and Merri and Willie spot Bick and gesture him over to the bar. Willie is wearing a black suit and a T-shirt featuring the face of David Cassidy with I THINK I LOVE YOU written underneath. October knows Merri and Willie and they exchange greetings and count along.

"Ten, nine . . ."

Over the din Willie says, "If one more person tells me they like the rain because it reminds them of New York, I'm going to carve out their eyes with my car keys."

Bick hops on a stool next to Willie while noticing many girls with black net stockings and garters, apparently the look of the season. The night is feeling better after the first hit of champagne.

"THREE, TWO, ONE! HAPPY NEW YEAR!"

And horns blow and everyone yells and hugs and kisses.

October gives Bick a big smack and rotates into the kissing swirl. Though the kissing is pretty liberal and generous, it still seems restrained to Bick compared with New Year's past, compared with New Year's before AIDS.

"Wait, wait," a loud actor yells, "that was premature. Look at the TV—it's not the new year yet! Look!" On MTV they're still counting down. People around the TV laughingly begin another countdown. *"Twenty-nine, twenty-eight . . ."* And soon everyone joins in and the whole *"HAPPY NEW YEAR!"* thing starts again and again there're horns and hugs and kisses and champagne spraying.

When it dies out, someone turns the stereo radio on and the deejay is counting down, *"Nineteen, eighteen . . ."* Laughter rolls through the whole party.

"One more time!"

"Fourteen, thirteen . . ."

And everyone joins in, smiling, laughing, and this time when the *"HAPPY NEW YEAR!"* comes people go berserk—louder horns and longer kisses and

louder laughter and champagne spraying everywhere as they desperately try to top the last two.

Several minutes after midnight Bick and Willie are alone together at the bar while many others are still copping kisses.

"This is a group with a serious commitment to drama," Willie says.

"Guess I'm not drunk enough," Bick says.

"I know the feeling."

Willie grabs a bottle of bourbon and hands it back to Bick. He less cheerfully grabs a bottle of Evian for himself. They pour, toast, drink. They're about the only two not wildly exhibiting their enthusiasm for the new year, Bick because he's not the demonstrative type and Willie because he has taken leave of booze and drugs.

A girl in black kisses them each and moves on.

"You fuck her," Willie asks.

Bick doesn't answer.

"I hope you didn't fuck her." He inhales deeply on his cigarette, then slowly exhales. "She used to be a porn actress. She has AIDS."

Bick stares back.

"Joke," Willie says. "Have you seen her in that horror movie? The one where she gets decapitated while she's giving head?"

Bick's not sure if he's joking.

"You should see it," Willie says seriously. "Everyone who's in it has sex."

"Always a plus."

"They have sex, then they die."

"Cool."

"Merri took me to see it," he says and looks around. "Where is the loving one?"

They both look. No sign of Merri.

"Have you seen Lee," Bick asks.

"Blond Ambition?" Willie says. "The scourge of cinema?"

"The very one."

"I think he went to Justine's."

"Of course."

"There aren't enough hot young stars here for him. I don't know what *I'm* doing here. I guess I just had this sentimental whim to be with friends on New Year's Eve."

"No wonder you're on the W Out list."

"Yeah, I'm trying to torpedo my career. First it was the booze and drugs, now it's my choice of parties."

"Smash cut to Willie John Paul, lying drunk on Hollywood Boulevard, washed up at twenty-five, vomiting on Tom Cruise's star."

"Could happen."

"One way to please everyone."

"This is the reason writers and actors get along so well, we know how much we're hated by them."

Willie can say these things and get away with it because his air of self-amusement keeps others amused no matter what he babbles. Something he learned doing bad movies, Bick figures.

"They don't hate us," Bick says. "It's just general ill will."

Willie laughs. "To quote one of my favorite movies—"

"Easy Rider," Bick says, knowing what's coming.

"'They're not afraid of you,'" Willie says in a perfect young Jack Nicholson, "'they're afraid of what you represent.'" Then he switches to an uncanny stoned Dennis Hopper, "'Hey man, all we represent to them, man, is a couple guys who need a haircut, man.'" Back to Nicholson, "'No, what you represent to them is freedom,'" and then Dennis Hopper, "'Freedom, man, that's what it's all about, man.'" Rolling now, he's Nicholson, "'Yeah, but saying it and doing it are two different things. It's awful hard to be free when you're bought and sold in the marketplace.'" He switches back to his own voice. "It upsets me I'm not drinking."

They both laugh and drink.

"I'm retiring," Bick says.

Willie laughs, "Yeah, me too, cool idea."

"It's my New Year's resolution."

Willie keeps laughing and lights a new cigarette off the one he's smoking. "I've been meaning to tell you," he says through a thick cloud of smoke, "you should give up writing realistic scripts. The world is too fucked up for realistic fiction."

Bick reaches over the bar for a clear plastic cup and ice cubes for the bourbon.

"Sci-fi is what you should do."

The bourbon tastes better on ice, but the cubes leave one of his hands wet and cold and he has nothing to dry off with.

"Like the kind of sci-fi Kurt Vonnegut writes," Willie adds.

"He doesn't write just sci-fi."

"There's aliens and time travel and the future is always really twisted. Sci-fi. Spielberg and Lucas understand."

"I'll think about this." He dries his hand on his untucked shirttail.

"Will you?"

"Yeah. But not too much."

"I'm serious about this."

"I believe you." Bick lights a cigarette. "Merri said you bought a new sled."

"Yeah. Aston Martin. You know, like James Bond in *Goldfinger.*"

"Right."

"I'd take you for a spin, but it's in the shop. I drove it onto one of those freeway ramp-divider things."

"Say what?"

"I couldn't decide whether to take the exit or not, so I ended up in between."

A girl suddenly kisses Willie. It becomes a long strangulation-style kiss.

"Thank you," Willie says after she lets him go.

She glances at Bick, giggles nervously, then moves on. Bick looks at Willie. Willie laughs.

"What are you two losers laughing about?" It's Oscar.

"Your movie," Willie says.

"Don't laugh. Weep."

Oscar's eyes are glassy with exhaustion and the usual dark circles underneath seem to be spreading. Oscar is the most upbeat person Bick knows and truly talented, but his edge is a revolutionary-like ability to focus solely on his work and this, Bick suspects, may be costing him.

"Who's the girl with the black leather Little Bo Peep thing," Oscar asks.

"Which one," Willie asks.

"Good point. So why aren't you two running around swapping AIDS-positive saliva with the guests?"

"Is that what you've been doing?"

"I'm a lonely guy. I can't afford to pass up opportunities." Oscar's voice, despite his appearance, is even more animated than Willie's. "Is there beer here?"

"Somewhere," Bick answers, "there's got to be beer." His own voice sounds as though he has throat cancer.

"Minifridge," Willie says, flopping himself over the bar. "Ah-ha!" A moment later a beer is tossed up in the air.

Oscar snags the can. "Thanks. Now," he asks when Willie pulls himself back onto a stool, "who's this Little Bo Peep girl?"

"She has syphilis, or gonorrhea," Willie says. "Or maybe chlamydia."

"All bacterial infections," Bick points out, "easily curable."

"Who's that," Oscar asks, gesturing with his beer.

"Playmate of a couple months ago," Willie answers. "A real bowwow without an airbrush, huh?"

"I don't know. She's not bad."

"Tell her you're directing a movie, she'd be yours."

"Naw, I need a girl who could be a girlfriend."

"So find one."

"Don't have time," Oscar says. "I work for a living."

"We all work for a living," Willie says, then turns to Bick. "Sci-fi."

But Oscar apparently hears "high five" and repeats it back and they both have to high-five him.

Someone switches the radio off and there's the familiar sound of a needle cuing onto a worn record and U2's "New Year's Day" bursts out, volume rising. Bick notes the way the rhythms of conversations seem to unconsciously catch the beat. He pours himself some more bourbon.

Libby and Merri come over and kiss Bick and Willie.

Oscar stands silently pointing at himself with a questioning look. Libby and Merri both kiss him. "If you guys had any sense," he says to the girls, "you'd leave these losers and be with me. Both of you."

"You're right about that," Libby says.

Bick and Willie nod to each other in a show of agreement. Merri looks at Bick.

Libby takes Merri by the hand and swings her into a sixties-style dance that seems especially absurd with U2 playing. They break loose of each other and begin thrashing about in a sexy improvised dance that resembles treading water. They're a total spectacle.

"That's our girls," Willie says.

Among those observing is a rock-video director who for years has been trying to persuade anyone who works in feature films to take him seriously. After he got his chance and made his first feature, he assumed such an attitude, acting superior to anyone not semifamous, he's now more of a joke than when he was just a rock-video director. Next to him is an older guy with long hair who was supposed to be a directing genius two years ago but can't get work now. Bick wonders if these two are together, another unholy Hollywood alliance.

"I expect y'all to have a good time tonight," Libby says, stopping the dance inches from Bick, resuming her hostess persona. "And stay *very late.*" "Y'all" is all that remains of her Texas accent. Her acting teacher and her voice coach did a job and only when she's drunk does she turn the accent back on. Bick likes it, or maybe he just likes her drunk. She points her finger at him. "*You* don't try to escape early." With a flourish she splits off into the crowd.

"Cuts into your options," Willie says. "Huh?"

"Yeah," Bick nods.

"I know the feeling."

Merri elbows him.

A young lean guy out on the patio near Libby starts taking off his shirt. "Danny's been drinking kamikazes," Merri says.

Danny tosses his shirt and takes off his shoes, socks, and pants. He is not wearing any underwear.

"Actors," Oscar says to Bick.

A few people whistle.

Danny hops onto the diving board, jumps a few times for attention, and then cartwheels across the board and through the air and splashes into the brightly lighted swimming pool. The crowd claps and cheers and then returns to party chat.

Merri mentions that she was shocked to see a girl driving with a personalized license plate that said CUMONME. Bick argues a new interpretation, suggesting that maybe the girl was ambitious, that the "come on me" was just an exhortation to higher levels of achievement. Merri doesn't buy this. Willie says he saw a bumper sticker that said WITHOUT MUSIC THE WORLD BE A MISTAKE. It took him five stop lights to get it. Oscar mentions his favorite, WHERE WERE YOU WHEN I WAS LONELY AND POOR? Bick tells about the COVER ME HONEY—I'M CHANGING LANES! bumper sticker.

"Literacy is a beautiful thing," Willie says.

Eventually Willie and Merri and Oscar venture out into the crowd, but Bick stays alone at his bar stool because almost everyone at the party comes to the bar at one time or another and the amount of time it takes to get a cocktail is his idea of the perfect amount of time for a party conversation.

A girl he recognizes from a taco commercial tells him with airy earnestness he should buy some spiritual books at the Bodhi Tree, to discover his road. Bick nods. An agent he vaguely knows asks if he's in synchronicity with his current agent. Bick asks what time it is. A studio executive who everyone knows is going to be fired next week asks if he would be interested in doing some dialogue polish on a script about an alien who mates with a human and leaves Earth but then comes back and wants custody of the child, sort of a *Close Encounters of the Third Kind* meets *Kramer vs. Kramer* that just needs to be commercialized with an access character and Bick starts to miss the girl who talked about lost souls and discovering roads.

A young drunk girl, attractive in a mud-wrestler sort of way, approaches and asks the standard "What do you do?"

He tells her he's a hack.

"Oh. What kind of stuff do you write about?"

"I write screenplays. Mostly do rewrite work these days."

"Have any been made?"

"Yes."

"What?"

"Mostly ones that shouldn't have been."

"Like what?" she persists. "Anything I'd recognize?"

He tells her, leaving out the one about the white slave trade.

It seems to Bick that strangers are fucking more than ever these days, contrary to all reason. She seems like this kind of stranger.

"That must be a really satisfying experience," she says. "Actually seeing something you wrote on the big screen and everything. I'd go to the theater every night and scream and point at the screen and make a scene."

"It's never really what I wrote," Bick says. "Just bits and pieces, moments, usually surrounded by shit."

"It's still something."

"Maybe, but I'm retiring."

"Huh," she says. "Why?"

She loses interest rapidly when it becomes obvious that his future is dubious. He doesn't blame her. She's just trying to find her ticket into that colorific world featured in movies and magazines and commercials, *a world,* he thinks, *where an Uneducated Girl from nowhere can fulfill her fantasies and meet Nikki Sixx of Motley Crüe and overdose in a poorly kept up Beverly Hills mansion and Tom Petty can play at her funeral, "She was an American girl, raised on promises. . . ."* While he pictures her ugly early death, she asks if he's friends with Willie Paul. He admits he is. She's impressed. Suddenly word gets out that Julian Lennon is having people over and there's a mass exodus the suspected mud wrestler excuses herself to join.

Mona and Joy find Bick smoking under the LET THE GOOD TIMES ROLL poster. They are both pale and wearing all black as usual, but Joy has a white flower poking from her breast pocket. "Happy New Year," Joy says, kissing him, spilling her champagne.

He turns to Mona, who flicks her cigarette into the Korbel bottle she's holding by the neck. Bick smiles and kisses her quickly.

"Late even for a funeral," Mona says.

Bick looks at Joy and is about to apologize, but Joy cuts him off, "I should *thank* you for being late," she says. "It was the only thing that made me smile, because it was like *familiar.*"

"And I decided not to come to the, uh—"

"I know, I shouldn't have gone either. It was full of phony fucks who hardly knew Tim pretending to be his friend because they wanted to be part of the fucking event or something. You would have been sick to your stomach."

"Joy called this actress a cunt," Mona says, smiling.

"That was the best part." She puts her cigarette in Mona's bottle. "I have to go to the bathroom."

"Isn't New Year's the most miserable?" Mona says as Joy walks down the hall. "At least on a normal night you go out figuring there's a fifty-fifty chance you might have a decent time. But on New Year's what happens? Too much

shitty champagne, no incredible kiss, and you're like *obligated* to think, 'Another year's over and what have I done? I have no job, no money and nobody to love.'" She laughs. "The Angriest White Woman in America."

"But tomorrow you start a new year."

"With a hellish hangover."

"Things will have to get better then."

"I know you have drugs. Let's do them with Joy."

"All I have is half a joint."

"Shit. Nice New Year's."

This is the part about parties Libby likes best: almost everyone is gone except her closest friends, who are gathered around the swimming pool by the Jacuzzi: Merri and Willie, Mona and Joy, Bick and Oscar. Party hats and bottles and butts are floating in the still pool, a twisted lawn chair rests on the bottom of the deep end, but there's nothing that can't be cleaned up tomorrow while Libby sleeps. The Jacuzzi gives off misty heat into the cool wet night and she thinks of it as a Californian-modern version of a campfire. She slips her hand into the rip above the knee in Bick's Levi's.

Willie is doing his Dr. Strangelove imitation of Slim Pickens riding the big bomb into Russia—"Yahoo!"—and everyone's laughing.

"I can't understand why he killed himself," Joy suddenly says. Libby's not sure what drug Joy is on tonight, but it's making her even more maudlin than usual. "I don't understand why he did it with a *gun?*" Joy says.

"Because he had one," Mona says, leaning back in the chaise longue chain-smoking.

The others look for Joy's reaction. There isn't much of one, just a horrible uncomfortable silence. The first times they were together after it happened they said all the things people say in such situations, but the next few times the group seemed to realize that they weren't feeling or voicing anything new. Repeating the obvious seemed to lessen the importance of it all.

There's a popping in the distance, firecrackers or gunshots.

"He called me the week before," Bick says, "and asked me to buy his gun." *This* is a new revelation, a new twist, at least to Libby, and she notices it seems to be new to everyone else as well. "I told him I didn't want a gun. I told him to call Willie."

Eyes shift warily to Willie.

"I told him I didn't need another gun," Willie says. He lights another cigarette, shakes his head. "I had no fuckin' idea."

"Neither did I," Bick says.

Everyone is still a little stunned.

"He wanted to kill himself," Oscar finally says. "Wouldn't have mattered if he didn't have a gun."

"I know," Willie says, "but I should have heard what he was saying."

"How could you?" Merri says. "He was acting like everything was fine."

"No," Willie says. "No. He was hypersensitive to the way all his friends were starting to do whatever while he was still fucked up. I mean fucked up more than average. We talked about it some that night." He blows smoke. "I think he just felt like everyone around him was ... *doing* things."

"What about *me*?" Joy says, setting off nervous laughter.

"He was only twenty-four," Libby says.

"Twenty-five."

"Still."

"I should have heard."

Libby wishes somebody would say something to put this to rest.

Merri puts her hand on one of Willie's shoulders. "He should have been fine," Merri says. "He had friends."

Libby smiles. Only Merri can say something like this and mean it.

"Maybe he didn't see *It's a Wonderful Life*," Mona says.

"Fuck off, Mona," Joy says.

"He was getting real insecure about his friendships," Willie says. "He had this weird idea, I think, that if he didn't keep up—"

"He thought we'd like lose interest in him," Joy fills in. "If he wasn't, you know, keeping up."

Libby considers her own lack of professional success. She has been training for about a year with the best teachers and coaches and she's well connected, but all she's landed is an Alf part, referred to in the script as Bitchin' Babe. This was certainly not what Daddy had in mind when he died six years ago and left his seventeen-year-old only daughter over three million dollars.

"Tim's job wasn't *that* bad," Merri says. "A lot of people his age would kill for that job."

"He didn't want to work as a copywriter anymore," Joy says.

"Quitting to work as a doorman at twenty-fucking-something wasn't exactly a step up," Mona notes.

"He wanted . . ."

"What?"

"I'm not sure."

Libby doesn't like the way this is all starting to sound familiar. She can tell Bick feels the same way. She wants him to say something.

"What the fuck is success, anyway?" Oscar says, and finishes his drink.

"Not killing yourself?" Mona offers.

Nobody laughs.

"He didn't have a passion," Joy says.

"He had you," Merri says.

Wrong thing to say, because Tim and Joy had broken up—again—about a week before Christmas and Joy's eyes are glassing over.

Merri quickly realizes what she's said and turns to Libby with a pained helpless look. Libby turns to Bick.

"I think there's a moral here," Oscar volunteers. Oscar knew Tim the least of all of them. "If you're taking notice of how empty your life is and going out to clubs on coke all night," Oscar says drunkenly, lamely, "don't keep a loaded gun at home."

This time there's uncomfortable laughter as everyone checks each other's expressions. The laughter somehow builds. Libby assumes it's because everyone has had nights like that, nights they took Valium or Advil instead of a bullet, but in any case she's glad for the laughter because it serves as some kind of cue that tonight's dirge is concluded.

"Can we talk about New Year's resolutions," Libby asks.

They all look to Joy for her tacit approval.

"I could use one of those," Joy says.

"I think we should all announce what we want for New Year's," Libby says.

"I don't want to be the voice of reason," Bick says.

"Don't worry, you're not."

"But New Year's resolutions aren't supposed to be about *wants* but about changes, improvements. Like 'I won't smoke anymore.'" He's smoking and quickly adds, "that's just an example, of course."

Libby considers. "That could translate as 'I *want* to be a nonsmoker.'" Bick laughs. "Seriously," Libby continues, "it all comes down to what you want. Doesn't it?"

Bick just laughs. Expecting something else from him, more of a rebuttal, more of *something*, Libby is vaguely disappointed.

"Tell her what you want for New Year's, Bick," Willie says.

"I have one for you," Mona says, still leaning back in her chaise longue

chain-smoking. "Save Drew Barrymore. Save her from the dizzying spiral of substance abuse that has cursed her since *E.T.* days."

"No," Willie says, "Bick's retiring."

"Retiring?" Libby says.

"Thanks, Willie," Bick says.

Willie grins.

"Retiring?" Libby repeats.

"I'm thinking of moving back to the Northwest. I thought I'd try a normal life. A more religious life."

"What the hell are you talking about, Bick?" Oscar says.

"He doesn't love us anymore," Willie says.

Libby stares at Bick, knowing he's joking but wondering how serious the joke is.

"A more religious life," Mona says, laughing.

"A *normal* more religious life," Willie says, also laughing.

"This isn't normal?" Merri says, not joking.

"What the *hell* are you talking about," Oscar asks again.

"He just said," Mona says.

Libby smiles at Bick and digs her fingernails into the flesh below his kneecap.

"Thanks again, Willie," Bick says.

"Now, what's yours, Merri?"

"Let me think for a moment," Merri says. "Someone else go."

"Oscar."

"Ask Mona."

"No, be my guest," Mona says to Oscar.

"Women first," Oscar says.

"Eat me," Mona says.

Willie leans toward Mona with an unlit cigarette in his mouth. She lights it for him.

"A girlfriend," Oscar says. "To find a girlfriend." Oscar turns to Mona.

"I don't believe in New Year's resolutions."

"Hey," Oscar says, "that could be the beauty of it."

"We're all making New Year's resolutions," Libby says. "That's what we're doing."

"I don't believe in them."

"Make one anyway," Joy says. "Pretend you believe."

"You must have some goal for the new year," Oscar says.

"To find a job," Mona snaps back.

"That's it," Libby says. "That's your resolution."

"You know what you want," Joy says. "That's good."

"What's yours going to be," Libby asks.

"Mine is," Joy pauses, "to have one. I've never had a New Year's resolution before."

"But what is it?"

"To come up with one before next New Year's."

"I'm not sure that counts."

"Of course it counts," Willie says.

"It's very realistic," Bick says.

"True."

"I've got mine," Merri declares with a smile.

"Maybe you should keep it to yourself," Willie suggests. "Maybe it won't come true unless you keep it to yourself."

"This is the year we grow up," Merri says. Willie contorts his face. "We're going to buy that house we've been looking at," she continues. "And we're going to move in, buy a dog, read the newspaper in the morning and you're not going to drink. And I'm going to wear hats all the time."

"I'm not going to drink and you're going to wear hats all the time," Willie says. "Let me picture this."

"So what exactly is your official New Year's resolution?" Libby says.

"We grow up." Merri turns to Willie. "You quit drinking."

"Quit drinking? Grown-ups drink. The whole idea of becoming a grown-up is so that you can drink whenever you want."

"Grown-ups don't do the kinds of things you do when you're drunk."

"What do I do when I'm drunk," he asks innocently. The group groans. "OK," he says, "never mind. But I can't just stop."

"You already have. You haven't had a drink since—"

"Yeah, but, I can't just stop indefinitely." He looks around desperately. "I think we need to rewrite this resolution. Bick? Help me out here?"

"Maybe you can resolve to quit drinking to excess."

"Excellent. Good vague promise." He turns to Merri. "Will that do? If I quit drinking to excess?"

"Anything you do you do to excess."

"But I can *try* not to. Isn't that the whole idea of a New Year's resolution? To try? Bick?"

"Yes. That's the spirit."

"Absolutely," Oscar contributes.

"If," Merri says, "if you really mean it."

"I mean it. I'm going to try to be a grown-up."

"And you'll give up drugs," Merri adds.

"Drugs?" Willie says.

"That was quick," Mona says to Merri. "Nice move slipping that in."

"I've been trapped," Willie says to Bick.

"Run," Bick advises.

"No," Willie says. "I can do this."

"I have witnesses," Merri points out.

"I swear to God and my friends I'll try." Willie pulls his most charming trust-me pose.

Libby can't believe how happy Merri appears. Merri is so optimistic, even Libby sometimes wants to throw up. "OK," Libby says. "We're there. We've all got our resolutions."

"Don't we all feel very complete and goal oriented now?" Mona says.

"What's the ticking clock," Oscar says.

Bick laughs.

"What!?"

"The ticking clock," Oscar says. "Your goal has to be achieved by a certain time, the clock has to be ticking."

"USC really fucked you up," Mona says to him.

"Hey," he says, "you're the one who went to film school, not me."

"The clock's ticking anyway," Joy says. "Every day."

"Tick, tock," Mona says.

"No, he's right," Libby says. "We need a deadline. Pressure."

"*I* don't need any more pressure," Willie says.

"Yes you do," Merri says. "When you don't have pressure, something to do, you get in trouble. The devil finds work for idle hands."

"How do you know it's the devil?"

"How about one week," Oscar suggests.

"No," Merri says. "Why doom us with an impossible deadline?"

"Hey," Oscar says, "God made our world in a week."

Everyone stares back at Oscar.

"Good point," Oscar says.

"Two months."

"Too arbitrary," Oscar says. "Let's choose a date with some symbolic value."

"April Fools' Day?" Willie suggests.

Merri elbows him.

"Arbor Day?" Willie tries.

"What is Arbor Day?"

"A day for planting seeds, or trees, or something. Trees, yes, trees. I remember one Arbor Day helping my dad plant trees in the backyard. They all died within a month."

"Not bad," Oscar says. "When is it?"

"I don't know."

"Anyone know?"

Nobody seems to know.

"Valentine's Day," Merri suggests.

"Valentine's Day," Joy repeats, sounding unsure.

Joy's pause stops suggestions for a moment.

"How about Merri's thirtieth birthday party?" Willie tries.

"When is that," Oscar asks.

"March tenth."

"Yeah," Oscar says. "That should be 'bout right."

"Perfect," Libby says. "Good idea."

"Did I just suggest that," Willie asks Bick.

"What about jeopardy?" Bick says to Oscar.

Libby thinks Bick intends this dryly, but Oscar in his drunkenness seizes on it.

"Jeopardy!" he says. "We need jeopardy."

"My favorite game show," Mona says.

"Jeopardy," Oscar repeats. "High stakes."

"There's enough jeopardy every goddamn day," Joy says.

"She's right," Libby agrees.

"She doesn't even know what I'm talking about," Oscar says.

"Neither do you," Mona says.

"Good," Oscar says. "Conflict."

"Cut, cut, cut, stop," Libby says. "Well, y'all"—she brings her Texas accent to bear—"it's decided. Joy's resolution is to find a resolution, Oscar's is to find a girlfriend, Mona's is to find a job, Bick's is to begin a normal life. Merri and Willie are going to grow up. Mine is . . . to get a part. One with lines. All by Merri's thirtieth birthday."

"Sounds like a hellish year so far," Willie says. "Huh?"

Everyone laughs in agreement.

"We'll have a celebration," Merri says.

"I wonder what Tim's would have been," Joy says.

The laughter is again stifled.

"Hey," Oscar says, a little too loudly. "He doesn't *get* a New Year's resolution because he's dead! If he wanted a New Year's resolution he shouldn't be dead!"

Though Libby feels the same way, she wouldn't have said anything. Oscar, however, is allowed this. It's expected of him.

A breeze picks up and blows across the pool and wavy reflections of blue wash over everyone.

"He probably killed himself just to avoid this shitty party," Willie says.

Again the laughter builds and even Joy joins in, so Libby decides it's a good time to change locations. "It's really getting chilly," she says. "Let's move this inside."

Libby pulls Bick ahead of the others. "What are we going to do about Joy," she asks.

"I don't know what we can do."

When Bick made his joke about a more religious life, Libby considered telling him about what she'd thought listening to the minister at the funeral, but not in front of everyone.

"We'll kick 'em all out soon," she says as they step into the mess of the house.

"I've gotta go," he says walking toward the door.

"I'll kick them out now."

"I really have to go home."

Bick can be charming and witty or he can just be broodish and boring. When Libby was first getting to know him, he seemed so bright. Then as they became better acquainted, he started acting like a total cretin, confused by some of her simplest sentences. She realized it was because he wasn't listening, wasn't concentrating on her, but she has learned how to catch his attention.

"I've got this rough diamond rock of cocaine about the size of a Ritz cracker," she says, smiling.

"I don't want to donate money to the contras."

"Actually, I bought this from a *Weekly* critic."

"He probably bought it straight from Noriega."

"He said he bought it from George Bush."

"Probably baby laxative, then."

Bick's lack of interest surprises her. She bought the blow just to be a good hostess and he must know she has no desire to do it alone. "Well," she says. "I have a few other surprises. I recently went on a shopping spree at The Pleasure Chest."

This makes him smile. "You think you can lure me with drugs and sex?"

They stop in the foyer. The glass squares around the door light up as a car passes. "And I just bought The Eagles' *Hotel California* on CD," she throws in for good measure.

"Drugs, sex, rock and roll."

"They're out of fashion, but—"

"I'm a traditional guy."

"I count on that."

"But I've gotta go."

"You're getting old."

"I know," he sighs.

"The old Bick, the *young* Bick, he avoided sleep like the plague. Didn't want to miss a moment."

"Sorry, but the new Bick is almost thirty and becoming human. He requires sleep. Talking about suicide for an hour grinds him down."

"I don't want to talk about that any more than you do," she says. "Prom-

ise." Libby points to their reflection in one of the foil stars slowly swaying above the mess. "You like the stars?"

"It was a good party," he says too politely. "Thank you."

"Come on," she says. "You don't want to go home and start the new year alone, brooding in sleazy Venice?"

"Yes I do."

Libby knows to be not serious with Bick, not possessive, not threatening, not frightening. Boys scare so easy, like horses, you have to be gentle and sly. Her acting teacher's words come to mind: *What people want isn't usually interesting, what's interesting is how you try to get it.* She had told Bick this, thinking he'd find it a somehow romantic notion. He'd said her acting teacher was ripping off Brecht.

"Excuse me," he says, "I'm going to use the bathroom. Then I've gotta go."

"Fine," she says, and smiles. "Guess I'll just fuck one of the other guys tonight."

"Cool."

Bick locks the bathroom door behind him. Right now he's tired of interpreting the group's language. He puts down the toilet lid and sits and picks up the telephone. Sarah's answering machine comes on.

"Sorry," Bick says, "but I just want to wish you a happy new year and—"

"Hi, Bick," she says picking up the phone.

"Happy New Year."

"Happy New Year."

"What are you doing?"

"Lying in bed. Reading."

"Scripts."

"Yep."

"You shouldn't be working tonight."

"I went to a party, but there were too many writers."

"I think I better come over."

"You want to come over?"

"Yeah."

"You OK?"

"Yeah."

"You at home?"

"No."

"You're with Libby and those people."

"Yeah."

"If you're here within ten minutes, OK."

"See you soon."

He hangs up and walks out into the main room to say good-bye. The group is singing a pop song drunkenly and badly, as they often do this time of night.

"I wah-wah-wah-wah wonder . . ."

"Runaway" is one of the group's favorites, because of the lyrics and the way it lends itself to their over-the-top vocals and theatrics—Willie runs in place during the "run-run-run runaway" part.

Bick doesn't join in.

"Watching the planes fly by, some live and some die . . ." They sing the version from the TV show.

When they finish, Bick says good night. His slow exit with air kisses and hugs is like numerous other nights of drunken parting.

Libby somehow gathered the group together a few years ago, when they were all broke except for her and Merri. They have a history. When Merri lost a lead movie part she badly wanted and wondered if her life was forever changed for the worse, Libby and Bick showed her how to make Manhattans. When Willie threw up the night the movie he was proudest of stiffed at a screening, Bick smoked outside the bathroom stall door. They've walked out of dozens of movies together, including a few that one or more of them had worked on. There have been successes too, but the whole town wants to be your friend after a success and so sometimes it was the worst times that became the best times, memorable for the healing emotion of wild ideas and plans and promises and, inescapably, shared hangovers on painfully sunny mornings.

Something strong was shared once and this matters, Bick thinks as he walks to his car, *and whatever the reasons—we're stuck with each other now.*

J oy closes the front door stealthily. She and Mona tiptoe across the dark living-room floor. Something in the near blackness crackles under Mona's shoe.

"Shhh," Joy says.

"Sorry."

Just outside the kitchen Joy picks up two large fly swatters. She hands one to Mona.

"Ready?" she whispers.

"Ready."

"Listen."

There's a scratching sound.

"Hear that?" she whispers.

"Yeah," Mona whispers back. "They're there."

"Time for Godspeed."

"Time for Godspeed."

Joy takes an extremely soft step into the kitchen, moves her left hand on the wall, finds the light switch and clicks it on.

"Aiiiiiiiiiii!" they scream and run into the room swinging their weapons crazily. Snap, crackle, pop, splat, the swatters squash their victims.

"Nowhere to run, baby, nowhere to hide," Joy sings the Motown tune from some chopper-attack scene from some Vietnam movie of which she remembers nothing else.

The cockroaches, caught in the light, scramble for cover, but she and Mona are swift with both their swatters and their shoes.

"Nowhere to run to, baby, nowhere to hide . . ."

Splat, splat.

"Nowhere to run to, baby, nowhere to hide . . ."

Splat, splat.

In seconds almost a dozen die.

They ritualistically cross swatters. The instruments are customized with gaffer's tape wrapped around the hitting surface. The tape is peppered with pin-sized airholes to improve aerodynamics. Written in childish scrawl across each is GODSPEED BUG KILLER.

"I think we taught them a lesson this time."

"No, they never learn."

As they undress in the bedroom, Joy says, "Did I ever make a New Year's resolution?"

"Your resolution was to make a resolution."

"Right."

On the wall are Joy's drawings: charcoal sketches of stretched curvy human bodies, impressionistic visions of perfect apartments, a portrait of Tim.

"What was yours," Joy asks.

"To find a job. It was assigned to me."

"That wouldn't be hard if you weren't so goddamn picky."

"But I *am* picky."

"You could have worked as an assistant to Harry. That might have been OK."

"He wanted to fuck me."

"Is that what's called a fringe benefit?"

"I wouldn't mind working as an assistant if I could find a producer I could work with in a healthy atmosphere of apprenticeship and mutual respect. It's totally unrealistic, I know."

"What do you think about Merri and Willie? Getting a house?"

"Him not abusing chemicals?"

"Growing up."

"I don't believe in miracles," Mona says, hanging up her blazer.

"What about Oscar?"

"What was his?"

"A girlfriend. To find a girlfriend."

"That's right, many miracles were asked for tonight."

"He's successful and smart, why should it take a miracle for him to find a girlfriend?"

"Because he has a crew cut."

"He can grow it out."

"And he doesn't really want a girlfriend."

"I would think that would better his odds."

Mona tosses her tights onto the pile of clothes and turns off the light. Though Joy is still struggling out of her tights and could use the light, she doesn't say anything. She knocks her shin against the closet door.

"Is it just me," Joy asks, "or is Libby acting strange lately?"

"It's just you," Mona answers from one of the twin mattresses on the floor.

"Yeah. Probably." She thinks. "You think Bick'll really go back home? Isn't that what he said?"

"He was joking, Joy."

"I don't know."

"Believe me."

Joy suspects she shouldn't judge in her condition. She knows she's seeing things somehow differently now. Once when she was a kid, her father dragged her to a museum with a series of illustrations demonstrating the relativity of perception, a man standing straight next to a slanted wall that made him seem to lean, a midget in a small room that made him seem a giant. She felt discombobulated for several minutes afterward. Now she feels discombobulated pretty constantly. On Christmas Eve when Tim shot himself she woke up with a piercing headache. She gets headaches sometimes, but this was the only one to awaken her in the middle of the night. It took four Halcions with wine to put her back to sleep. When she found out about Tim the next day, she knew there was a connection, a connection that confused her with its suggestion of further strange connections. She wants to tell someone about this, but she's afraid it makes her sound crazy. She can tell everyone's already a little worried about her. She forgets Mona's question.

"Where am I going to find a New Year's resolution," she asks.

Bick turns down La Cienega off Sunset and turns again onto a street with motellike modern apartment buildings built a few feet from older buildings with dramatically angled roofs and a few conspicuous and useless chimneys. This stretch is sometimes referred to as D-girl row.

D-girl is shorthand for a woman who works in development. Her job is to find writers with good scripts or good ideas for sale and when she finds something she can love she persuades her employer to buy and if successful she nurtures the writer along until the script is presentable. Then the employer, a producer or a studio, decides either to abort or go forward with what is now called a project. In either case the D-girl is suddenly disconnected, as Sarah says, like an unfit mother. This is what Sarah does, but "D-girl" is not an expression Bick uses, especially in front of her.

"You're late," Sarah says through the security phone after his third buzz.

"I stopped at 7-Eleven to get you something."

"It's been almost an hour."

"It took me a while to find an open store and parking was hard to find. . . . " Sarah doesn't say anything. He knows his charm for her is largely based on her limited time and how little he demands and he shouldn't have been late. The phone starts ticking. "Sarah?"

She buzzes him in. After two flights of stairs he is winded. He pauses a

couple moments outside her door so he can enter with the appearance of some vigor, then knocks.

"It's open."

He locks the door behind himself and walks through the main room, past the fluffy comfortable couches, and through the absolutely immaculate kitchen to the bedroom, which is all baby blues and pinks.

"What took so long," she asks from her bed, a flannel sheet pulled up to her tanless belly, a screenplay blocking his view of her breasts. "Did you park in Pasadena?"

"I guess I was driving around for a while."

She sniffs. "Been smoking the devil weed?"

"Just a bit. I'm weaning myself off."

She sighs, then smiles. "What did you bring me?"

"Your favorite." He comes over and kisses her and hands her an Almond Joy.

She sets down the screenplay and pulls up the sheet. "It'll keep me awake all night."

"My kiss or the chocolate?"

"Have you been drinking a lot tonight?"

"Not enough."

Bick goes back into the kitchen and pours himself a highball from a bottle of Jim Beam she keeps exclusively for him—or at least so she has told him. After a couple sips his breathing slows back to normal.

"Could you bring me a bottle of Evian?" she says, already started on the chocolate.

He brings her the bottle and then kicks off his penny loafers and sits on the bed next to her and lights a cigarette. She doesn't smoke but keeps a Spago ashtray around for him. He checks the titles on the screenplays piled in tidy stacks.

"How's life at the factory?"

"Pretty slow, which is good. I feel like I'm finally catching up on my reading."

"Reading anything good?"

"No, it's really frustrating."

He looks at the Susan Sontag book on her nightstand, *Against Interpretation.* "Weren't you supposed to read that shit in college?"

"I was a business major, what's your excuse?"

"I was too busy getting drunk in college," he says, and has another swallow. "I did all my heavy reading the year after."

"You should read this."

"I have."

"Sure."

"The 'Against Interpretation' essay ends with 'We need an erotics of art.'"

Sarah puts half of the Almond Joy back in the wrapper and picks up the book to check. "Lucky guess," she says. "I didn't realize you were a closet Susan Sontag reader."

"Don't tell anyone."

Bick thinks about all the books he once read and how rarely they lessened despair and even when they did, it was not as satisfyingly as drunkenness or another's warm body. Still, he reads. Sometimes a good book will increase his appreciation of drunkenness and warm bodies.

"Here's something to amuse you," she says, flipping pages. "Blah, blah, blah, here, 'Tolerate qualities in a lover—moodiness,' blah, blah, blah, '—that they would never countenance in a husband, in return for excitement, an infusion of intense feeling.'"

"Not applicable. We're not lovers."

"We're *not?*"

"No."

"We're not lovers?"

"Making out like teenagers does not make us lovers."

"No?"

"Not technically."

"Why not?"

"We don't fuck."

She sets down the book. "What are you getting at?"

"Maybe we should change things."

"Change what exactly?"

"Maybe we should be lovers, in a technical sense."

"Are you going to continue fucking club sluts?"

"No, I don't think so."

"Whoa. Am I hearing a pledge of monogamy?"

"With all the sluts in Los Angeles," Bick says, "how do I end up with a girl who thinks she's a virgin?"

"I *am* a virgin. If you go without sex for a year, you can reclaim your virginity. It's common knowledge."

"You could be my first."

"Sorry," she says. "I'm really not interested in making love with someone who's also fucking club sluts. It's demeaning. And dangerous."

"I didn't come here for abuse," he says, taking off his blazer. "At least not with my clothes still on."

"You didn't answer the question. Are you making a pledge of monogamy?"

"I'm not sure."

"Explain."

"It's my New Year's resolution."

"What is?"

"To begin a normal life."

"Why couldn't you have a normal New Year's resolution, like to quit smoking?"

"I like smoking."

"I must say, this is your most ambitious approach so far."

"What? You think I'm saying this just to talk you into having sex with me?"

"At least you didn't say 'fuck.'"

"Sarah, forget the sex thing for a second. Can you do that?"

"Bick, be realistic. We've been doing this for months and if anything more was going to develop between us, it would have by now."

After a long drink he says, "You sure?"

"Yes."

He nods.

"This is it," she continues. "And you don't really want it to change. And neither do I. Because it's not going to."

"That's awfully unromantic," he says, smiling now.

She laughs.

"Don't you think it's sort of mutually torturous," he asks.

"Yeah."

They both nod, not quite smiling.

"But for now . . . " She hands him a down pillow. "Come to bed."

He undresses and slides under the sheets with her and she turns off the bedside lamp. As though darkness is their cue, they instantly kiss. She starts kissing his neck, kissing up toward his ear, and that warm wet tongue is right there and she's breathing and the sound sends the much-heralded shivers twanging down his spine and his own hands are moving on her moving breasts, closing in on nipples that are reaching out and she's breathing in quicker bursts now and the sound of the warm wet breath makes him feel just like he remembers feeling as a teenager discovering sex—when it was so intense it fogged your brain better than a twelve-pack of Mickey Big Mouth Malt Liquor—and her hand is on him and his hand is inside her cotton panties and it's warm and wet like the breath in his ear that's building quicker and louder, fogging his brain back to sixteen, which is all he thinks he wants at this point and all either of them is going to get.

After sex Willie can't sleep. He's been having trouble sleeping since he quit drinking. Merri, on her side of the bed, is already breathing quietly like a baby. She had a couple glasses of champagne.

Willie nudges her. "Merri?"

"Hmmm?"

"I can't sleep."

"Good night."

She pats him and curls back into the fetal position.

"I said I can't sleep."

"Go to sleep."

He stares into the darkness. Somewhere out there people are drinking, doing drugs, cranking themselves up on sensation, getting in trouble, hurting themselves, enjoying life. It's so early, not even three.

Tonight wasn't so bad, he tells himself, considering he was sober. Then he moans, suddenly remembering the New Year's resolution he made, *Merri* made, and how happy she was.

"Shit."

"Mmmm?"

"Nothing."

What kind of promises has he made now? The house thing is livable, they were eventually going to do that anyway, but how did it come as a package

deal, with him as a nondrinking element? Thinking about it makes him want to get drunk.

Matt Turbov is having a party downtown in some warehouse, he remembers, Wall Street and Pico or somewhere like that. He'll find it. It's probably just starting to happen about now. Bick probably went there. There will be booze and girls and maybe drugs. He has to go out. His herpes has just cleared up and he has to go out.

He'll leave Merri a note saying Bick called and needed a, uh, tow or something. *It's possible.* She knows Bick sometimes drives around all night like an idiot. Bick will cover for him.

He eases out from under the sheets. He puts on his Levi's, not bothering with underwear. Then he puts on his shirt and picks up his jacket and shoes and quietly steps toward the door. He looks back at her. She looks so sweet, so cute, so trusting curled up like that. He takes another two steps and slowly turns the door handle. He opens it and light from the hall streams in, making him squint.

"Willie," she says.

"Yeah?"

"Where are you going?"

"Just to . . . make some hot chocolate."

She sits up. "What are you doing with your jacket and shoes?"

He looks at his jacket and shoes. "I'm going to put them on."

"To get hot chocolate?"

"I was going to get it at the store."

"There's plenty in the cabinet above the microwave."

"Is there? I didn't know. I thought I'd bring my shoes and jacket just in case."

"Close the door."

He does and the room is dark again.

"You were going to get something to drink."

"Right. Hot chocolate. Cocoa."

"You know they don't sell alcohol here after two."

"I know that. I was just going out for hot chocolate. Really."

"Is there an after-hours club or something tonight?"

He feels guilty. "Yes," he admits.

"You can't sleep?"

"No."

"Thinking about Tim?"

"I guess. Sort of."

She comes out from under the sheets toward him. He notices again how good her body is. Everything he can think of, her body to her brain, her style, her humor, her care, everything about her appeals to him. He is lucky to have

a girl like this, he knows. He shouldn't want to head out in search of trouble. She takes his hand and leads him back toward the bed.

"You need sleep," she says.

"I know."

"It's going to be a good year."

He nods.

She seats him on the bed and unbuttons his shirt and takes it off. Folding it, she sets it on a chair. He checks his stomach and sits straighter. When she unbuttons his Levi's, he watches himself, but she ignores this and folds the Levi's and puts them by the shirt.

"Do you really want some hot chocolate," she asks.

"No."

She reaches out her hands for his and he stands to reach her. Then she pulls back the sheets and steers him into bed. He cooperates, wondering exactly what this might be leading up to. Something kinky? She tucks him in. His arms are at his side and he imagines he's in a straitjacket. There's a rising bump in the middle. *Bump*, he remembers, is what his publicist calls a blast of cocaine, as in *"Want a bump?"*

She's leaving the room.

"Where are you going," he asks.

She opens the door, smiles as the light comes in and steps out, closing it behind.

Merri is good sex. She enjoys it, she's passionate and loving. But she's not kinky. So he doesn't understand what she could be brewing. What if she returns wearing some new sexy lingerie she wants his opinion on? He'll shred it. What if she returns with honey dripping all over her body? He'll get toast.

She returns with a book.

A sex manual he hopes but knows better.

She climbs into bed on her side and turns on the night-table lamp. The book is *Go, Dog, Go!*—his favorite children's story.

"Cool," he says. It's been weeks since she read this to him. He doesn't really want to go downtown now that he thinks about it. Bad things await him out there. Her hand smooths the hair from his forehead back. Memories of childhood soak over him—he always had trouble sleeping, or maybe he had trouble so his mother would have to read to him, rub his shoulders, whisper senseless things. . . .

"'Dog,'" she reads, and points to the illustration. He looks at the dog on roller skates.

She turns the page, "'Big dog, little dog.'" A big dog sits regally in a wagon being pulled by a little dog, which appears to be sweating. As a kid he saw a whole story in that image, picturing himself as the little dog. "Dogs don't

sweat," his mother explained. "They breath hard and salivate instead." Nonetheless, he sees himself as the little dog, sweating.

She turns the pages. A pink poodle is greeting a large yellow dog on two legs. "'Hello,'" Merri reads in the pink poodle's voice, female, sexy.

"'Hello,'" she answers in the large yellow dog's voice, male, gruff.

"'Do you like my hat,'" asks the pink poodle.

"'I do not,'" answers the yellow dog.

"'Good-bye.'"

"'Good-bye.'"

This exchange is the book's leitmotiv.

"See how she handles herself," Willie interrupts. "He doesn't like her hat at first, but she passes the test, she doesn't go home and slit her paws or anything."

Merri laughs and continues reading.

"Cut to the party," Willie says.

Merri shakes her head and reads one page at a time, even slowing down the pace.

"Look at you," she says, stopping at a page with twenty-one dogs tucked in asleep on a big bed, the whole page washed in a soothing blue except for the white of the moon and the white of one wide-awake dog's eyes.

When she gets to the climax, Willie's favorite part, she holds the book open between them and there it is: "A BIG DOG PARTY!" On top of a tree with foliage like a golfing green are dozens of dogs, red dogs and blue dogs and yellow dogs and green dogs and black dogs, eating cake, blowing horns, flying out of cannons, flying out of cannons into cake, running, skipping, swinging, sleeping, and one white dog opening presents, apparently disappointed. Willie can still stare at it for a long time. He doesn't know why. It just looks so good and involving, so desirous. The closest he's come to realizing such chaotic joy was a week in New York on crystal meth that didn't end well.

Hot white video-camera light beams swing through the room in bluish tunnels of twisting smoky air. Hundreds of people are packed in a gymnasium-sized warehouse, some dancing, some staring at the seminaked people of suspect sexual identity dancing on pedestals, some talking, most not talking, most just posing.

All the leather and metal spikes and road-warrior costuming would have a menacing feel if it didn't seem so much to Oscar like an art director's idea of danger.

He chugs beer from a plastic cup. He came thinking he would know people, which he doesn't seem to, and figuring Bick would probably be here, which he doesn't seem to be. Also, he came for the girls. As he looks around, however, he realizes he can't muster much interest in girls who remind him of the actress who played the mother on "The Munsters."

Mostly he needs to think about his movie's ending. He doesn't know what makes him think he can think here, but at least the music's good, a Cowboy Junkies cover of The Velvet Underground. He listens for his favorite verse but doesn't hear it. He can't help but wonder what these people do for a living. Aware that it would be uncool to ask the rainbow-haired girl with WHITE GIRL tattooed on her pale shoulder where she works, he still wants to know. She just stands there, apparently alone, not doing anything but smoking.

Does she go to movies? Romantic comedies or action pictures? Would she

like his movie? What does she want from movies, from boys, from life? She must have desires and dreams like everybody else, but what are they, except maybe to decide on a single hair color?

"Excuse me," he says, tapping the tattooed shoulder.

She turns, checks him out cautiously.

"Where do you work?"

"Huh?"

"For a living? Where do you work?"

"You mean like a job?"

"Yeah."

"Why? You writing a book?"

"No."

One of the lights passes over them.

"I was just wondering. If we'd met?"

"What do *you* do?"

"I'm a, uh, nothing," he says. "I don't do anything."

"That's the same thing I do."

"How do you pay rent?"

"How do *you?*"

"I, uh, live in my parents' guest house." This is at least true but would be even more embarrassing if she knew what he did and how much he's paid to do it.

"I live with my parents too. They don't have a guest house, though. That must be all right."

Something about the way she says this makes him like her, but he's not sure how.

"Yeah," he nods. "It's all right."

"Where do they live?"

"Hancock Park."

"Do they have a pool?"

"Yeah."

"That must be all right. How old are you?"

"Twenty-five." He lies by two years for some insane reason. "You?"

"Twenty."

"You have time."

"For what," she asks.

He thinks. "For what?" he repeats. He doesn't know. He takes a sip of his beer to stall, to think up an answer, preferably witty, but no answer is forthcoming. "I'm going to get another beer," he finally says. "You want one?"

"Yeah, sure."

As they make their way through the dark crowd toward the beer table, he imagines she would be interesting sex and knows it won't happen. Five years

ago it would have been a given—a couple shared moments and soon you're fucking. What's changed, besides the sexual climate, is him. There will be no sex tonight, even if she should turn out to be a nymph, because—and he hates to admit this—she's not in his league. He is a twenty-seven-year-old feature film director who has had obsequious articles written about him in *American Film* and *Vanity Fair*. She is a sexy twenty-year-old with a colorful tattoo. He is looking for a girlfriend. She is not it. He's looking for someone on his level or, better yet, above. Career-mating types disgust him and he doesn't want to be like that. He truly wants to be more romantic but can't seem to find the time.

He worked for success because he wanted sex with girls he didn't know and now he's successful and he doesn't want that kind of sex.

This all reminds him the ending of his movie needs irony.

Bick dreams he's smothered in an earthquake. He wakes up and it's still dark and the room isn't shaking. He's been dreaming a lot about earthquakes lately. After a long time of restlessness, he gets up and goes into the bathroom and masturbates quickly and effectively and comes back to bed next to Sarah. Then he falls asleep and dreams more earthquake dreams.

In the morning, with far too much dull daylight coming through the Levolor blinds for Bick's taste, he's in her bed alone, flipping through channels, mostly going back and forth between the ending of a movie he's already seen and a rock-video channel. He's only mildly hungover, but he's annoyed because when he was younger he never used to get any kind of a hangover.

"Shouldn't you be watching football, affirming your virility?" Sarah asks, bringing in orange juice and bagels and butter on a tray, wearing a plaid flannel robe.

"I thought I did that last night."

"You tried," she smiles, getting in bed and setting the tray between them.

"Cable TV is a godsend," he says, switching channels.

"Bick, I think you need a vacation. You've been working like a madman for the last five years."

"I need something," he agrees.

"I'd travel all night just to get back home," says Bon Jovi in a black-and-white rock video of "Wanted Dead or Alive."

"This is an inspired song," he says.

Sarah watches for a few seconds. She's horrified. "This is adolescent trash," she says.

"It's brilliant," Bick says, sort of serious and sort of not. The song reminds him of music he listened to in high school, a touch of Lynyrd Skynyrd's "Tuesday's Gone" and Bad Company's theme song and other songs he can't quite place. "Classic adolescent mythology."

"According to the twenty-eight-year-old."

"You're not an overage adolescent?"

"I've got a *job,* rent, phone bills, a subscription to *Harper's Bazaar.* I bought the Pursuit of Happiness album, *Love Junk.* I'm an adult."

"When your parents were our age, they had *us.* I was five when my father was twenty-eight. My little brother was two."

Sarah thinks for a moment. "I was nine when my mother was twenty-eight."

"Depressing, isn't it?"

"It's so wonderful to wake up with you. Starts my whole day with a smile."

Bick laughs. "Sorry," he says.

It's strange, he thinks, he was building to something, he was going to ask her something, but he doesn't know what. He watches Bon Jovi load into their Lear jet.

"Finish your breakfast," Sarah says.

"What are you doing today?"

"Work, I've got three scripts that have to be read."

He has one bite of the bagel, watches the rest of the Bon Jovi video and then offers to leave.

"Let's go see a movie this week," Sarah says. "I haven't seen *The Boost* yet."

"I'd rather be tortured by Colombian drug dealers."

Sarah laughs. "I could see *Working Girl* again."

"I'll call you later this week."

He dresses without showering, slowing down only to brush his teeth with a toothbrush he carries in his blazer at all times.

J oy wakes up at about one o'clock, tired, and lies in bed for half an hour or so before deciding to rise for a cup of coffee.

Mona is in the kitchen reading *The Village Voice.*

"Anything good happening in New York," Joy asks as she starts up Mr. Coffee.

"Just the usual shit. Crazy people freezing and starving in the streets. Some good plays."

"What are you doing today?"

"Probably go see a movie. You?"

"Same as yesterday," she answers, lighting her first cigarette of the morning. "Same as tomorrow."

"Nothing?"

"Right."

Joy picks up a week-old copy of *The Star.* Mr. Coffee gurgles.

"Want to go see a movie," Mona asks.

"What's playing? Anything good?"

"Nothing we haven't seen, I don't think."

"Maybe I'll buy some new CDs today. Want me to get you anything?"

Mona thinks. "A job application."

"You're not that desperate yet."

"Not yet. But maybe by later this afternoon."

"You might have to lower your expectations some."

"That's insightful advice, especially coming from someone who's never had a job."

"I had a job. I worked—"

"I know, you worked on one of your dad's movies."

"It's time you started using your connections. That's how people get jobs here. That's how people get jobs everywhere."

"*What* connections?"

"I'll talk to my father anytime you want."

"Your father and I don't really get along."

"He doesn't really get along with anybody, but I'm sure he'd help you out."

"No, I'll find something. Don't worry. Like you said, I'm not that desperate yet."

"What about Oscar?"

"*Oscar?*"

"He's extremely well connected. I'm sure he'd be happy to help you out."

"I'm sure he'd be happy to *not* help me out."

"You're one of his closest friends."

"No, I'm friends with his closest friends."

"He *likes* you, Mona, despite the fact that you're usually a bitch to him."

"Thanks, Joy, that's nice of you to say. Now why don't you go record shopping."

"I guess you just can't help anyone these days."

Mona begins to bounce one back but stops herself.

Joy wasn't referring to Tim with her last remark, at least not consciously, but she suddenly realizes that's what it is.

"Thanks," Mona says, "I know you want to help, but I'm going to be fine." She smiles. "I'll have a job long before Merri's birthday."

"Oh no," Joy says, tensing up. "Is Tower Records open on New Year's Day?"

"Yeah, I think it is."

"Thank God."

Joy starts crying in the rock-and-roll cassette section. She sets down the Blondie *Parallel Lines* tape and puts on her sunglasses and wipes the tears from her cheeks and continues crying. Almost every third album on the rack reminds her of Tim, but this one in particular. *Parallel Lines* was the summer they were most in love. The album had been out since the late seventies New Wave, but for some reason it was what they listened to that summer, in his convertible, at his apartment, at parties.

That summer he confessed to occasional thoughts of suicide. She said she understood. She told him how well she understood. It was a windy night parked by the beach, under a yellowish moon she still remembers. Together they fashioned their shared feelings into something romantic, something to intensify the desperate adolescent notion of this-may-be-all-we-get. If nothing else, it made for amazing sex.

Somebody last night said Tim needed a passion and Joy realizes she was his only passion and she doesn't know why she kept pushing and pushing him to break up with her. Was she that goddamn bored? She couldn't help herself. He shouldn't have loved her as blindly as he did. She needed a passion too, but her only passion for the last couple years was breaking up with him monthly, but maybe if . . . She doesn't know. He's dead and she has to stop crying. She wanders out of the cassette section into LPs, where she picks up whatever moves her and takes these selections to the check-out-counter line.

"Full of holiday cheer today, huh Joy?" It's Bick.

"Oh, hi. How are you?"

"I'm OK. How are you?"

"Just buying some music."

"I can see that. You OK?"

"Fine. Good. Great."

He doesn't seem to believe her.

"I'm fine, really."

"OK," he says, and checks out the albums she's carrying. "Bauhaus, Blue Oyster Cult, Blondie, Love and Rockets, Smiths, Joy Division, Jane's Addiction, Tones on Tail, Christian Death? Planning a pretty festive party?"

She suddenly realizes she's gone with some dark tunes here, but maybe it's funny, since Bick seems amused. She looks at his purchases: the new Social Distortion album and a Bon Jovi maxisingle cassette of "Wanted Dead or Alive." "Who's that for," she asks.

"Me."

"You're in worse shape than I am."

Bick laughs and Joy realizes she actually made a joke, the first in a long time. Maybe this is a good sign even if it was unintentional. As they exit, about to part to their separate cars, she grabs him. She hadn't planned to do this, but she's holding his arm very firmly. "I'm glad you're going away," she says.

"What?"

"I mean I'm not *glad*, we'll all miss you and everything, but I mean it's probably best for you."

He puts his sunglasses on with his free hand.

"I need a ride to Bakersfield," she says.

He studies her curiously.

"I'm kidding." She tries to laugh but doesn't do it very well. She releases

his arm. "When you go, let me know. So we can say good-bye properly and everything." She wishes she didn't sound so *desperate.*

He's still looking at her curiously. "Joy, you want to get together and talk?"

"No, I'm kind of busy this week. Maybe next week."

"Let's go get some coffee or something."

"I quit coffee."

"You could have a cold long milkshake."

"That sounds good."

"Let's do it."

"No, but it sounds good."

"Joy?"

"Really, I'm fine. Thanks. And I've got this meeting I've gotta go to."

He nods, obviously not believing her. "Call me anytime," he says. "OK?"

"OK. Thanks. I'm parked by Book Soup." She starts to walk backward in that direction. "Don't leave without saying good-bye."

"Watch it—"

She bangs her back into a Mercedes grill. He moves toward her to help. She puts her hands out, "I'm OK, I'm OK." She doesn't feel hurt and tries to laugh, but it still doesn't sound right. "Really, I'm OK."

Driving down Sunset toward the 405, Bick has a delayed laugh at the realization Joy was the only one who took seriously his threat to leave town.

He wasn't sure what to say, she seemed so totally unhinged. It's understandable, he supposes, something she'll get over on her own, which, he's afraid, is the only way to get over such things. Bick never really knew Tim because when Joy was with Tim she didn't want to be with the group and when he saw Tim without Joy at a club or a party, it was friendly but just as acquaintances. Since Bick has been in LA, he has known almost a dozen people besides Tim who have either killed themselves or OD'd or died in some other ugly circumstance, but like seeing a nun on roller skates on Sunset Boulevard or a man in a convertible walking his dog by tying the leash to the driver's door handle, it doesn't seem remarkable.

He takes the San Diego Freeway south to the Santa Monica Freeway west, the air seeming cleaner and lighter as the road drops toward sea level after the Twenty-sixth Street exit. He gets off at Fourth Street and takes Pacific to his large studio apartment on the top of a building on the beach.

One wall, almost all window, looks over the boardwalk light poles and palm trees and ocean and is tinted and slanted so it seems part of the outside blueness. The other three walls are black and cracked from earthquakes. There's a desk and a couple futons, one is laid out for sleep and the other

folded up as a reading couch and surrounded by books stacked on the hard-wood floor.

The answering machine is blinking and he hits the play button when he enters. "Hi," a girl's voice says after a long rewind. "I just wanted to know if you were coming to Lesley's tonight, but you're probably going to Justine's or Libby's. Maybe I'll see you somewhere. Hope so. Bye. And Happy New Year."

Beep.

He steps over to the kitchen space and pulls out a bottle of bourbon and ice and a glass.

"Bick, it's Liz. I was feeling kind of depressed so I thought I'd call you."

"Thanks," Bick says back to the machine as he pours.

"I'm sure you're out somewhere," she continues, sounding very down. "I hope you're having fun."

Beep.

"Bick, you *better* come over here." Libby.

Beep.

"I'm on the way to Justine's." Lee is calling from his car phone. "Come by. Should be happening."

Beep.

He sits on the folded futon with his drink and studies a stack of books.

"Hey, Bick, wake up!" Lee is calling again from his car phone, must be the next morning. "Get your overpriced ass out of bed!" Pause. "OK, forget it, you're probably still boning Libby, or some other wench. I heard about your New Year's resolution, pretty funny. Call me when you get home. I have something you want."

Beep.

Bick can't decide whether to read the *Tao Te Ching,* always a good choice in times of confusion, or some Carver or Yeats.

"Bick, James Jankman, Lee tells me you're talking some craziness about retiring." Bick's agent's voice is as distinctive as Walter Cronkite's but he always identifies himself by his full name, which Bick admires. "I hope you were just drunk. Call me at home."

Beep.

"Good morning," Willie says. "Good morning!" Merri yells in the back-ground. "We're just checking on you," Willie says. "Call us," Merri says. "We're at her place," Willie says. "Bye!" Merri yells.

Beep.

Bick decides on Yeats but waits for the messages to end.

"Hi," Libby says. "Call me."

Beep.

"Pick it up, you bum," Mona says. "*You're* the one without a job," Joy yells at her. "Eat me," Mona responds and then says back into the phone, "We

just talked to Willie and Merri and we're all going to have a late lunch at Hugo's. Join us. I'm sure it'll be the shits." As Mona hangs up Joy is yelling, "How can you be a bitch before brunch?"

Beep.

"Bick!" Lee again, from his car phone. "Bick, I know you're there. . . . Pick up. I've got something I know you'll want. . . ."

Beep.

Bick sincerely doubts Lee has something he wants.

"Bick, it's Mother. Haven't spoken with you in a while, so we thought we'd check in. . . . Call us. Good-bye."

Beep.

Bick doesn't know what to say to his parents. They are good and intelligent people with no understanding of what he's doing with his life. If he's writing movies, why isn't he credited on most of these movies? "It's all a mystery to me," Bick always answers. He doesn't measure his success against his peers' but by what he might have done as compared with what he has done. What he's done is make over a million dollars in the last four years. His parents think this is insane. Bick doesn't disagree.

As the machine is rewinding, the phone rings.

"Hello?"

"Got ya."

"Hello, Lee."

"I've lined up Jayne."

"What?"

"I've set up a meeting with her tonight at the West Beach Café. I told her you lived only a couple blocks away. She thought that was cool. She also lives in Venice. I told her you were talking about retirement. She thought that was hilarious. I think she likes the fact that you're playing hard to get."

"I'm not playing anything, Lee."

"Just come meet her. She's got three movies coming out in the next nine months and when these movies are out, she's going to be finger-scorching hot. You've got a chance to work with her before the pressure of it all makes her totally crazy and useless."

Bick can hear traffic over the cellular airwaves.

"Bick?"

"Yeah."

"Just come meet her. What's the worst that could happen?"

What's the worst that could happen, he asks himself, and decides not to answer.

M‌ona leaves the apartment when Joy comes back. She thinks avoiding each other during the day is in the best interest of their friendship. Neither needs to be reminded by the other how directionless her life is, how unemployed she is. It seems worst during the day.

She walks to Hollywood Boulevard and down to the Mann Chinese. As always there are tourists with their cameras gawking at the stars on the sidewalk. She thinks they ought to be arrested. *The Naked Gun* is playing in half an hour, but there's already a line and she's already seen it. *January Man* is playing in an hour, but she thinks John Patrick Shanley is a sham and she'd rather just keep moving down the street to the Mann Vogue, where *Pumpkinhead* is playing. She lights a cigarette as she walks past the stores with windows full of neon and posters and Hollywood icons, *junk*.

A job is what she needs. The plan was to graduate, secure a job as a reader at a studio, make contacts, quickly ascend the ranks to president and be fired and start an independent production company. She told fellow film students she was going to be Irving Thalberg with tits. The plan has gone wrong at stage one. Thousands of people are applying for reader jobs and a film degree means what her parents always told her it would mean: nothing. Now she needs money so bad she's willing to settle for a job outside the industry, but even a decent waitressing job is hard to come by in this town. As she continues down the sidewalk, she sees more tourists with cameras, kids without futures and unemployed people like herself.

She's strolling by a long row of magazine racks when the answer screams from one of the skin rags: phone sex. People always tell her what a sexy throaty voice she has. She'll be a natural. It'll pay the rent until she finds a real job. She drops her cigarette without stepping on it and for three quarters buys a copy of the *Hollywood Press*. A scraggly man with sunglasses and a beard watches her do this and so she moves on quickly, feeling like a pervert.

Stopping at a coffee shop she's never been in before, she sits at a table for two and orders soup and a Coke and peruses the *Hollywood Press*. The front page is in color, featuring a Spanish girl with bleached blond hair and abnormally large breasts. Much to Mona's amazement there's an article about Jim Henson and The Muppets on page 3. She turns the page to movie reviews of legitimate films. She suspects she's been gypped, but the next page has a letters section called "Masturbatory Mail Bag" and the page after that is chock-full of naked tramps in ads for 976 numbers and she knows she's reading the right paper.

The "Job Offers" section mostly offers opportunities for nude "modeling." This is followed by blatant ads for prostitutes. The girls all claim to be eighteen and are interested in "generous gentlemen."

The next section, "Specialties," has ads with subtitles like GOLDEN SHOWERS, PRIVATE ENEMAS and EMASCULATING HUMILIATION as well as abbreviated sex-act expressions Mona can't decipher.

Her soup and Coke arrive. The old waitress does not seem to notice Mona's reading material. Sipping the Coke, Mona spots the line she's looking for: POSITIONS AVAILABLE. Cum Talk is the name of the live phone-sex company with positions available. Mona can hear the party conversation now:

"What do you do?"

"I work for Cum Talk."

This makes her smile and helps her get out of the chair and go to the phone in back. For some reason she doesn't want to make this call from home. Standing next to a mop and a bucket, she dials. After Mona explains she's interested in a job, she is forwarded to "Brooke." Brooke is very polite, with a vaguely New England accent. Brooke asks Mona simple questions, like how long has she been in her current residence. Mona says, "Seven months," and this impresses Brooke. It seems they look for girls who stay in one place for a time because Cum Talk installs a separate phone line and other costly equipment and often girls just get up and leave after Cum Talk has made this investment.

"I moved out here after I graduated from NYU," Mona tells her.

"What did you study?"

It's just like meeting parents' friends. "Psychology," Mona lies clumsily. "I'm going to grad school at UCLA."

"This should be interesting for you, then."

"I'm looking forward to it."

"Let me give you some information."

Brooke explains that the men call on the line Cum Talk will install. Mona can work as many or as few hours as she likes, leaving a message when she's off duty. Cum Talk will pay Mona a flat fee plus a percentage. If Mona does her job well, she can expect to make between eighty and one hundred dollars in a nine-hour day, before taxes.

"Sounds OK," Mona says.

Then Brooke asks Mona how she feels about intercourse and oral sex and such.

"Fine," Mona says. "Normal."

"Anal sex?"

"Over the phone it'll be OK."

Brooke laughs. "Some of the men will sound real creepy," she warns. "You can just disconnect them if they bother you. But remember, the creepy ones are sometimes the most profitable. They become regulars and regulars are your bread and butter."

Mona doesn't expect phone calls from Prince Charles, but if the guys sound too creepy she certainly intends to disconnect them and probably tell them to fuck off, but she just says, "Uh, huh."

"You have a terrific voice," Brooke says. "You'd probably be good with B and D."

"B and D?"

"Bondage and domination. Submissives."

"Right."

"How do you feel about rape?"

"Rape?"

"Rape fantasies are fairly common."

"I'm not real keen on rape."

There's a pause. "Can you deal with that kind of fantasy?"

In a state of horrified fascination Mona makes it through the rest of the conversation. Finally she takes down the address of Cum Talk and says she needs to think it over. Brooke understands.

It takes Mona about two more sips of her Coke to decide there's no way in hell she can do this. It would soon cease to be funny. It could make her hate men for the rest of her life. It could make her hate humans for the rest of her life.

She pays the bill and exits, leaving *Hollywood Press* behind. As she walks back down Hollywood Boulevard, she wonders why the street depresses her so, why she can't see anything glamorous in the decadence and ruin, why she can't be excited by the possibilities of life the way people like Oscar are. Easy for Oscar to be excited by life, she tells herself, he has a job.

O scar is worried he's going crazy. He has been watching the final scenes over and over and over on the Steenbeck and it's doing nothing for him. The guy gets the buxom blond cheerleader and it doesn't work.

It must be almost night outside. "Tell me something, John," he says.

The phone rings and startles him.

He picks up on the second ring, "Hello?"

"There's a friend of yours here to see you," his secretary says. "Mona Cohen."

"Oh." *What the hell does she want?* "Send her down."

"She's already on her way."

"OK, thanks for the warning. By the way, what time is it?"

"A little after six."

"Go home."

"You don't need anything?"

"Go home."

"OK, good night."

"Good night."

As he hangs up, there's a knock on the door.

"Come in."

Mona enters and looks around, smoking. He stays at his seat in front of the Steenbeck.

"Nice equipment," she says. She regards the image on the screen, the boy and girl about to kiss, and says, "You busy? In the middle of a porn film?"

"No, I lock the door when I'm screening porn."

"You ever fuck in here?"

He smiles, "Mona, I'm flattered."

She makes the face he expects. "Don't be. You have an ashtray in here?"

"No."

"Why don't you smoke?"

"I don't have time."

She uses the floor for an ashtray.

"What is it you want?"

"Well, first I wanted to establish some bond with you, I know you guys are into bonding. That's why I asked if you've ever fucked in here. I thought maybe we had something in common we hadn't thought of before. We used to fuck like bunnies in the NYU cutting rooms."

"Seriously?"

"It's very sexy, fucking alongside your movie."

"Maybe I should have gone to film school."

She pulls up one of the other chairs. "I'm looking for a job," she says, lighting another cigarette.

"Why would you want a job? They're overrated."

"It's my New Year resolution, remember?"

This makes him think of that girl . . . fuck, he forgets her name, the White Girl.

"I've been out here a couple months and the only leads I've gotten so far have been for Indie-prod D-girl jobs for men I despise, PA jobs which I've already done and despise, and the free advice that if I get too desperate I should polish up my blow jobs."

"That's good advice."

"I need to find something. Something worthy of someone with my skills and résumé. Head of a studio would be about right, I think, but I'll take almost any job if it's with a producer I could respect and learn from and wouldn't try to fuck me. I don't know. I thought you might be able to suggest somebody I could talk to, a lead."

"You need a job," he says, considering.

"That's genius the way you so succinctly summed up my dilemma."

"Insult me some more. It helps me think."

"That's a nice shot," she says, gesturing to the screen, surprising him with what sounds like a sincere compliment, "but that girl has nothing but Jell-O behind her eyes."

He inspects the girl's eyes, *Jell-O.* This has to be a big part of the problem

with the movie's ending and he saw it before and knew it but didn't quite. "You're right," he admits to her.

"May I," she says, reaching for the control switch.

"Please."

She studies the scene. He watches also, wincing at times, turning to see her reaction.

"Who's the girl in the background," she asks. "The one wistfully gawking at your lead."

"Wally."

"Her name's Wally?"

"The lead's name is Wally. Her name is Anne Ryder. Or do you mean the character?"

Mona nods.

"She plays Wally's confidante."

"Is she hot for him?"

"Yeah, but he's hot for the blond cheerleader."

"Realism, huh."

"I'll screen what I have for you tomorrow."

"That's OK, I think I've seen enough to know the whole story."

"You should see the whole thing if you're going to work on it."

She swivels her chair. "Work on it?"

"You just got the job. Assistant editor *extraordinaire.*"

"No thanks."

"You came looking for a job, and you just got one. Thank me."

"Eat me. I don't want a job as an editing assistant."

"We'll call it something else, then. Assistant vice-president in charge of creative splicing."

"Your other assistants quit when they realized you've got mental problems?"

"I only had one assistant. I do most of my own editing, but the job is pretty much done and I'm working alone now, just cleaning up. I need somebody to be here to help edit but mostly to use as a sounding board."

"Sounding board? You really know how to sweet-talk a woman. No wonder you can't find a girlfriend."

"You know what I mean."

"I'm sure there are plenty of people out there you can pay to tell you you're brilliant."

"Yeah, but you're the only one I can pay to tell me I'm stupid."

"I'll tell you you're stupid for free."

"Listen, I'm serious about this. I'm obviously desperate." He lowers his voice. "I'll tell you a secret: I've got the makings of minor disaster on my hands."

"That's no secret," she says.

"Shit. Really?"

"Everyone knows those hacks wrote a cheesy script. Everyone's looking forward to you flopping with it."

He knows this must be true and it gives him extra incentive. "I'm not going to flop, but I've got a lot of work still to do and I could use some help from someone I can trust. And you need a job. We'll be finished in a month or so. You'll make money and just hanging out here, you'll meet people and if you help me out now, I'll owe you." He pauses. "This is what's called an opportunity."

"Oscar, we don't like each other."

"Of course we like each other, we like the same friends who like us, so there must be something about us that we both must like."

"That made no sense."

"We're friends. Even if you're always on the rag, we're still friends. I trust you. I even almost respect you."

"Oscar, we don't get along!"

"I know!" he yells back. "That's what's brilliant about it."

II

II

*I*t's her, Bick thinks as a taxi pulls up and confuses the red-vested valets. Through the window and across all the white linen and bowed heads he can't really see the person stepping out of the taxi but knows it's her. He has never seen anyone come to a restaurant in LA via taxi. He's sure it's been done before, still it's a good touch.

Just inside the front door she stops suddenly, raising a finger to her mouth and squinting. Bick notices others glancing up at her. Her hair is different from in the movie, though he's not sure how. She is wearing an off-white skirt and T-shirt under a man's black dinner jacket and her socks are red and her legs are very pale. There's a bruise on her shin. Her eyes spot Bick, move to Lee, come back to Bick, seem to open wider and she smiles. Bick smiles and then lights a cigarette. By the time the cigarette is lighted, she's in front of them. Lee air-kisses her. She extends her hand to Bick, "Hi."

"Hello," Bick says, with a half-rise.

He focuses on how very white the hand is and then looks up and her face comes to him in three separate images, red lips, black hair, surprisingly light blue eyes.

She slips in next to Lee. He is nervously stroking his short blond ponytail between his thumb and forefinger. His face is blotchy. "You look great," he says.

"Thank you." Her eyes stay fixed on Bick. "Could I have a cigarette?"

"They're unfiltered," he says and holds up the Camel pack.

"Mmm-hmm." She knows.

He shakes a cigarette out and she takes it and taps it a few times on her big boy's watch and licks her lips before putting it in her mouth, showing him she's smoked these before. He lights a match. She touches his hand and sucks in the tip of the yellow flame and to Bick her moves seem drawn out, slow and stylized. Smoke wafts out of her mouth.

Lips like a remembered kiss.

He isn't sure where he first heard or read the phrase. He makes a mental note to use it in the script but then reminds himself he doesn't want to take this job.

The lack of conversation makes Lee anxious. "Drinks," he says. "Bick can't talk until he's had a drink." He hails a waitress. "Jim Beam and rocks for you," he says to Bick.

"Yes."

"Gin on the rocks," Jayne says.

"Perrier for me," Lee quickly adds.

Bick thinks how easily he could love a girl who orders gin on the rocks.

The waitress asks to see her ID. "I don't have a driver's license," Jayne says. "I don't drive."

The waitress asks if she has some other kind of ID.

"Is this really necessary?" Bick says.

"Sorry," she says. "We had a problem last week."

"I know Jimmy," Lee says indignantly.

"Who's Jimmy," the waitress asks.

"I'll just have water," Jayne says. She smiles at Bick and shrugs. Though she's embarrassed, she somehow uses the awkwardness to her advantage.

"Did you like the script," she asks as soon as the waitress steps away.

"Yes."

"Did you *love* it?"

"I like it."

"I know, but did you *love* it? *Could* you love it?"

Bick just smiles at her enthusiasm.

"*I* could love it," she says. "I just think it needs to be more romantic, especially the ending. The story and characters are great, well, *he's* great, but she needs work. Anyway, I agree with the studio—for a change—that everything's too dark. I told them I'd do it if the script were rewritten with more romance and wit and I've read some of your work so I told them you were the one they wanted."

Scripts are often rewritten to suit an actor, because the right cast can turn a script like *Rain Man*—which almost every writer in town was paid to fuck

with—into blockbuster Academy Award material, but Bick wonders if this is what this young actress wants or what the studio has told her she wants.

"What do you mean by more romantic," he asks.

"Moments," she says. "I like the edginess and sexiness of the script, but I think it could use some more romantic moments, romance instead of just lust. Also, the ending. I *don't* think it's a romantic honeymoon when he throws the heater in the bathtub and fries her."

"How about when he dives in to join her corpse?"

Jayne shakes her head, making a face.

"Honest enough way to end the story," Bick says.

"And now the writer's in jail with tattooed love boys."

He smiles. "What do you think would be a more romantic way to end this story?"

"Maybe if he kills just himself," she says, watching his reaction, then laughs and says, "No, I think they should be together in the end, together and alive. They want and need each other and they belong together, right?"

Bick nods.

"So he should forgive her and they should get back together. Then it would be a comedy instead of a tragedy and that's what we want, isn't it?"

He's not sure what she means by "we" but doesn't ask because he's concentrating on the way her red lips are manipulating her cigarette, forties movie-star style.

"Can you do it," she asks.

"What?"

"The rewrite."

"Yeah."

She smiles, he smiles back. He feels like they're communicating but has no idea what they're saying.

"That's it," Lee jokes nervously. "Done deal."

"What did you think of the scene where she tries to seduce him into not going to that party," she asks, ignoring Lee. "And he freaks out and tells her not to use herself that way."

The waitress brings the drinks. Bick shakes his glass and has a long swallow. He scrutinizes the Surf Christmas artwork and wonders why it's still up and what will come next.

Jayne says something about sex and pain—he refocuses on her. What exactly she says doesn't matter much because he already knows what she wants in *Till Death Do Us Part.* He realizes she sees herself the actress as the adolescent girl in the story throwing tantrums to be loved, and he knows that what she wants in the script is what she wants and not necessarily what the studio wants, a potential problem, but she's making amazingly effective eye contact

with him at the right moments, hinting at the possibility of promises fulfilled. She's nothing if not a pro. Bick knows but doesn't mind.

"What's the difference between BMWs and porcupines," Jayne asks as the valet pulls up in Bick's car. "With porcupines," she smiles, "the pricks are on the outside."

The valet opens the passenger door. She gets in and Bick pays the valet, who hustles around to his side after staring at Jayne's legs.

"Lee told me you were talking about retiring," she says when he climbs inside. "But I just assumed he was lying."

"He tells the truth occasionally," Bick says, shifting into gear. "Just to confuse us."

"He's one of the most uncool people I've ever met."

Bick nods.

"But he can be helpful, dealing with the studio."

"Except they don't take him seriously," Bick says, "since he's never produced a decent movie."

"Doesn't matter," she says, "all they care about is if you've done *something,* no matter how bad."

Bick reminds himself that this girl may be younger but has been in the business half her life and knows it better than he.

"Where to," he asks as they turn onto Pacific.

"Left on Venice Way. You did the rewrite on Lee's one hit, didn't you?"

Bick nods.

"What's your full name?"

"Lyle Milton Smith. Thanks Mom, Dad."

"Bick," she says. "I guess it's an improvement. Who came up with it?"

"High-school friends. Shortly before I moved down here. It's a long story."

And instead of asking him to explain, she says, "Wanna know where I got my name?"

He nods. If she would rather talk about herself than him, that makes two of them.

"Kiss the Sky," she says. "Which I changed to Jayne Sky. Jayne with a *y.*"

"Kiss the sky? Your parents eat a lot of acid?"

"Yeah. It's from 'Purple Haze.'"

"I know," he says. "'Acting funny but I don't know why, excuse me while I kiss the sky.' When I was young, a friend told me Hendrix was a fag and the line was 'excuse me while I kiss this guy.'"

She laughs. "Did you believe him?"

"No."

"How old were you?"

"I don't remember, pretty young."

"You look pretty young now. How old are you?"

"I'm almost thirty." He doesn't want to scare her, so he adds, "twenty-eight."

"You're still young. My parents are a lot older than you and they're still infants."

"How old are you," he asks.

Lee has told him twenty-one, but that was probably a lie. Bick would've guessed around eighteen.

"Doesn't matter," she says, turning on the radio.

Bick imagines she'll be the type to try every station the buttons offer in five seconds. She immediately turns the radio back off.

"Take a right here," she says.

He does and takes the opportunity to look both ways and catch a good profile of her lips.

"I really appreciate this," she says.

"My pleasure."

"This is it."

She lives in a house on one of the Venice canals, a one-story with bars on the windows. He idles outside the front door.

"Are you coming in?"

"Right."

Unlocking two locks she leads him in the front and he's not unexcited. "I want you to do something," she says, closing the door behind him.

"Oh?"

He looks around as she leads him in. There's an American flag on the wall, multicolored paint, wicker furniture and lots of books and records, the old vinyl kind. The focal point of the room is a big rainbow bong. *My God*, he thinks, *this is a hippie house.*

"It's my parents'," Jayne says. "Kinda groovy, huh?"

"Kind of historical."

"They're spending the year in Marrakech," she says, "or someplace else from a Crosby, Stills, Nash and Young song."

Bick doesn't see anything that could be hers.

"I'm just living here temporarily," she explains as she steps over to a book-shelf, "while my house is being worked on."

She pulls out a hardcover. Bick is jolted—it's the collection of short stories he wrote before he knew about real money. She hands it to him.

"I've already read it," he says.

"Sign it."

He takes out a razor-point felt pen from his blazer and has no idea what to write.

"It's a first edition," she says.

"I'm not even sure *I* have a first edition."

"My parents bought it. They were really into it."

"Hmmm." Bick makes a show of surveying the room. "Your parents have interesting taste."

She laughs.

He opens the book to the contents page. "I haven't signed one of these in five years."

"I read it a long time ago," she says. "A couple of the stories were among the best I've ever read."

"Don't read much, huh?"

She smiles. "I read a lot. They were good stories."

"No, some weren't."

"But some were. I totally *loved* 'To Want and Want and Want.'"

"Thank you," he says. "But there was a fourth want."

"'To Want and Want and Want and *Want*'?"

"Right."

"Why so many stories about karate and Zen and drugs and stuff?"

"Lack of imagination."

She laughs. He thinks it's sincere, but he's not sure.

"It's what I was doing at the time," he says.

"You're Catholic?"

"Yes."

"And you're a black belt?"

"Not anymore, I don't train anymore. If I returned to the dojo I would wear a white belt."

"Until the *sensei* thinks you've earned the right to wear your old black belt."

"Right."

"See. I remember from your stories."

"Yes."

"And why all the drugs?"

"Metaphor."

She laughs. "Sign it."

He stares at the page.

"Your *name*," she says. "Sign your name."

Inspired by his surroundings, he writes, "Love and Peace, Bick Smith," and thinks there ought to be a typeface that implies cynicism and facetiousness so that future generations can understand the dominant tone of the times.

"Thank you," she says and puts it back on the shelf without opening it to check what he wrote.

Stepping up just behind, he looks over her shoulder at the books. He is always shocked to see his book between Salinger and Steinbeck.

"I should alphabetize my library someday," he says.

"Do you have a lot of books?"

She is staying very close to him.

"Yeah," he says.

"How do you find a book you're looking for?"

"I have the order sort of memorized."

They are still close. He is staring at book spines and not seeing a single title.

"Did you always want to be a writer?"

"No, I wanted to be a drug dealer, but things changed."

"Too bad. Do you still write stories?"

"No, just scripts."

"Are you going to write a novel?"

"No."

"No?"

"Even F. Scott Fitzgerald said movies had greater potential than the novel. Turned out to be wrong, of course, but still, as you know, the movies pay wonderfully."

"Money can't be that important to you."

"Of course it can. I'm a good American."

"No," she insists, "money's not that important to you."

He turns to face her. "You've known me how long? A couple hours?"

"I can tell," she says. "Am I wrong?"

But she's not waiting for an answer. She picks up a book and opens it in the middle and nudges her nose inside and sniffs deeply. "Mmmmmm," she says. "I just love the smell of old books." She puts the book in front of his face.

"Drugs in there," he asks.

She laughs and pushes the paper closer to his nose. He sniffs. He's not sure what he smells, aged pages, or her perfume, or her, but he's sure he's smelling sex in some way and his heart is beating fast like he's just sucked up a gram. She pulls the book away and her face is right there.

She wants you to kiss her, he says to himself. *And you want to kiss her in a way you haven't wanted to kiss in a long time.*

"I wish we could just stay up all night and watch the sun rise," she says, her voice suddenly resonating with the possibility of unspeakable sensations.

"Sounds good."

"But I have to get up for some stupid meeting early tomorrow morning."

He feels like she just slipped in a quick kick to his balls. There's no sensible reason for this feeling and he shows no reaction.

She puts the musky book back on the shelf and steps away. "I'm going to twentysomething tomorrow night with some friends," she says. "Are you going to be there?"

"I hadn't planned on it."

"You know where it is?"

"Oh yeah."

"Come."

"Maybe."

They are walking back to the front door.

"I hope you do," she says and suddenly kisses him on the lips, quickly, but long enough for him to taste her and suffer. "We'll talk about the script. Or something."

"Uh-huh," he says.

He'd like the "or something" to be their lives together.

"Good night," she says.

"Good night."

She closes the door on her smile.

He walks to his car, dazed. He puts the key in the ignition but doesn't turn it. Instead he clasps his hands together on the top of the steering wheel. He doesn't want to go home. His usually well-controlled senses have been stirred up and they're famished.

Libby's lying on her king-sized bed watching "The Love Connection." A vibrator lies on the other side of the bed. A heavily made-up girl on the giant Mitsubishi TV is describing her ideal man. *"I like blonds, good bodies, money's good too, but mostly I just want someone who really, really, really loves me."* Libby feels a combination of pity and envy. The phone rings and she turns the sound off with the remote and answers, "Hello."

"Hello, it's me."

"Who?" It's a bad connection.

"Who do you think?" It's Bick.

"Where are you? I can hardly hear you."

"I'm close. I'm at a phone booth on Sunset."

He wants to come over. "Why?" she says.

"You want to meet for a drink somewhere?"

"I'm in bed."

"That's as good a place to meet as any."

She laughs, knowing she should say no and not wanting to say no.

"I'm coming over," he says.

She hangs up and turns off the TV.

They both know what he's doing here so the first greeting kiss becomes a greeting grope right there in the hall, with the front door still open. Suddenly he unbuttons her button-down and takes it off and she has no bra. She unbut-

tons his button-down. Her breasts press against his ribs. A car's headlights flash by, lighting the scene. He makes a move to close the front door and she stops him by grabbing his belt and undoing it and unbuttons his Levi's while he unbuttons hers. His boxers are white and her legs are tan and his aren't. Another pair of headlights flash by fast. Two pairs of white underwear are on the cool marble floor along with four hands in front of her face and several drops of sweat despite the night air and there's a siren growing louder and screaming over Libby's own voice. White and red and blue lights flash by. When the siren fades away, Libby moans, starting to notice the pain in her knees.

"You're such a slut," she says to him.

They're sitting in the steaming Jacuzzi. He knows he shouldn't have done this and Jayne shouldn't be on his mind.

"I'm not a slut," he says, and rests his head on her shoulder.

"*I'm* a slut," she continues. "I just let you come over here and fuck me."

"I came over here for affection," he says, lifting his head. "And I was raped."

She laughs. He reaches over for his beer. The steam rising into the clear night clouds his view of the city lights. She's drinking Evian. He toasts her with his beer can.

"What are we drinking to," she asks.

"The new year, I guess."

"How's your New Year's resolution coming?"

"I'm doing another studio assignment."

She smiles. "A rewrite or an original?"

"Rewrite."

"What?"

"Called *Till Death Do Us Part*."

"Haven't heard of it. What's it about?"

"Love story, two people torturing each other."

"I'm glad you're going to be around for a while."

He puts his arms back on the ledge and lifts and tries to float his body on the bubbles.

"I think my New Year's resolution should have been to quit acting," Libby says.

"What *was* your New Year's resolution?"

"To get a part. Looks like I'm already dropping out of the resolutions race."

"Why are you suddenly thinking about quitting?"

"It's not sudden. I've just been thinking, if a boyfriend treated me the way my career has, I'd break up with him."

Bick laughs.

"I was at this audition today," she says, "for a small part. One line."

"One line?"

"But the character's in this party scene, so it would be like a two-week shoot and the star's Chevy Chase and maybe if they like me in the audition, they'll consider me for a larger part, right? Anyway, I'm there and I read my one line for the producers and the casting director. Fine. They've seen me. They've heard me. Time to go home? No. They make me read this *one line* about ten times. And these cretins are sitting there watching me, like they're *pondering* this big character. It's one line!" She's laughing. "OK," she continues, "I do it sexy, I do it bitchy, I do it humorous, I do it loud, I do it quiet and cool, hard and soft, deadpan, you name it. I even try just screeching psychotically. Finally one of the producers looks at me, real serious, and he says, 'How do you look in glasses?' I couldn't even answer. I just burst out laughing and they started laughing too, thank God. I think the absurdity of it all finally occurred to them. These grown men spending their day listening to me deliver one line. Like it really fucking *matters*."

"You'll probably get the part."

"No," she says. "*No*. I don't *want* the part. I don't want to spend my life that way. You know what the one line was?"

"How would I?"

"Guess."

"How many words?"

"Four."

"Four words." He remembers a song. "'Let's go to bed?'"

"No," she says, shaking her head, about to laugh some more. "'Get a real life.'"

And they both laugh and shake their heads.

"Yeah," he finally says, "I could see how you could take that as a cue."

"I don't know why I ever wanted to be an actress anyway. I don't need the money, obviously."

"What was it, then? I've wondered."

"Don't you know, these days you have to be rich *and* famous." She's laughing and he's grateful for that. "What happened to the good old days when it was enough to just be rich?"

Bick doesn't respond to this.

"Something to do," she says, "I guess."

She climbs up out of the Jacuzzi and throws her wet dark-blond hair back and he watches the water drip off at the top of her thighs and, from his low angle, catches a quick cut of her pudenda. She turns around, smiling, obviously aware he's watching. Her extraordinarily good skin is goose-pimpling in the light breeze.

"'Get a real life,'" she says, still laughing but not as truly.

Whenever Willie enters a bank he thinks about robbing it. He cases the joint: several circuit video cameras, no armed guard in sight. It wouldn't be difficult to whip out a pistol and yell for everyone to drop and then leap the cashier's wall and fill a bag with money from all the drawers. Some do-gooder would probably trigger a silent alarm, but he would still have at least a minute to collect the cash and split. This would probably be the quickest and best way. However, he imagines a better scenario from a dramatic standpoint: he and his heavily armed comrades burst in spewing bullets and revolutionary slogans and hold everybody hostage for a week and demand in the name of the People and the Revolution that "Charles in Charge" never appear on television ever again.

"Let's see, who are we supposed to talk to?"

"You asking me?" Willie says. "I don't know. Fuck."

"I know what's going on here, don't panic."

He and Merri are standing just inside the busy lobby. They are here for a home loan and he hasn't the vaguest idea what this involves. Merri, he assumes, does. Willie suggested they let their business managers handle it, but Merri insisted on doing it this way, for the experience.

When she took him with a real estate broker to check out houses, he pretended to like the one she liked because it obviously made her so happy. He didn't realize it would make her want to buy the damn thing.

"I hope we don't have to get in line," Willie says.

"No," Merri assures him. "And get rid of that candy bar and take off your sunglasses. Look serious."

He takes off the sunglasses and drops the candy wrapper in an ashtray and lights a cigarette. He has been craving sugar and cigarettes since he quit drinking. She leads him over to the side of the big fluorescent-lighted room where there are older men and women sitting behind desks. Willie feels like people are starting to stare. He doesn't know if this is because people recognize him or Merri or because the two of them look so confused.

"Can I help you," a woman behind a desk asks.

"We would like to speak with someone regarding a home loan," Merri says in a voice Willie hardly recognizes.

"Mr. Warner will be happy to help you," the woman says, gesturing to an older man who's on the phone. There are two chairs in front of his desk. "Why don't you sit down there and I'm sure he'll be with you shortly."

"Thank you," Merri says.

"Thanks," Willie says.

The woman smiles insincerely and looks back down at her paperwork.

Merri and Willie hover over to Mr. Warner's desk and Mr. Warner gestures for them to sit while he continues to talk on the phone. They sit. Mr. Warner is saying something about debt-to-obligation ratios. Willie notices the American flag in a corner beneath one of the video cameras. The big clock on the wall reminds him of a grammar-school clock. Merri nudges him and points to a picture of a woman and a little boy and little girl in a photo on the desk, Mr. Warner's family. Inside, Willie shudders at the thought, but he smiles and nods. Merri rubs her hands nervously on her dress, a very prim and not very attractive dress he has never seen her wear before. She insisted he wear a blue blazer. He said he didn't have one. She told him to borrow one from Bick. Bick told him to go to Brooks Brothers, where he bought a three-button model off the rack. It's heavy and baggy and doesn't fit quite right. *So,* he thinks, *we're just sitting in this horribly lit room in ill-fitting clothes in front of a man with anchors on his tie.*

Mr. Warner finally hangs up. "Sorry about that," he says and rises and sticks out his hand to shake. "Hello." Willie and Merri rise and shake his hand and then the three of them sit back down in quick one, two, three order.

"What can I help you with," Mr. Warner asks.

"Do you have an ashtray?" Willie says.

"Uh, yes, certainly," Mr. Warner pulls an ashtray out of his drawer. It looks brand-new.

"Thank you," Willie says.

"Anything else I can help you with?" Mr. Warner smiles.

Willie thinks about asking for something to drink, but Merri speaks up too

quickly. "We're buying a house," she says. "We've picked it out, but we haven't made an offer yet, but the broker told us how much we can get it for and it's still for sale, so we thought we should see about a loan." She sounds a little nervous, but business-like.

"You want to secure financing before you make an offer, then, is that correct?"

Willie looks at Merri.

"Yes." She nods.

Mr. Warner reaches into a drawer and pulls out some forms, which he puts in front of Willie and Merri, closer to Willie. Willie shoves them over to Merri.

"We start by filling out that form," Mr. Warner says. "You can do it here, or take it home and fill it out at your leisure."

"Let's take it home," Willie says to Merri.

Merri is looking at the form. "Wait," she says to Willie. She looks up at Mr. Warner. "Maybe we should do it here so we can ask you questions if necessary. If that's OK?"

"That'll be fine." He hands her a pen. "You can use this desk. I'll be back in a moment to answer any of your questions."

"One quick question. Can you tell me exactly how much more our monthly payments will be if we put, say, thirty percent down instead of fifty? Or maybe even forty percent down?"

"Of course," he says, picking up a little book. "How much did the broker expect you'll have to pay for this house."

"Three and a quarter. It's optimistic, but that's how much we're going to offer."

"Let's start with how much your payments would be if you put down twenty percent. Eighty percent of three twenty-five would be . . ." he punches it into a desk calculator. "Two hundred and sixty thousand." He refers to the book. "A thirty year loan at—" He looks up.

"Excuse me," Merri says, "but when I said three and a quarter I didn't mean three hundred and twenty-five thousand."

"What did you mean?"

"Three and a quarter million."

"You want to buy a house for three and a quarter million dollars," he says slowly. "That would require a down payment of at least—" he puts the numbers into the calculator—"six hundred and fifty thousand dollars."

"Our business manager says we should do something with the money."

"Otherwise it gets blown on drugs," Willie says.

Merri jams her heel into his arch. "He's kidding," she says to Mr. Warner.

"What we should do now," Mr. Warner says, neutrally, "is fill out the form and take it from there."

She fills in the amount on the form but stops at the next question. After a

few moments she looks up at Willie. "What's my phone number?" Then she turns to Mr. Warner, who looks suddenly uncomfortable. "I just changed it because of psycho phone calls."

Mr. Warner nods, apparently deciding to stay and watch Merri labor over the form.

Willie rests his chin on her shoulder. "This looks like a really hard test," he says.

Merri pushes him away, but he can tell there was almost a giggle. She fills in the easy details quickly, address, Social Security number, profession.

"Banking relationships," she says, "credit experiences?"

"Just fill in where you bank and the account numbers," Mr. Warner advises. "Under credit experiences list your credit cards and any other loans you've had."

Merri nods. "Assets?"

"Comic timing," Willie says and Merri suddenly giggles and he laughs.

"Maybe it would be a good idea if you went over the application at your leisure, at home," Mr. Warner suggests, "or with your business manager."

Merri refuses to talk to Willie as they walk through the parking lot. She seems angrier now than the time he fucked her little sister.

"I'm sorry," he tries. "I didn't realize this was so important to you, that you were so serious about it."

She steps ahead of him.

"We're still going to get the loan, you know. And we can buy the goddamn house even if we *don't* get a loan."

"That's not the point."

"What *is* the point?"

She won't tell him.

When they pull the Jaguar convertible Willie bought for her last birthday to the gate, they realize they forgot to get their parking ticket validated.

"Twelve dollars," the man in the booth says.

"Fuck that," Willie says.

He jumps out of the car and runs into the bank and asks a youngish not-bad-looking girl at a desk to stamp his ticket. He had noticed her watching him on his way out.

"Are you Willie John Paul," she asks, taking the ticket.

"Willie Paul," he corrects her. "The John is just for SAG."

"I'm a big fan of yours."

"Thank you." He smiles. She's cute and he can see down her blouse.

"Your last movie really sucked though."

He nods. She's not wrong, but this is not a good time for "At the Movies."

"You were great anyway," she adds.

"Thank you."

"Was that your girlfriend you were in here with," she asks. She has made no motion to stamp the ticket.

"Yeah."

"What's she do?"

"She's an actress."

"What's she been in?"

"Her car. She's waiting for me in the car right now."

She smiles, then writes some numbers on the ticket and stamps it. Happening to lick something off her lips as she hands the ticket back to him, she says, "I think you're really funny. And sexy."

"Thank you." He practically has to jerk the ticket out of her hand. "Be good." He quickly exits.

Merri has moved the car out of line. He hands her the ticket.

"What's this," Merri says, looking at the numbers on the ticket as she pulls the car up to the gate.

"Phone number, I suppose."

"Whose?"

"The girl who stamped my ticket."

"Not a bright girl," Merri says, handing the ticket to the man in the booth.

$\mathbf{B}$ick is trying to keep the day out. His blinds are closed and the room is dark except for the gray light of the black-and-white movie playing on the VCR. He's on the futon watching *Baby Doll* for the third time, remote control in one hand and a glass of bourbon in the other.

Eli Wallach and Carroll Baker rock gently on a porch swing. He asks about her husband, she's uncomfortable. He edges from his side to hers, his left hand grasping a pole, his right sliding around her shoulder onto her bare arm. Talk turns to her, the rocking slows. The camera cuts in tighter, now her hand is on the pole. His left hand caresses the skin above her breasts, his right hand is out of view and something sexy seems to be steaming outside the frame, because Baker's breath is erratic, her lips open.

Bick read somewhere the scene was shot on a cold winter day.

When they rise from the swing the seduction continues, but Bick sets down his bourbon and the remote and picks up a Venus no. 2 pencil. There is something about how sex is used in *Baby Doll* he thinks he can use in *Till Death Do Us Part.* He jots notes on a yellow legal pad. ***Feelings of isolation and longing. Desire against b.g. of decaying country. Microcosm. Save themselves?***

He feels he needs to know Jayne better to do this well. Somehow he feels

if he becomes close enough to her, he might know and understand her secrets, the sort of secrets he always suspects are linked to larger secrets, the secret truths of love and sex and existence itself.

He sets down the pencil and picks up the bourbon.

The screen goes dark and Oscar and Mona sit silently. It pained him to watch the movie again. He had to avert his eyes during several scenes.

"You did some really interesting things," Mona finally says. "Some incredible images and camera moves."

"It's a flat failure."

"Right."

"You don't feel anything for him and her at the end?"

"No."

"Fuck."

"You don't feel anything for anybody."

"Nobody?"

"You've stripped these characters of any humanity."

"Any?"

"They're just props for you."

"I think you're overdoing this."

"I don't want you to underestimate just how totally this movie misses."

"Thanks."

After a long pause she asks seriously, "What went wrong?"

"I don't know," he says. "There was a time when so many people were

telling me so much shit and . . . I don't know, I fucked up. This is the movie I thought I should make next. I was out of my goddamn mind."

"Must have been."

"Hey, it's not like I was being offered the next Nicholson and Streep movie. I didn't turn down Hoffman and Cruise and *Rain Man*. I was being offered more high-school movies."

"I thought you were *hot*," Mona says, laughing.

"Fuck off."

"OK. Who's seen this so far?"

"Just people who worked on it, and a couple executives I trust. And my agent."

"What did they think?"

"They said it's brilliant as is."

"They're wrong."

"I know."

"Has Bick seen it?"

Oscar shakes his head.

"Why don't you find out what he thinks?"

"I know what he'll think. He'll think I should have hired him to rewrite it."

"How about Willie and Merri?"

"They'll think the same thing. Plus they'll think they should have played the leads."

"That would have helped."

"All three of them were busy at the time and I couldn't afford them anyway." He pulls his feet off the chair in front. "We'll all have a chance to work together later if I can figure out a way to not end my career with this turkey."

"Is someone going to turn on the lights?"

Oscar doesn't answer.

Mona uses the ashtray built into the arm of the chair. "Screening rooms remind me of New York," she says. "The thing I love about New York is you can smoke in the theaters."

"What the fuck am I going to do?"

"How soon do you have before the test screening?"

"A few weeks."

"Plenty of time."

"To what? Choose a new career?"

"Reshoot the ending. So Wally ends up with the cool geeky girl rather than the bimbo cheerleader."

Though Mona is not telling him anything he didn't know, he needs to hear it anyway. He needs to believe the importance of this strongly so he can sell it

to the studio executives, who have to make the money decisions. He needs to psych up his confidence. He wishes he hadn't thrown away the White Girl's phone number.

"I'll story-board a new ending tonight," he says. "I've got nothing else to do."

Mona parks Joy's car in the mini-mall parking lot. They light cigarettes as they walk across the deserted side street to the unmarked twentysomething entrance, where people stand loosely lined up in front of the graffiti-littered brick wall.

"What I've always liked most about this," Mona says, "is that it's a perfect place for a drive-by shooting."

Joy starts shaking as they step into line, but she doesn't let Mona see. She had been preparing herself for the fact that Tim would not be at the door to usher them inside, but still. She hates this.

"Don't they know who I am," one girl jokes. "I'm a first cousin of Imelda Marcos."

"I'm Cher's gynecologist," a guy answers.

"This is insane," Mona says.

Joy nods, "Maybe we should have gone to Java or that other place, the Pick You Up."

"Coffee makes me fucking insane. I need a drink."

"I wonder if the others are already here?"

"Well, at least the Beverly Hills chapter of Hell's Angels is here." Mona tosses her cigarette butt toward a row of shiny Harleys on the sidewalk, then lights another. "Why are boys such *nimrods?*"

"I don't know. What exactly is a nimrod?"

"I don't know."

Mona starts talking about Oscar's movie, but Joy doesn't listen. She knows Mona is trying to distract her and the effort is nice even if it's not working. She doesn't know why she suggested everyone meet here. A reward flier on the building wall offers $$$ for information leading to the arrest of the driver of a jeep who ran down a motorcyclist.

"The kind of guy who would drive a jeep probably has the kind of friend that will turn him in for a reward," Mona says, reading over Joy's shoulder.

"What a shitty way to die," Joy says.

"Joy, Mona!" One of the owners, Brad, comes out and sees them and mercifully motions them inside.

They go down the stairs without paying and into the cavernous smoky basementlike space. Young and not-so-young people, actors to lawyers, black leather to white button-downs, all are standing around talking and drinking or dancing under a small mirrored disco ball to vintage early eighties Soft Cell, "Tainted Love."

The room smells, as usual, dank.

Dank is how Tim described it to Joy.

At the bar a tall Star Wars cooler bubbles with the Scary Blue Fluid. Some people drink this. Mona and Joy don't. Mona asks the hyper guy behind the bar for a beer. It's served from a keg in plastic cups. It's free and Joy leaves a dollar tip.

They say hello to a few people Joy vaguely knows and make their way to the steps. As they wind up the stairs through pairs conversing, they pass Clock Girl, who Joy always finds spooky for some reason. Upstairs is better lighted and less crowded and there are tables.

Merri and Willie are here with Libby, Bick and Oscar. Bick and Willie pull up chairs for Mona and Joy. Merri wears a bizarre hat with floppy daisies. Willie is drinking water, or straight vodka.

They all talk about Willie and Merri buying a house and Bick staying in town for another job and though Joy isn't surprised he's not leaving right away, this bothers her. The music is very loud. Mona calls Glenn Frey a totally soulless moron for doing some commercial. Not everyone is convinced he's a totally soulless moron, but they do agree Frey was much cooler with his seventies look and find it disturbing that a coauthor of "Hotel California" now looks like a professional wrestler. Politics comes up. Oscar starts in on CAA, saying CAA and the Republicans are the same kind of animal—wanting power for power's sake, not knowing how to do any good with it. Willie says George Bush will be a good president because to prove he's not a wimp he'll probably blow up the world and this, Joy agrees, is the right thing to do. Willie repeats a Dan Quayle joke from David Letterman. Merri and Libby joke about registering voters on college campuses and being asked which political party Ronald

Reagan belongs to. They decide music and movies and books are more interesting and important and tell more about the country than politics because more people they know buy records and go to movies than vote. For some reason this makes Joy think about doing laundry. Cal, Brad's boyfriend and co owner of the club, comes by and says hello. A young actress comes by to pontificate about AA, "the only club worth joining." Mona has a coughing fit. Cal chuckles and moves on to the next table.

Joy tries to remember what she used to like about coming here, then remembers: leaving. She liked being with Tim and going someplace where it was just the two of them.

"Let's go to Canter's," she says. She can't stand being here another minute. Food sounds good, just picking up the fork and stabbing the food and putting it in your mouth over and over.

Everyone agrees except for Bick, who says he has to stay because he's waiting for someone.

"Who," Mona asks.

"Jesus Christ," Bick says.

"Oh," Merri says. "Get his autograph for my mom."

"If he's boring," Mona says. "Come to Canter's for potato pancakes."

Joy has killed a thousand nights at Canter's, but tonight she notices how truly horrific the ceiling is—what she had always thought was just bad abstract art is actually a tree branch with leaves. Dozens of brightly lighted squares overflow with the same fucking tree branch. She can't stand staring at it and returns her attention to the table.

"He shot Ronald Reagan," Libby is saying.

"I heard about that," Crispin says. "But I forgot the name."

"Loves Jodie Foster," Libby adds.

"Kelly McGillis?" Crispin answers.

"Let's try a different approach," Libby says. "First name. Star of . . ."

"What? What? Star of . . . how about a hint here?" Crispin is frantic.

"A religious star. Star of . . ."

"'The Jim and Tammy Bakker Show.'"

Libby shakes her head, Crispin is not even warm.

They are playing Celebrity. The group is divided into three teams of two. There's Merri and Willie, Mona and Joy, and Libby and Crispin Glover, whom Libby recruited from a nearby table. Libby has picked a name from a bowl that was full of Mona's matzo-ball soup a few minutes ago but now contains the names of semicelebrities written on folded slips of ripped napkin. The idea is to identify as many names as possible per one-minute round, but Libby and Crispin are still struggling with their first.

"A religious star," Libby repeats. "The kind in the sky. Star of . . ."

"Bethlehem!"

"Keep coming."

"Uh—"

"Jewish icon."

"Star of David! David—"

"Second name. Two syllables. Second syllable is the first name of the person we know as Blond Ambition."

"Lee Chassler."

"Lee. Right."

"Hey," Mona says.

"What?" Libby says. "He had it."

"Come on!" Crispin says, squirming.

"First syllable, rhymes with 'pink.'"

"David blank Lee," Crispin says, clutching his head.

"Ten seconds," Mona says.

"Rhymes with 'pink,'" Libby repeats.

"Sink. David Sinklee!"

"Keep coming!"

"OK, OK, OK." He shakes his dark hair over his face. "I'm almost there."

"Five seconds."

"Come on!"

"I'm almost there!"

"Time," Mona says.

"David Hinckley," Libby says.

"I knew it!" Crispin bangs his hands on the table.

The others are laughing.

"It's *John* Hinckley," Mona says.

"It is?" Libby says.

"Yes."

"Oh."

"I *knew* there was something wrong," Crispin says and bangs his hands on the table again, harder. A knife rattles off onto the floor.

Joy stares at the knife, thinking if she cared any less about this game her eyes would pop out of her skull.

Bick hangs out at twentysomething for hours, drinking and smoking and talking to various acquaintances. Dunphy, who is reluctantly writing a sequel to *Ernest Goes to Camp,* pulls up a chair. Dunphy is hilarious and welcome. He wears a T-shirt stenciled with the faces of the "Brady Bunch" girls: Marcia, Jan, and Cindy. He stops attractive girls and gives them his version of a personality test by asking which is their favorite Brady girl. They usually look back suspiciously, but he persists and his friendliness is so surprising it works.

Dunphy improvises but generally if a girl says Marcia, he tells her she's domineering, possibly sadistic. If she says Jan, he tells her she's confused and lost. If she says Cindy, he just shakes his head. "You're going to have a sad life." After several amusing conversations Dunphy exits with a girl who says she's the real sister of Eve Plumb, the actress who played Jan.

Later, an actor who has just returned from an ashram in India joins Bick. He bums a cigarette and they discuss the difficulty of applying Eastern principles to Western life, particularly in this town. "Or any principles at all for that matter," Bick says.

The actor laughs, agreeing. He still plans to continue his meditating though. "It's like washing your car even though it gets dirty again," he says.

Others come to the table, say what they have to say and then go say it to someone else. An actress kisses and hugs Bick and tells him about her new

lover. "We were in bed and he told me he loved me and I laughed," she says. "Do you think that was wrong?" Bick is glad to see these friends once or twice a month.

By about 5:00 A.M., Bick is alone in a corner downstairs sitting on a wooden bench. He is halfway through his second pack of cigarettes and finally comfortably drunk. He's watching a pop star dance to his latest record, which, presumably, the deejay is playing in the pop star's honor. Bick is impressed the pop star likes his own work so much.

About three dozen people remain, the weirdest, the drunkest, the most lost and fucked-up, or maybe just the most possessed. Bick is not particularly proud to be counted among them. He decides it's time to exit. He has given up hope of making contact tonight and Jayne's obviously a no-show. Just then the deejay puts on The Pretenders' "Precious," and Bick decides to stay the three minutes just to hear Chrissie Hynde.

"Trapped in a world that they never made"—and suddenly Chrissie's cool strong voice is buried beneath the yelling of drunks on the dance floor—*"but not me, baby, I'm too precious so fuck off."*

Bick notices a girl on the other side of the room with shredded Levi's not unlike his own. They look better on her. He thinks she's been looking at him. He's usually right about such things, but he has to consider the possibility that she's looking at the young actor nearby known for antidrug public service announcements noisily snorting coke from a car key or, more likely these days, heroin.

The actor gets up and jerkily makes for the bar. Bick watches the girl to see if she's watching the actor. She looks right back. Bick shrugs, a "what the hell are we doing here" shrug. She answers in kind.

When the music segues to a Smiths song, the dynamics of the dance floor shift and the girl and Bick lose each other for a moment.

Bick goes to the bar, hoping she will join him in neutral territory. She's already half there when he spots her again. "Hello," he says.

"Hi."

He immediately senses sex. It's a strange kick and he has never really understood how he knows, but sometimes he feels it and he feels it now. He asks the dancing fool of a bartender for a beer and since the girl is drinking the blue shit he asks the bartender for one of those too.

"Are you Bick Smith," she asks.

Bick nods.

"I thought you looked familiar," she says. "We've met. I'm a friend of Denise's."

"Oh, how is Denise?" Bick has not seen Denise in months. He tries to remember if they had sex the last time they were together.

"She's fine. We met at the Bangles show. Backstage."

"Oh, yeah," he says, wondering how drunk he was that night. The drinks come and Bick gives the guy a buck.

"You never called," she says.

"You sure?"

"Aren't you going to say you lost the number?"

"No," he says, "I don't even remember you giving me the number. When did you do that?"

Honesty has never benefited Bick much, but he sticks with it anyway.

"When do you *think* I gave it to you," she asks, smiling.

"I don't know."

"After sex."

Bick is caught for just a moment.

"Just kidding," she says. "You'd remember *that.* I promise you."

"Oh?"

"You're not an actor, right?"

"No, I'm not." He isn't sure if she's glad or disappointed.

"I'd consider having sex with you, then."

"That's, um, awfully good of you." He assumes this is just a joke.

"What do you do," she asks.

"I'm retired."

"Seriously. What do you do? You're a writer."

"Close enough."

"I'm in real estate. I sell dirt."

He nods.

"That must sound really boring to you."

"No more so than anything else."

"Well," she says. "It *is* boring."

"OK."

The beer is flat and warm.

"You should have called," she says.

"I've been known to make mistakes."

"Like being here at 5:00 A.M."

"It's not five yet. Is it?"

"Almost."

"Well, I'm almost sober enough to drive," he says, killing his beer. "Maybe I should drive home before the sun comes up."

"You alone?"

"Yeah, I was with friends earlier, but they left and then I was going to meet someone here."

"You still waiting," she asks.

He laughs. "Not tonight."

The anticipation is still stirring. Sex is one thing that almost never bores him, thank God, and he hasn't had an opportunity like this in a long while. Still, he wonders whether he wants the horror of waking up in a stranger's bed, or worse, waking up with a stranger in *his* bed, and then feels old for wondering this. "You want to go some place?"

"Where?" she says and smiles.

The smile is all he needs at this point.

"Home," he says.

"Whose home?"

"Where do you live?"

"A few blocks away."

"Yours."

"You have a condom?"

"Yes," Bick says, reaching over to his blue blazer, which he had left within arm's reach of the bed. She continues sucking on his neck. He tears open the Trojan package.

"Want me to put it on," she asks.

"I think it makes more sense if I wear it."

She giggles. "You know what I mean."

"I can handle it," he says, though he hates doing this. At least he's erect, which is a plus, since it's nearly goddamn impossible to put a condom on otherwise. He starts rolling the puppy on, but it gets stuck.

"Want me to help?"

"No, that won't be necessary."

In the dreaded dawn light that's filtering through her yellow curtains her body is well shaped and nicely textured and reminds him why he's doing this. Sex with a stranger may not be any more emotionally satisfying than masturbating, but it's far more aesthetically pleasing. He wonders where Jayne is. She sucks a bit harder on his neck. He continues working the sticky condom and it's rolling on lopsided.

"Fuck."

Now he's losing the erection, and the safe-sex device is jammed less than halfway down. He starts laughing because he doesn't know what else to do. She giggles. Suddenly the room seems horribly light.

"This isn't working," he says.

She's a trouper and tries to help. However, this just makes the condom jumble up again and she giggles. He looks down at himself.

"Looks like a circus machine, huh?" she says. "For like inflating balloons."

He briefly considers suggesting oral sex, but they're laughing and now the morning light seems to be *burning* through the window and Bick doesn't want to do things that are against the law in some states.

"Sorry," she says.

"It's not your fault."

"I should get a diaphragm or something."

"Condoms are a good idea. It's just too bad they don't work."

She pulls the condom off and tosses it at the curtain. It sticks for a moment and then slides off. They both laugh tiredly. "You want to sleep?" she says.

"No. What time is it?"

She stretches to check a watch on the bedside table. For the first time he notices the screenplay there. "About six thirty," she says. He calculates he has just squandered almost ten hours of his life. "The paper is probably here by now. *The New York Times* comes earlier than the LA papers."

He's surprised she subscribes, almost impressed. Now that he thinks about it, breaking a few archaic sex laws in the morning light doesn't seem really wrong. On the other hand, he should practice resisting temptation. He knows they'll hate each other and themselves much less if they don't have sex. In the last couple years it has become increasingly difficult and anxiety-inciting for Bick to have sex with a girl knowing she's not the one. Besides, this is a girl who subscribes to *The New York Times.* "Fuck it," he says. "Let's do the cross-word puzzle."

"What do you mean, 'no'?"

"I mean no."

"No," Oscar says, "I can't take no for an answer." Oscar is on his feet, leaning over Steele's desk, thoughts on strangulation.

"Even if I agreed that the change you're suggesting would make a better ending—and I'm not agreeing—but even if I were in agreement, the money thing is a major problem."

"OK. How much can you give me?"

"What do you mean?"

"If you can't give me what I'm asking, how much can you?"

"You're not hearing me. Let me phrase it differently. We're, uh, we aren't giving you any money for a reshoot."

"I can do it for less than you spent on the fucking bad art in this office!"

"No, Oscar."

"Can you say anything other than no?"

"No." Steele may see the humor in his reply since he's actually smiling.

"Fuck you," Oscar says.

"I realize it's your style to get so worked up and I respect that but—"

"Fuck you," Oscar says.

"What is the problem? There's no problem. You've made a brilliant movie, there's signs of sheer genius. We're all happy here. . . ."

Oscar stares back into his eyes and the man stammers a bit but stumbles on—"you don't realize how good a job you've done. . . ."—and what Oscar sees in Steele's eyes is fear. The fear is masked but unmistakable and seems out of sync with the dynamics. Steele is a very successful president of production and Oscar is just a kid filmmaker begging a favor, but the man is obviously afraid and even though Oscar doesn't quite get this, he starts to like it and stares back harder. Steele rises from his chair, losing his power sphere. He paces around the stark room, avoiding Oscar's eyes. Oscar looks out the window and sees a crew setting up to shoot on the lot far below across the parking lot, reflector boards flashing. This angers him further and he turns back to Steele.

"You're going to have an incredible career. . . ."

Oscar figures it out: the man is afraid of who Oscar might become. Steele's sense of self depends on the deference others show him, but it's not him they're deferring to, it's the power his job carries. Oscar even feels some sympathy, because the man is smart enough to appreciate the situation. *The man doesn't give a shit about movies, he certainly doesn't give a shit about art, he probably has no sense of values, no real sense of self, no real friends, just allies who help him hold onto his goddamn job.*

"We're going to work together a lot. . . ."

And Steele wants to count Oscar among his allies, but Oscar knows how Steele bullies and manipulates and uses his allies. They take it because they're also using him.

"Fuck you," Oscar says and walks.

Slamming the door behind him, he repeats, "fuck you." He is definitely going to reshoot the ending. The straightforward approach was a mistake. Steele lied. It's not a matter of money but of who controls the movie. Oscar knows he should have set up a power play first with his agent and his lawyer and his friends. Now he'll have to come up with a plan of attack. He would rather use his energy on the new ending, but there will be no change if he doesn't play the game. He's so angry and disgusted he can't even think about what he'll do if he wins. He storms through the reception area to the elevator.

"Oscar!"

It's Lee. *What a slime.*

"Hello," Oscar says curtly, then notices Bick. "Hi, how ya doing?"

"Same," Bick says, "how about you?"

"Not great," he says. "What are you doing here?"

"Meeting with Wanda Dillady."

Wanda is typical of Steele's allies. Oscar's anger becomes pity for a moment. "Bring earplugs?" he says to Bick.

"Just a beer." Bick holds one up.

The elevator opens and an oddly attractive young girl steps out. She looks familiar.

"Hi," she says, apparently to Bick and Lee. Lee air-kisses her. She looks at Bick's beer. "Inspired idea," she says. "You have one for me?"

Bick pulls a beer out of his doctor's satchel.

"Thanks," she says, popping it open, licking the foam off the rim. "Great."

"Great," Lee says. "Now you're contributing to the delinquency of a minor."

The girl smiles at Oscar.

"Oscar," Bick says. "Do you know Jayne?"

Oscar shakes his head.

"Jayne, Oscar Foreman," Bick says. "Oscar Foreman, Jayne Sky."

"Jayne with a *y*," the girl says. Her hand moves up to her mouth and then drops into her purse. She pulls out a pack of cigarettes, the same brand Bick smokes, and then puts it back.

A secretary enters and says, "Wanda's ready to see you."

"Good luck," Oscar says. "Nice meeting you, Jayne with a *y*."

"Nice meeting you."

"I'll call you later, Bick."

Oscar wonders what's happening between Bick and the young girl, who must be the actress he's been hearing about, but by the time the elevator opens he's planning how to leverage the money for a reshoot.

Bick and Jayne and Lee follow the secretary down a hall, past posters of various movies the studio made in better years. The offices were recently moved off the old lot after a corporate takeover and the halls are still jammed with unopened boxes.

"Let's make this quick and painless," Bick says. "I want to get back and write."

He wants to get back and drink. He has worked with smart producers and valuable executives, but he has more often worked with people like Lee and Wanda. This meeting is a useless political exercise but, as James said, it would be a nice gesture to include a meeting for the one hundred and sixty-five thousand they're paying.

"Are you bringing those beers," Lee asks.

Bick and Jayne both nod.

"Wanda will have a hemorrhage," Lee says quietly. "She hates writers who won't kiss her cottage-cheese ass and if you're not going to kiss her ass, at least don't kick it."

"I'm just drinking a beer."

"You're doing this just to piss her off."

"No," Bick says, "I don't care enough about her to piss her off."

"Why are we meeting with this woman," Jayne says, "instead of Benji or someone else important?"

"Because it's no big deal," Lee says. "This is just a formality to include Wanda. They pay her, they have to do something with her. What we try to do is make her feel involved and excited about the project, the more people who are excited about it the better. You know how these things are." He lowers his voice again. "Too bad she hates Bick and me."

"I don't blame her for hating you," Bick says. "But why should she hate me? She doesn't know me."

"She hates anyone who's younger and better looking," Lee says, still in a low voice.

"That's almost all of LA."

"Fortunately she hates women more than men." Lee glances at Jayne. "Don't worry. She's going to be perfectly nice to you two because she's afraid of you and Bick and his friends."

"I know," Jayne says.

"And then the cunt's going to take it out on *me.*"

The secretary opens a conference-room door and says Wanda's office is in disrepair so the meeting will be here. The room has dirty gray walls and closed gray curtains and a big rectangular table with black chairs. She asks if they would like anything to drink while waiting.

"Perrier," Lee says.

Bick and Jayne hold up their beers to show they're OK. The secretary smiles at this as she turns and leaves.

"I hate fluorescent lighting," Jayne says.

Lee points at chairs. "I'll sit on this side. Bick you're on that side. Jayne, you sit at the head there."

"I *hate* power seating," Jayne says.

"This just forces them to mingle with us," Lee says. "So we don't get in a situation where we're sitting on opposite sides of the table."

Bick and Jayne shrug and take their assigned seats and immediately light cigarettes.

"This room is really empty and ugly," Jayne says.

"Should we open the curtains?"

"No, I'd spend the whole time spacing out the window."

"What did you end up doing Saturday night," Bick casually asks.

"I don't remember, why?"

Apparently he overestimated the earnestness of their date. "I went to twentysomething," he says. "I thought you were going to be there."

"Oh, yeah, I was going to go there, and . . . didn't get there. How was it?"

"Same as always."

"Yeah?"

"Yeah."

There's nothing else he wants to say. He kills his beer. He decides baiting

Wanda with a Bud is not very sporting and tosses his can into one of the cardboard boxes.

"Two points," Lee says.

"Three points," Bick says.

Lee looks confused.

"I thought we were going to use the cans for ashtrays," Jayne says.

"We'll use yours."

"OK." She guzzles what's left.

Wanda enters. "Sorry, the world's running late today." She's wearing black stockings and a short green skirt and shouldn't be. They all shake hands and exchange greetings. Wanda is friendly, frowning only for a split second at the beer-can ashtray. She sits exactly where Lee has arranged that she should.

A junior executive will be joining the meeting, she says. Bick thinks she says the guy's name is Bobo and he doesn't ask for a confirmation as she and Lee launch into a serious discussion of shopping. It seems they both buy their clothes at Agnès B.

"Sandra Bernhard was there," Wanda says, "clowning around with a leather something or other wrapped around her head like a blindfold."

"Was Madonna with her," Lee asks.

"No," Wanda says, not hiding her disappointment.

When Bobo enters, more greetings are exchanged and it turns out his name is Boyd O'Something. Boyd is the ex-houseboy of a major producer who's a good friend of the studio president. Boyd sits where Lee has arranged that he should.

"Gale just called," Boyd says to Wanda. "She says Don Henley was with Fawn Hall at the Ivy last night."

"You sure she didn't mean Donna Rice," Wanda asks.

"Yeah," Lee answers, "that was the night Dweezil Zappa was there with Walter Mondale's daughter. I hear he's porking her."

Lee laughs and looks at Bick and winks. Bick nods as he knocks his ashes into the beer can. He has to admit Lee can be hilarious sometimes.

Gossip continues until Wanda notices that Bick and Jayne are chain-smoking and not paying attention.

"I guess we should get started," Wanda says.

"Give us your thoughts," Lee says.

Wanda looks up at the lights and then back at the table, blinking. "I think the important thing here is that we keep in mind what we're trying to do. When I was at Yale, Christopher Durang and Sigourney and I used to talk about character arc. Like it or not, audiences prefer characters who can put on a happy face. Now, realism is fine, even effective, as long as it doesn't get depressing . . ."

Boyd nods as Wanda continues. Lee feigns intense interest, chin on knuck-

les. Jayne slides her watch up and down her wrist. Bick is starting to fade out when Jayne lights another cigarette and whispers, "Jesus Christ, the woman sounds like the teacher in Charlie Brown–'Blah, blah, blah.'"

Wanda stares, recovering after a moment. "My main concern," she says to Jayne, forcing a friendly expression, "is when your character dabbles in prostitution."

"Dabbles," Jayne says.

"The audience needs to love her," Wanda says, reaching out a hand across the table toward Jayne. "She needs to be a more sympathetic character. Prostitution, even out of desperation or as a lark or whatever the case is, it's not a sympathetic activity."

Jayne looks at Bick.

"Neither is lounging in your parents' swimming pool all day, getting up at night only to fuck your father's law partner's wife," Bick says, lazily synopsizing *The Graduate,* one of his favorite movies. "But if the character is real and going through true emotions the audience understands and maybe shares, anything can be a sympathetic activity."

"Uh-huh, right, but, uh," Wanda says, "but why does she do it?"

Fair question, Bick thinks.

"Because," Jayne says, "she gets something from it she isn't getting anywhere else."

"Yes," Wanda says, surprised, "but, um . . ."

Even Bick is thrown by the sudden conviction in Jayne's voice.

"The thing is," Wanda says, "though I do see your point. I mean, I feel what you're saying. Hmmm." She stares at her hand out on the table and brings it back.

Boyd seizes the pause. He's sure the American public doesn't want to watch unbridled lust and perversion unless it's presented with a positive arc, particularly not the good people in the Midwest.

Jayne and Boyd exchange stares of sheer contempt. She stuffs her cigarette butt into the beer can. Bick feels like asking Boyd how a guy who's spent his adult life as a professional sodomist in LA knows what the good people in the Midwest want to watch.

"We hear what you're saying." Lee jumps in and parrots what they've said back to them, then adds, "I think Bick's point was that this movie's potentially massive appeal lies in the love story's ability to, uh, suck people into the, uh, emotions of the characters and though they may not seem sympathetic on the surface, they are in fact sympathetic because what they're going through is what everyone goes through, except our two are more extreme. And because of the way they love each other."

The beer can is smoking like a dry-ice machine.

"My point was even more simple," Bick says. "I don't want you to expect

one thing when the script is going to be something else." He has learned people like Wanda can't tell the difference between a good script and a bad script, but they can tell the difference between what they expect and what they get.

"Uh, yes, right, exactly," Lee says. "What Bick is going to do is, uh, to write a new ending so they are together, together and alive. This, of course, will mean rewriting the whole script so the characters aren't so serious and, uh, self-destructive. There will be more comedy and romance." He glances at Bick and Bick nods for him to continue. "It will still be a realistic edgy love story, but they'll be looking for beauty in the ugliness. Instead of killing each other they'll save each other." Lee looks around proudly after this improvisation based loosely on what Bick told him over the phone several days ago. "I really believe Bick's going to do the script of his life here. And what Jayne can do with a role this juicy . . ." Lee's expression suggests it's too incredible for words. "You'll have all the hot directors in town killing each other for a chance to do this movie."

"OK," Wanda says, "I feel good about this. Let's do it."

"That's it," Boyd agrees, "let's do it."

Wanda frowns at Boyd.

Bick looks over at Jayne and her eyes roll so far back into her head it puts him in mind of a horror movie.

In the elevator Lee pushes the down button. "They're involved now," he says. "They're excited. They're with us now."

"Bullshit," Bick says. "If Wanda had any power, we would have been kicked out of her office and the project would be dead."

"No," Lee says, "we left on a good note."

"I think so too," Jayne says. "I think it was the beer."

"We're off to the races," Lee says. "Now the reins are in your hands, Bick."

"Giddy-up," Jayne says, smirking.

"How'd you get here," Bick asks her.

"I drove."

"I thought you didn't drive."

"I don't have a license. But I sometimes drive. I borrowed a car from a friend."

"You two want to get a drink somewhere," Bick asks, hoping Lee is too busy.

"Sure," Lee says.

"Thanks," Jayne says. "But I've gotta get this car back to my friend."

The elevator opens to a cold steel and cement lobby.

"I'm parked on the street," Jayne says. "I'll talk to you two later?"

"I'll call you," Lee says.

"Bye-bye," she says, smiling at Bick, and walks out through the glass lobby door.

"Where should we get a drink," Lee asks as they exit into the parking garage.

"I don't want to get a drink with you," Bick says as though he's joking.

"Actually," Lee says, looking at his watch, "I don't really have time, I have—"

Suddenly Bick bolts out of the parking garage, into the daylight. He doesn't know what kind of car Jayne's in, so he quickly scans the whole block. Cars drive by, a BMW, a Mercedes, a BMW, a Honda, a BMW, something American, but no sign of Jayne. He walks back into the parking garage, wondering what he would have said to her.

Lee is still waiting for his car.

"What the hell was that about," Lee asks.

"I remembered I wanted to ask her a couple questions," Bick says, handing his ticket to the valet.

"What?"

"I'm not sure."

"Be careful," Lee says, "sex will sap your strength."

The valet pulls up in Lee's yellow Mercedes 450 SL.

"I need her phone number," Bick says.

"I'll leave it on your machine," Lee says. "You should talk to her while you're writing. Involve her in the process."

"Uh-huh."

"How's the script coming?"

"It's coming."

He hasn't written a single page yet.

O scar arrives uninvited at the office of one of the most powerful writer-producers in town. The man is busy twirling a very large globe but takes a moment for Oscar since Oscar's father was his best friend at UCLA in the fifties. Oscar's parents never had anything more than middling success in this town, his mother as an actress and his father as a director, but they do have a few powerful friends.

Oscar tells him the problem quickly and angrily.

"Cool your jets," his father's friend says. "You'll eventually learn not to care too much. You'll get jaded."

"No, I won't," Oscar snaps.

His father's friend smiles and runs a hand through his long thin hair.

Oscar continues to explain why the reshoot is necessary, why it's important. He's not sure what he's saying, but he means it.

His father's friend cuts him off and picks up the phone. He tells his secretary to get the president concerned on the phone. This happens almost immediately. He begins by joking with Mr. Steele about last night's Trivial Pursuit game.

Oscar looks up at the movie posters mounted on the wall, most of which have the name of his father's friend above the title. Oscar only likes a couple of the movies, but he tries to respect the fact that the nine movies add up to almost a billion gross dollars, counting worldwide merchandising. This is not

something he envies, not something he aspires to, because Father's friend blew it. He had won a prestigious fellowship as a young writer and was off to a good start, but, like Bick, he decided to write one quick screenplay for the money. Then he wrote a few more. Then he became a producer. He often tells Oscar that he doesn't regret the choices he's made. He usually says so while wistfully staring into space.

Father's friend finally informs Mr. Steele that he thinks it would be a good idea to do a reshoot on Oscar's movie. He hangs up a moment later. "Done."

Oscar has to admit there's a flash of something like happiness in Father's friend's smile.

J̲oy can't sleep even though it's nearly 3:00 A.M. As she got up sometime just before sunset and has done absolutely nothing since, this is not surprising. She is glad Mona has a job with Oscar but misses late-nights talks. MTV bores and depresses her because she doesn't recognize the bands anymore. She picks up the *TV Guide*. One program, which bills itself as "an unscripted show about real people," just started, so she turns to the channel.

Dr. Someone, the show's host, is grilling a real person, a mother, about her nine-year-old son. The boy has AIDS. After the doctor presses the mother to admit "what she's really feeling," he asks her what the boy's feeling. *"How much does he know?"*

She tells the doctor that the boy once asked, "Am I going to die?" And she and the father told him yes. The mother is close to tears.

"What are you going to do," the doctor asks.

"Love him the best we can," the mother says.

The camera cuts to the live studio audience—close shots of people wiping tears.

A commercial break: tomorrow Oprah Winfrey will interview unloved children who grew up and killed people. *"I'm not only the Hair Club President,"* a man with a toupee says after a pitch for hairpieces, *"I'm also a client."* He reveals an old photo of himself bald.

118

The show's next segment focuses on a woman who complains about how dreary her love life has become. She blames the eighties. The doctor badgers her into agreeing it's her own fault. *"I guess I'm scared,"* she admits.

The doctor turns to the audience and says, *"Scared."*

The audience applauds.

The doctor turns to the camera and advises everyone, *"Don't be afraid. We'll be right back after these messages."*

The TV speaker distorts with the swell of an overly lush John Williams score. Joy winces. A boy reaches out and touches E.T.'s leprous finger and suddenly there's the goddamn Pepsi logo and Joy wishes Mona were here because it's obvious the end of the world is near. She can hear the trumpets of the archangels.

Bick points the remote and the TV goes black. He feels lucky. Maybe if he weren't a writer he would have the compulsion to express himself in a much more embarrassing manner. At least as a writer you can always say, *Fuck off, it's fiction.*

He takes a bottle of water from the refrigerator and sits at his desk, determined to work before he sleeps, determined to atone. His desk faces a bare black wall. His chair is an old wooden banker's chair. His computer is an old IBM XT desk model he feels attached to and he removes the cover from the keyboard and touches a couple keys lightly. The water washes the taste of bourbon down his throat. He lights a cigarette. He touches the keys again and picks up a Venus no. 2 pencil and puts it behind his ear and picks up a yellow legal pad and rises and paces. He stops in front of the windows facing the ocean but does not look out. He sits on a stool with the pencil and the yellow legal pad, hoping to jot down some thoughts that will mean he's really begun. Instead, he writes his name and hers inside a heart.

He reels back, shakes his head, looks out the window. Beyond the boardwalk lights the waves are breaking in long stretches of white in the clear night and this isn't working.

He returns to his desk and stares at the computer. He touches the keys. He puts out a cigarette. He lights a cigarette.

After a while the phone rings and the machine picks up.

"Hello, please leave a message at the tone, thank you."

Beep.

"Bick, it's me." Libby with crowd noise in the background. "I'm at Rebecca's" she says, "and I've had a couple margaritas and it's closing and since I'm in the neighborhood . . . Bick?"

She's at a restaurant just down the street, her Texas accent slipping out, drunk.

He decides to pick up. "Hello."

"Hi, what are you doing?"

"Working."

"I'm bored. I want to see you."

"That's certainly flattering."

She laughs. "Sorry. Can I come over?"

"Sure."

"I won't if you don't want me to."

"No, I'd like to see you."

"Good."

You're a sucker for sex, he thinks as they fuck, *but why shouldn't you be?*

He puts his moist hands on her moist shoulders and they gently roll over and he's back on top and it's building now, he feels that back arch—

And the phone rings.

She doesn't notice.

"Hello, please leave a message at the tone, thank you."

Beep.

Bick wishes he'd remembered to turn off the sound, which he usually does when he has a girl over.

"Bick, please be there," Jayne says. "Bick?"

Libby opens her eyes, either responding to the phone call or Bick's sudden lack of focus.

Bick tries to pretend he's ignoring the call.

"Bick," Jayne is pleading, sounding desperately scared. "Please be there, please, please, please."

Bick pulls out and reaches for the phone.

"Hello, what's wrong."

"Jesus fucking Christ, I'm glad you're there," Jayne says.

"What's wrong?"

"You've gotta come over."

Bick looks at Libby. Her mouth is open in shock.

"Jayne, tell me what's wrong."

"Please come over right now."

"What's wrong?"

"Bick, please."

"OK, I'll be right there."

"Hurry."

He hangs up and looks at Libby and shrugs as he starts dressing.

"Are you fucking kidding me?" she says.

"A friend's in trouble."

"Are you fucking kidding?"

"No, a friend's in trouble."

"Who the hell is calling you at 3:00 A.M.?"

"Stay here," he says. "I'll be right back."

"Stay here?"

"Why not?" He buttons every other button of his untucked shirt. "You've been drinking. You don't want to drive all the way back to Hollywood."

"I'm sober *now.*"

"Stay," he says, reaching over and kissing her. "I'll be right back. I just have to help out this friend."

"What's this girl's problem?"

"I don't know what her problem is." He slips his feet into his loafers. "I'll tell you about it when I get back."

He kisses her again and heads out.

Driving the few blocks to Jayne's house, he's in such a hurry he doesn't conjure up any specific images of what to expect.

"Who is it?" she says through the closed door.

"Me. Bick."

She opens the door and suddenly hugs him. "Thanks." She grabs his hand and leads him into the main room, which is trashed. Books are scattered all over, lamps are on the floor, the bong is broken, the coffee table leans upside down in a corner. "This guy turned psycho on me."

"How'd he get in?"

"I let him in. He's sort of a friend. An old boyfriend."

Her face is full of confusing expressions. She's shaking. She suddenly seems very young and uncertain. "Lately he's become kind of crazy."

Bick wonders what he's gotten into here.

"I'm afraid he might come back," she says, still holding Bick's hand.

"How'd you get him out?"

"He just left. I was trying to stop him from breaking stuff and he threw me down and then he said he had to leave because he knew he'd hurt me really bad if he stayed and he didn't want to do that."

"Uh-huh."

"He's not a bad guy."

Bick examines her expression.

"Seriously," she says. "He's just really fucked up."

"No shit."

"But he won't hurt me or anything."

"How do you know?"

"He's obsessed with me. He *loves* me."

Bick shakes his head. He notices his own book on the couch, spine cracked. He lets go of her hand and starts putting books back on the shelves. She starts cleaning up also.

"Did you call the police," he asks.

"No, I called you."

"Has this sort of thing happened before?"

"Not like this," she says.

"What do you mean?"

"He's been getting really psycho lately, but this is the first time he's *done* anything really weird."

Bick knows she's not telling everything and this makes him even more curious than he would be otherwise.

"What was he doing over here," he asks.

"He came over to get his car. I borrowed it."

"Why are you borrowing this guy's car?"

"He used to be a friend. Before."

"Come on. You must have a *lot* of money. Why don't you *buy* a car?"

"I don't like cars."

"Cars are one of the best things about this city."

"I don't like this city."

"If you're going to live here, you need a car," Bick says. "You definitely can't borrow this guy's car anymore."

"I know." She laughs. She has calmed down considerably.

Bick tries to piece the bong back together. "What is this guy's story," he asks.

"He's crazy sometimes."

"What's he want from you?"

"Who the hell knows?" she says, righting a broken lamp. "To be my boyfriend, I guess. To have sex with me. I don't know. He said he was gay until he met me."

"Oh no."

"Yeah."

"Do you like this guy at all?"

"Just as a friend. He'd be OK if he weren't obsessed with me."

"Does he *realize* you don't like him, as anything more than a friend?"

"Of course. That's why he broke all this stuff."

"Of course."

They continue to right things.

"I really appreciate you coming over," she says. "You really helped. I feel a lot better now." She whirls toward the window. "What was that?"

"What?"

"That."

"What?"

He follows her gaze to the window. All he sees is a hedge and some plants and the canal in the background.

"Probably just one of the neighbors' cats," she says. "They've got these insane cats."

She's moved close to him.

He continues looking out the window, noticing their reflection, befuddled boy with scared girl, wondering what he should do or say next.

"I don't want to sleep here," she says and holds his hand. "Let's get out of here."

"Well, do you want to go get some coffee or something?"

"No, I want to sleep. Can we go to your place?"

"What?"

"Your place, let's go there."

"Well, we could."

"I'll get some stuff," she says, and goes into the bedroom.

Bick slowly realizes what is happening. They are going to his place—*where Libby is sleeping or awake waiting.* He picks up the phone. There's no dial tone.

"He threw it against the wall," she says, coming back into the room with a bag. "I'll get a new one tomorrow."

Oh, fuck, Bick thinks.

"Who were you going to call now? It's almost four."

"You sure you don't want to go to Zucky's or something? Have breakfast?"

"I'm really . . . I don't know. I just want to sleep somewhere safe."

Bick wishes he knew somewhere safe.

On the way home he stops the car at a phone booth with what appear to be bullet holes in the glass. He picks up the receiver. The cord has been severed.

"Who were you gonna call," she asks when he gets back in the car.

"Checking my messages. I was going to check my messages, I guess."

Jayne considers his answer. "Is this gonna cause a problem for you?"

"It'll be OK."

"Do you have a girl over at your apartment?"

He nods.

"Is this girl like a girlfriend?"

"No, she's not really a girlfriend."

"What's she doing sleeping over," she asks, smiling. "Is she staying with you for a while?"

"Just the night."

"Are you having sex with her?" she says.

After a pause, Bick nods.

"This should be entertaining."

Libby is stunned. Bick and Jayne are just a couple steps into the room and Libby is staring at them.

"Libby, Jayne," Bick says. "Jayne, Libby."

"Hi," Jayne says.

Libby stares.

The Matchmaker is on TV.

"I would have called," Bick says, "but Jayne's phone was disconnected. She's had a really weird night. Some psycho trashed her house and she needs a place to stay tonight."

Libby weighs this story, her eyes narrowing.

Bick decides he better keep talking. "I'll roll out the futon," he says, gesturing to the folded-up mattress that serves as a couch of sorts. "And I'll sleep there and the two of you can share the, uh—" He suddenly realizes this is not such a hot suggestion.

"No, I'll take the futon," Jayne says. "And you don't have to roll it out or anything. I'm skinny."

"I think I'll be leaving," Libby says.

"That's not necessary," Bick says.

"Where's the bathroom?" Jayne says.

Bick points to the door across the room.

As Jayne closes the bathroom door and the fan turns on, Libby whispers harshly, "What is wrong with you?"

"She needs a place to stay," he whispers back.

"What is she? A teenage runaway?"

Bick laughs, trying to keep it light.

"I try to be pretty liberal with you," Libby says, "but this is absurd." She starts picking up her clothes from various places in the room.

"You don't have to leave."

"I'm not into three-ways."

"I'm glad you're showing some levity here."

Libby makes a face at him, not one of levity, and quickly begins dressing. She wads up her hose and stuffs it in her purse.

There are no sounds coming from the bathroom.

"I'll walk you out."

"That won't be necessary. I'll be perfectly safe. You're the only person in your sleazy neighborhood who's still awake." She walks out the door.

"I'll be right back," he says toward the bathroom.

"Amazing," is all Libby says as they walk down the stairs. Bick wishes he could take this as a compliment.

They cross to the parking lot and everything's wet and still dark, but the blue light before dawn is beginning.

"You're right," Bick says. "Everyone else is asleep."

"Smarter people than us."

The crash and run of the ocean waves seem especially loud.

Libby suddenly stops, pulling her hands up to her chest. There's a dead seagull lying in a puddle. The bird's belly seems surprisingly clean and white. Its head is twisted to the side, the neck apparently broken.

"LATC is doing a production of Chekhov's *Seagull*," Bick says. "Judd Nelson plays Constantine."

Libby makes a terrible face at him and quickly steps around the dead seagull toward her jeep. He starts to follow, but she sprints and clicks off the alarm and unlocks the door and slams it shut, leaving him looking at her through the side window. She doesn't look back. Litter blows in the wake of the jeep speeding out of the parking lot and down the alley.

Jayne is in Bick's bed when he returns. The lights and the TV are off. He thinks she may be asleep and wonders what she's wearing underneath the sheets drawn up to her neck and where he's supposed to sleep. He quietly closes the door.

He slips off his shoes and hangs up his blue blazer in the open closet. Her shopping bag is on the floor and her black dress on a hanger. He takes off his shirt and Levi's and, standing there in his boxers, decides he's the sort of guy who lets the girl have his bed.

He starts rolling out the futon.

"What are you doing?" she says.

He turns around, faces her. "Sleeping on the futon."

"Why?"

Good question, he thinks.

"I don't want to hog your bed," she says. "There's plenty of room. And I don't snore or anything."

He starts rolling the futon back up.

"I knew you wore boxers," she says.

"Congratulations."

She laughs. "Why don't you own any stuff?"

"What do you mean? I've got books and a stereo and clothes."

"A dozen white shirts and a mattress on the floor."

"A futon."

"Aren't you old enough to start living like an adult?"

"No."

"I guess you really do like to travel light."

He nods.

"The kind of guy who can't even commit to a couch."

He turns, wondering where he can use her lines in the script.

"I'm wearing a T-shirt of yours," she says. The sheet has slipped down just below her breasts.

"Yes, I see."

"Hope you don't mind."

"No."

"Did I get you in trouble?"

"Yes."

"Do you two have good sex?"

"Say what?"

"You heard me."

"Yes."

"She doesn't look like she'd be good sex."

Bick doesn't respond.

"But I'm sure she's perfectly *decent*," Jayne adds. "Have you seen *Moonstruck?*"

"Yeah?"

"One of the characters said something about how guys chase girls because they're afraid of death. What do you think of that?"

"I've heard it said once or twice." He finishes rolling up the futon.

"Bring a bedtime book with you," she says.

"Pardon?"

"You heard me. Bring a bedtime book, something to read aloud. A bedtime story."

"What did you have in mind?"

"What kind of bedtime stories do you usually read?"

"Late-night movies." He lies in bed, a safe distance from her.

"Do you have any poetry?"

Bick remembers when he was that age and actually read poetry because he wanted to. He still has the books if not the devotion.

"Right there," he says.

She looks over at the stacks of books on the floor and reaches for a beat-up black and white *Tao Te Ching*. She skims it. "Mmmm," she says a few times. "'Fame or self: Which matters more? Self or wealth: Which is more precious? Gain or loss: Which is more painful?'" She looks up. "Pretty basic stuff, huh?"

"The more things change . . ."

"Yeah." She puts the *Tao* back. "Oh, Yeats. Great, *perfect.*" He's a bit spooked, because he has been recently rereading "The Second Coming," a poem in the collection she pulls out. "Does this have 'The Circus Animals Desertion,'" she asks, checking.

"I don't know."

"It does!" She hands it to him with the page open. "Read it to me."

"I think reading should be done silently, alone."

"Please." She quickly kisses him. He looks at her and she smiles and closes her eyes and leans back on the pillow. "Read."

He leans against the wall beside her. "'I sought . . .'" She adjusts her head, letting her bobbed hair barely touch his shoulder. "'And this brought forth a dream and soon enough this dream itself had all my thought and love. . . .'"

Reading in bed alone at night has always been a good thing for Bick and now he finds reading aloud and not alone is still a good thing, possibly better. He reads until she falls asleep.

When Bick awakes, Jayne is gone.

Next to the Yeats is a note:

> Dear Bick,
> Thanks. I will work it out with you know who today. He'll
> be OK when he comes down from the drugs and it's day
> and everything. I'll call you and let you know what
> happens. . . . Thanks again.
> > > Love, Jayne XXXOOO

Even though he knows her phone is broken, he tries calling. It just rings and rings. He decides he had better call Libby. Her answering machine picks up and he leaves a message. "Good morning. Sorry about last night. Please give me a call. Thanks."

Though he doesn't usually accomplish much work in the day, he thinks he should try, since he hasn't been getting much work done at night. On his way to his desk the phone rings. He picks it up for a change, and just as he says, "Jayne?" it occurs to him it must be Libby, who was probably home when he called.

"*Jayne,*" she says.

"Sarah?"

"Did you say 'Jayne'?"

"Yeah."

"Your little starlet calls you now?"

"'Who told you about it?"

"You kidding?"

He should know a private life is not possible in this town. "So, what else is new?" He's surprised because Sarah almost never calls him.

"I wanted to check on you. See what became of your New Year's resolution."

He laughs.

"But now I see—the starlet got her way with you."

"I'm just taking this last job."

"Sure."

"So what have you been up to?"

"Same old grind. I *hear* what you've been up to."

"Don't believe rumors."

"What if they're true?"

"Still don't believe them."

She laughs.

His call waiting blips. "Excuse me," he says, and clicks onto the other line. "Hello?"

"I haven't forgiven you yet." It's Libby.

"Good morning."

"Sleep well, did you?"

"Fine, thanks. Listen, I want to talk to you, but I have to finish up this other call. Are you at home?"

"Talking to her high-school principal?"

"Can I call you right back?"

"Fine."

"Thanks."

He clicks back over to Sarah.

"Sorry," he says.

"It's OK. I've got to go. I just wanted to check on you."

He suddenly feels guilty. He wants to make things right with her. His call waiting blips and he ignores it.

"You want to have dinner this week?" he says. "See a movie?"

"I've got dinners all week. I guess I could cancel one. What night?"

"I don't know."

"How about Friday?"

"Friday?"

"Never mind. I should know you don't like to book your Fridays. Something better might come up."

Since this is true, Bick laughs.

The call waiting blips again. "Take it," Sarah says.

"Hold on." He clicks over. "Libby?"

"Hi." It's Jayne.

"How are you?"

"I'm fine. I talked to him and everything's cool."

"Cool? How can everything be cool? He totally trashed your parents' house."

"He apologized."

"Apologized? That's nice, but—"

"He was really fucked up on coke. He's really not a bad guy."

"Are you kidding?"

"Thanks a lot for last night."

"Are you at home? Can I call you right back? I'm on the other line."

"No, I'm at his place."

"His?"

"Yeah."

"What are you doing there?"

"Talking. It's cool."

"Call me back in five minutes? Can you do that?"

"It's OK. Everything's cool. I'll call you back later tonight or something."

"You're OK?"

"Totally. I'm going to go buy a new phone. Then I'll call you."

"Hold on—"

"You're on the other line. I'll call you later."

"When?"

"Soon as I get a new phone."

"Get one today."

"OK. Work hard on the script."

"I'll talk to you this afternoon."

He clicks back over to Sarah. She's not there. "Fuck." He dials her office number. "Hi," he says to the secretary.

"Hi, Bick," she says. "Sarah's on another line."

"Tell her it's me, please."

"Hold on."

A moment later Sarah comes on the line. "What?"

"Sorry," he says, "I couldn't—"

"I'm on the other line."

"How about tomorrow?"

"Dinner?"

"Yeah."

There's the sound of shuffling paper. "Forget it, Bick," she says.

"Another night."

"I don't know. Call me later. I'm working."

"What's wrong."

"I'm on the other line and I've got people waiting in my office. Call me later." She's pissed.

"OK."

Sarah hangs up.

He calls Libby. "Hi," he says. "Sorry."

"We're just fuck buddies."

"Pardon?"

"It shouldn't bother me that you're fucking other girls."

"Libby . . ."

"I'm on the other line."

"You want me to call you back?"

"No."

"I'll call you back."

"Do whatever you want. I don't care."

Bick says nothing.

"I'm sorry I'm acting this way," she says, apparently sensing his surprise. "I know we're just fuck buddies."

He laughs, hoping this will lighten her up.

"Seriously," she says. "We were just fuck buddies and now we're not anymore. It's over. OK?"

"Well—"

"I'm sure we'll still be seeing plenty of each other."

"Yeah. Libby? I—"

His call waiting blips.

"Shit," she says. "Take it. I've still got this geek waiting on the other line."

"I'll talk to you later, OK?"

She hangs up.

Bick clicks over. It's Oscar. "Hey, guy."

"Hello."

"My secretary just reminded me I'm having dinner tonight with Blond Ambition. Guess where?"

"The ninth circle of hell?"

"Close. Helena's."

"Sorry to hear that."

"I told her to change it to Ivy at the Shore. I thought you'd join us. He's trying to talk me into getting involved with *Till Death Do Us Part*. Has he told you about this?"

"No." Bick is angry.

"Yesterday I ran into Canton at a screening and he told me he'd heard I'm in love with the script and dying to direct it. News to me, of course. I told him I knew nothing about it except you're rewriting it and you've barely started. Apparently your pal Lee has been telling people I'm attached."

Bick sighs.

"Listen, I know there's nothing you can do. You can't put a gag on the

guy. So I called him and told him to stop this shit, at least until you'd finished the fucking script and I'd read it."

"That seems reasonable."

"He said let's have dinner."

"With me?"

"That was my idea. I don't want to have dinner *alone* with him. Hey, it's a free meal."

Oscar and Bick both spent enough time after college broke that they haven't shaken their taste for free meals.

"We'll lose Lee afterward," Oscar adds.

"Sounds good," Bick says. "I could use some male bonding."

"**I** love eating pussy," Lee says, looking past Bick and Oscar at the hostess. Her white and pink and green cotton dress contributes to the restaurant's overwhelming white and pink and green design.

"The only thing better than eating pussy," Lee continues, "is butt-fucking."

This is not what Oscar thought Bick meant by male bonding.

Lee's blond hair is up in a short pony tail and he reaches back and feels it every few minutes. Oscar and Bick exchange glances and continue eating the swordfish they both ordered. Lee has been talking a lot but has yet to mention *Till Death Do Us Part.* Oscar is glad the restaurant is noisy enough nobody can overhear Lee.

They are sitting on the patio separated from the sidewalk and the headlights of cars by a body-height stucco wall topped with glass. Oscar can see the tops of the palm trees in the park across Ocean Boulevard and the brightly lit tip of the Santa Monica Pier Ferris wheel against the darkness of the ocean.

"The thing about butt-fucking," Lee says, "is that once you fuck 'em in the ass, they can never talk shit."

Oscar washes the swordfish down with a Corona. The fish and the beer both taste of lime.

"Blow jobs are good too," Lee adds.

"That's hard to argue with," Bick says.

Oscar nods, thinking he would be amiss in his maleness if he didn't.

"But I'd rather eat pussy," Lee says. "The thing about eating pussy is you have *power* over them."

Oscar looks up at the hot red coils of the metal boxes that keep customers warm from above. He can usually talk to ambitious people, but Lee's aspirations are so exceedingly superficial there's nothing there to talk about. Oscar does not share Bick's talent for detachment.

"You're all wrong," Bick says to Lee. "Control is the key." He slyly smiles at Oscar. "Wouldn't you agree?"

"With what?"

"Nothing," Bick says, picking up his knife and fork. "Never mind."

"I need a girlfriend," Lee says. "A girl who finds me as disgusting as I find myself. Then we'll have something in common." He laughs, playing a caricature of himself as though he were in a bad movie. If he were an actor, Oscar would fire him.

"Can I get you anything else," the waiter with white pants and a pink and green tie asks.

Lee orders another glass of champagne. Bick and Oscar order two more beers with lime. "I'd like to fuck her," Lee says, when the waiter steps away and crosses paths with the hostess. "She looks like a good fuck."

"Is there any other kind," Bick asks.

"No," Lee says and laughs.

"What about if you're in love?"

"A fuck is a fuck is a fuck," Lee laughs. "How's the script coming?"

"It's coming."

"You been involving Jayne in the process?"

"Yes."

"Good," Lee says, leering. "Good. And you've been working hard?"

"I'm working right now."

"Good."

Oscar expects Lee to use this as a transition to the *Till Death Do Us Part* situation. Lee turns to him. "Would you explain to me why the most boring abortion of a movie, *Accidental Tourist,* won the New York Film Critics' Award for Best Picture?"

Oscar answers, "Prestige cast, prestige director, based on a book said to be literary."

"And the dog," Bick adds.

"William Hurt gave the most one-note performance of his career," Lee says, "and yes, Bick, I realize he was supposed to be playing an emotional cripple and all, but he played it *autistic,* he should have been in *Rain Man.* And

Geena Davis? She's supposed to be the catalyst for Hurt's change, the life-force that opens his eyes—"

"And Kasdan starts shots at her fucking ankles," Oscar remembers.

"And the New York critics think this is art?" Lee is outraged. "And *Kathleen Turner.* She was totally miscast. The lush has fat lines on her neck! And what's her fucking *breathing* problem?"

"She and Kasdan are buddies, remember *Body Heat.*"

"Oh, yeah," Lee says, as though this at least makes sense.

"The kid was good," Bick says. "The little boy."

"And Bill Pullman was good as the editor," Oscar says.

"He was in a movie all of his own," Lee says.

"But he was good in it."

"Why are you two defending this amateurish shit?"

"It may be shit," Oscar says. "But it wasn't amateurish. Kasdan is a total pro. If he wants to make an odd movie from some book he liked, he's entitled."

"And Mike Nichols!" Lee turns to Bick. "The man must have sold his soul to the devil to get *The Graduate* made. *Heartburn* and coming soon *Postcards from the Edge.* You know the Big Red Guy wrote the fine print for those deals."

Oscar admires Nichols's talent and can't decide if Nichols's failing should be a source of solace or fear.

"I want to work with you two before you're so bored you turn to shit like that," Lee finishes his harangue. "After we're all rich, you can jerk off."

Oscar again expects Lee to mention the *Till Death Do Us Part* situation.

"Look," Lee says, nodding toward a nearby table. "Isn't that your agent being schmoozed?"

Oscar's agent is having his ass kissed by a movie critic–journalist–screenwriter who does nothing now but obsequious pieces on actors and agents and producers and studio presidents.

"Know who that writer is," Bick asks, lighting a cigarette.

Oscar frowns. "Remember when he was just an ignorant and bitter critic who trashed everything?"

"I liked him better then."

"He's growing up," Lee says. "Realizing he has to make some money."

"What are we doing here?" Oscar says, poking his food with his fork. "We're too young to be sitting around with these scum-sucking pigs."

"Speak for yourself," Lee says. "I'm not too young to sit around with scum-sucking pigs."

Oscar understands why Bick sometimes expresses a desire to leave town, but he'll settle for just leaving this restaurant. When the champagne and beer

arrive he asks for the check. The only good thing about the night so far is that it's on Lee.

Outside the restaurant Lee points to two older men with chest hair also waiting for the valets to bring their cars. "One used to be a mail-order scam artist," Lee says, "and the other was in porn. In the old days producers had to deal with all the shit of making movies, now they just have to pimp deals together." He laughs. Oscar can't understand why Bick's in business with this zero. "These guys are making hundreds of millions of dollars worth of decisions about the kinds of movies and TV people can see." Lee is pumping himself up. "They're affecting the consciousness of the whole country, or the whole *world*. And *we* will someday be in that position."

"I think he's trying to bond with us," Bick says to Oscar.

Lee laughs loudly.

"I'm mildly nauseous," Oscar says, "you think it was the fish?"

"No."

"No."

A police car cruises the park across the street, shining a spotlight on the homeless people trying to sleep. The crashing and hissing of the ocean below the cliff at the edge of the park mix with the traffic noise, but in moments of relative quiet Oscar can hear the bells of a merry-go-round playing somewhere in the lights of the amusement park on the pier.

The two moguls get into separate Mercedes sedans and pull into traffic. The valet pulls up Lee's Mercedes. "Where to now guys," he asks.

"Home," Oscar lies.

"You're kidding," Lee says.

The valet is waiting for Lee to take his car.

Lee looks at Bick. "What about you?"

"Work," Bick answers.

"You creative types work too hard," Lee says. "We'll all get together and talk business when the script's finished." He gets into the car as two worn women get out of a Datsun 240 Z. "Half-a-hookers," Lee says, closing his door and driving away.

"Half-a-hookers?" Oscar says. "That's a new one."

"No, it's not. Same old story. You pay their rent. They fuck you. A lot of big producers employ them, so Lee wants one."

"By the way, I thought Lee was gay."

"Not anymore. It's out of fashion."

"Why are you working with this guy? Why do you even *talk* to him?"

"He may be shallow and a liar and have no sense of honor, but he knows he is."

"Yeah, and he thinks he can get away with being a scum bag because he *knows* he's a scum bag and feels guilty about it, but that just makes him more loathsome."

"I can't be bothered by the Lee Chasslers."

"Maybe you should be."

"Maybe."

"He never even acknowledged he'd been using my name behind my back."

"Yes he did. He said, 'We'll talk business when the script's finished.' His way of saying he won't use your name anymore. At least not until the script's finished."

"Bick," Oscar says, concerned. "*Never* trust that pony-tailed weasel. He'll fuck you over if someone gives him the slightest reason. He's not a friend."

"You OK," Bick asks. "You seem unusually stressed out, even by your standards. Your face is all pinched up."

"Thanks. How are you? Your voice sounds like you've been gargling razor blades."

"What's happened with the movie?"

"I'm reshooting the ending."

"Want to talk about it?"

"Not until I'm finished."

The BMW comes to a quick stop beside them.

"Who knows," Bick says, tipping the valet, "he might be of some use to you someday."

"So we're using him."

"And he's using us."

"The way we all are. Including you and me?"

"Yeah, but at least we like each other." Bick gets in his car and rolls down the window. "Where are we going?"

"What do you want to do?"

"Go home to our work and our girlfriends."

"Great idea. Too bad we don't have girlfriends."

"Damn shame."

"Damn shame."

"Damn shame. Might as well go to The Luve Club."

Oscar nods. "Yeah, maybe we'll make contact there."

A valet pulls Oscar's old Porsche up behind the BMW.

At The Luve Club they stand on the patio warming themselves next to a surfboard-sized barbecue that reeks of lighting fluid. The night is cold with a wind circling through the palms above the patio, but the small abandoned the-

ater is crowded, so many people have come outside where there's space and a warm fire burning.

Oscar is admiring girls in black stockings and black skirts that come down barely below their butts. He never went to clubs until he met Bick at a party of Libby's. He didn't have much of a social life at all until he was sort of adopted by Libby. This happened at a time when he felt he *should* start having a social life, to reap the rewards of his labors.

"You looking for somebody in particular?" Bick asks.

"Yeah," Oscar admits, "I guess I am. Could you tell?"

"Who?"

"I don't know her name."

"OK."

"She never told me her name."

Oscar tells Bick the story of the tattooed White Girl, how they had this cool conversation about sad old movies and when she said she had to get home before her parents were up, she gave him her phone number and he had thrown it out because he didn't think she was important enough for him to seriously pursue. He adds that he doesn't know what makes him think he's such a big fucking deal he can't go out with a girl who isn't famous.

"Of course you do," Bick answers.

Oscar nods. "I've been thinking about her a lot lately," he admits. "I hope I run into her sometime."

"Small town. It's possible."

People all around are laughing, talking, watching each other. Often they're not laughing and talking with the same people they're watching.

"Look over there," Bick suggests.

Oscar stares at a girl in a black leather bodice warming her semiexposed flesh at the other end of the long barbecue.

"And look at the dark-haired girl's mouth," Bick adds.

"I don't like fat lips."

"*Pouty* lips."

"I don't like pouty girls."

"And look at her friend's eyes."

"Is that all you notice on women, mouths and eyes? What about breasts?"

"There's a couple." Bick points his beer at a girl in black with a cross hanging in the shadows of her large breasts.

"Who *are* these girls?"

The Luve Club happens whenever the owners, Connery and Antoinette, get the urge to send out invitations and it draws a large crowd of music people, young movie people, fashion people and ne'er-do-wells. Oscar knows this but still doesn't know who these girls are.

A young girl comes by and hands them fliers for another club and moves

on. This is the fourth flier for other clubs so far and they're only on their second round of beers. Oscar glances at the black and white and red postcard-sized advertisement. Bick puts his on the barbecue and watches it burn.

"Another new club," Bick says.

"This new place isn't a club," Oscar says, and shows Bick a line in the flier:

ARMAGEDDON IS NOT A CLUB.
WE ARE AN EVOLVING ENVIRONMENT
OF ART, ENTERTAINMENT AND PEOPLE.

Bick laughs. "It's good to know there's always going to be places people can congregate for drinking and music and the possibility of sex."

"Yeah, it's a comforting thought."

Oscar puts his flier in the barbecue.

"What about those two over there," Bick asks.

Oscar knows Bick would want the skinny brunet, which means he'll be stuck with the chunky blond, *but what the fuck.*

"Those look like fresh faces," Bick continues. "Possibly disease free."

"OK," Oscar says.

Bick shakes his head, then sets his beer on the side and warms both his hands over the glow. "I was just pointing them out for observation," he says, "I'm not interested."

"Something wrong?"

After a pause Bick says, "I'm sick of seeing pubic hairs in my bed and not knowing whose they are."

Oscar laughs. "OK. Then what the fuck are we doing here?"

"I don't know. I'm aspiring to a normal more religious life, remember, and none of the girls here fits into that picture."

"Nope."

"What if I fall in love?"

"What? What if you fall in love?"

"Yeah, what if?"

Oscar looks at him. "You're not?"

"Possibly."

Oscar turns away. "Naw. Big fucking deal. You've been in love more times than Warren Beatty has fucked actresses."

"No, you're the one who falls in love. I just get laid. I've *never* been in love."

Oscar makes a face.

"I've never been in love," Bick repeats, picking up his beer. "I've had moments of pretty good passion that were workable substitutes, but never love. You know that."

Oscar did not know.

"It's good actually," Bick says. "I still have the *hope* that someday I might be in love. It's what I live for. What if I were already in love? I'd have nothing to live for. It's like Woody Allen says, 'Marriage is the death of hope.'"

"We're talking about love, not marriage."

"Well, for now I'm just thinking about falling in love so I still have hope."

"Who," Oscar asks.

Bick hesitates.

"An actress," Oscar asks.

"Yeah."

"Trouble."

"A *young* actress."

"Major trouble."

"A young actress on the edge of stardom."

"Jayne Sky, the girl you're doing the script for."

"The very one."

"An actress. Oh, man." He shakes his head. "A girl becomes an actress for one reason—to be loved by millions."

Bick smiles. "And the love of truth and beauty."

"My God, Bick. Think about the kind of psychotic insecurity that would motivate a girl to seek out the adulation of millions."

"I have. I suspect it's the same psychosis that would motivate a person to become a writer or a movie director or a mass murderer."

"Writers and directors and mass murderers aren't loved by millions. Are you fucking kidding?"

"But they want their work to be."

"Yeah," Oscar says, "and there it is! Actresses *are* their work. They don't create anything, there's nothing they can separate themselves from. It's their whole sense of self. And they're always looking for The Better Gig." He's pointing his beer at Bick. "And they'll play any role to get The Better Gig. You know what I mean."

"I know," Bick says, "but isn't everyone looking for The Better Gig? The better car, the better whatever. Isn't that the rule these days?"

"Living in this town is twisting your sense of the world."

Bick shakes his head. "It's not the town."

"Listen—" Oscar starts to gesture with his beer bottle and notices it's empty.

"I'll get a couple cold ones," Bick volunteers.

Oscar stays at the barbecue, just glad to be away from the Steenbeck. He's worried about Bick.

Another girl comes by and hands him a flier. "Come to my club," she says and smiles and walks away.

Oscar looks at the flier. Under the club name, which is Read Peace, it states:

THE MONEY REQUIRED
TO PROVIDE ADEQUATE
FOOD, WATER, EDUCATION, HEALTH AND HOUSING
FOR EVERYONE IN THE WORLD FOR ONE YEAR
IS ABOUT AS MUCH AS THE WORLD SPENDS
ON THE ARMS RACE EVERY TWO WEEKS.

Oscar wonders where they get their figures.

When Bick comes back with two beers, Oscar hands him the flier. "I've read about this before," Bick says and puts the flier on the barbecue. "Long time ago."

"Now," Oscar says. "Jayne."

"Yeah."

"What's she got?"

"Hard to say. She's not really a classic beauty."

"I know. I met her."

"But she's . . . got these flaws that somehow come together beautifully. And eyes and a mouth."

"It's good she has eyes and a mouth."

"Her mouth sort of upstages her eyes. Her eyes are underrated."

"I'm worried about you."

"Pale blue."

"Just tell me if you're sleeping with her."

"She slept over one night, but nothing happened sexually."

"What do you mean by nothing? Heavy petting?"

"No. Just a quick kiss."

"Kisses mean nothing to girls like that."

Bick laughs. "Girls like that. Good title."

"After the kiss you should have jumped her bones."

"No, she was just over because she needed a place to sleep. I just read her some poetry and she fell asleep."

"You read her fucking poetry?" Oscar leans his face toward Bick's. "What kind of fag shit is that?"

"She asked me to."

"She fell asleep!"

"She was sleeping over because she was having trouble with some guy, he'd been bothering her and it didn't seem appropriate to jump her when she was weak."

"What could be a better time?"

Bick laughs. "We're just kind of friends at this point."

"Who's this other guy," Oscar asks.

"Just a friend of hers. Not a boyfriend."

"He's bothering her?"

"Just that particular night."

"Kick his ass. She'll love you for it."

"I don't kick ass."

"What, is that your karate motto?"

"No, it's just that I don't kick ass just to kick ass."

"But you have a reason. He was bothering her."

"They've made up."

"Too bad."

"I don't know."

"You gonna take the chance?"

"That's the question."

"Take it."

"Maybe she's the one who will make everything right?"

"Maybe."

"Then I'd be fucked."

Oscar laughs.

"Seriously," Bick says. "Then I'll have what I've always wanted. I'll have nothing to hope for."

"You can hope you don't fuck it up," Oscar says. "Bick, man, you see a girl and you think there's something there, you've gotta pursue it, you gotta get it in your hands and *touch* it and find out." Oscar's rolling. "That's what I did with Elaine, I met her at a party and the next day I tracked down her number through my agent and I called her in New York and did the phone foreplay bit and then I flew to New York and *bang*, that was it." He pauses, remembers. "And six months later the bitch dumped me for a forty-year-old dwarf movie star."

"Were you really in love with her?"

Oscar nods. "Definitely. Hate to admit it, but definitely."

"And your romantic ideals were crushed?"

"Oh yeah, the bitch danced them into the ground."

"So what do you have to hope for now?"

"That I'm stupid enough to fall in love again," he says and laughs. "Your heart heals," he says, thumping his chest.

"I'm really not into heartbreak."

"Well, that's what's most likely going to happen. But you gotta take the chance anyway. It's not that *bad.* It's an intense feeling. You gotta just tell yourself it doesn't hurt that bad and keep playing. If nothing else, you end up with a better sense of what you want from a girl, what you're looking for— you're getting closer—*you hone your desires.*"

"Hone your desires. Not bad phrasing for a director. You ought to take a poke at writing."

"No, then I'd have to listen to people instead of just telling them what to do."

Oscar believes Bick has never been badly burned by a girl. He thinks Bick needs to be torched. Suddenly Oscar asks something he has wondered about. "You and Merri ever, uh, ever?" Bick pauses and Oscar knows the answer. "When?"

"Just before she met Willie," Bick says. "I introduced them, as a matter of fact."

"What happened?"

"He flew her to Mazatlán about ninety minutes after they met. They came back a week later as the happy couple we know and love today."

"I mean between you and her."

"Nothing, really. And nothing was going to happen. I always knew that, so it was cool."

Oscar can't see how this could be cool. "Why not?" he says. "Why wasn't anything going to happen?"

"I think the best of Merri, she's the perfect girlfriend, loving, smart, witty, sensitive and politically aware, votes Democratic."

Oscar laughs. "Cut the shit."

"Merri wanted a movie star. Enter Willie, acting like a movie star long before he actually was one."

"True."

"No, it's more than that," Bick says. "I don't know. You can't explain these things." He lights another cigarette. "But Willie makes her pay for it."

"And pay and pay and pay."

Bick nods.

"Expect the worst," Oscar says, "hope for the best."

"Yeah, I've read that same bathroom wall."

Connery, one of the club owners, comes over. He's carrying a quart can of lighter fluid. "Hi, Bick, how you doing? Watch out."

Connery sprays the barbecue, squirting all the briquettes that aren't glowing and even some that are, and tall gaseous flames lash out in the wind, lighting people in a yellow glow. Oscar half-expects the flames to race right into the can of lighter fluid and blow it up in Connery's face.

Connery tosses the empty can into a garbage bin. "See ya." He waves.

Near the garbage two guys from a minor rock group are chatting up two skinny groupies who have glitter on their cheekbones and chests. Oscar overhears the guys telling the girls about wild days on drugs with their wacky friend Willie John Paul. "More fun than a barrel full of brain-damaged monkeys," one says.

Bick hears this as well. "Excuse me," he says, pivoting slightly, looking directly at the larger one. "You're not a friend of Willie Paul."

"Huh?"

"Because if you were a friend of his, you wouldn't be bragging about this shit," Bick says, dropping his cigarette, "and since you're not a friend of his, you ought to shut the fuck up."

Oscar has never seen Bick so edgy. The larger lummox-like rock and roller switches his beer bottle from one hand to the other. *Brawl*, Oscar thinks. *Thanks, Bick.* He clutches his own bottle. Bick is stone still. The lummox is flexing his shoulders, but his thin friend grabs his arm.

"Forget it, Dirk," the thin sensible one says. "We got beer, we got girls, who the hell is he?"

Dirk lets himself be turned around.

Oscar slaps Bick on the back. "And the night's still young."

T heater lights with cracked gels hang in the club. Red and white and blue lights beam down on the stage, where people are dancing, while in the audience people sit watching, talking, drinking, smoking and the waving stripes of smoke take on the appearance of a ghostly American flag. An old sixties love song is playing. Willie is up in the balcony, where the deejay and his friends hang out. Someone taps him on the shoulder. He looks over warily—Oscar and Bick.

"Hey. You guys just get here?"

"We were outside."

"Anything happening?"

"No. How about up here?"

"Same."

"How you doing?"

"I'm young, healthy, talented and drunk. Doing good." Neither of them comments on the beer in his hand, which Willie appreciates. "I've decided to become a recreational drinker," he explains. "I'm going to drink—I'm just not going to be championship-level competitive."

Willie does not consider himself an alcoholic, just a personality prone to excessive behavior, as Merri says. He isn't sure what his friends consider him, but Bick and Oscar seem pretty cool about it. He's glad they haven't asked him about Merri. "Do you think I should buy an old Jaguar XKE," he asks.

"No," Bick says.

"Why not? It's a classic."

"You'll kill yourself," Oscar answers.

"Don't you wish love were really like that?" Bick says.

"Like what," Willie asks.

"Like in this song."

"Oh." Willie realizes Bick has had a few beers himself. "This song isn't really about *love*," Willie says. "It's about *sex*, which *can* in fact make you happy. The song is supposed to read, 'sex can make you happy,' but they substituted the word 'love' because they got love and sex confused a lot in the sixties."

"Even sex isn't really that good," Oscar says. "Like everything else it only seems great when you don't have it."

"No," Willie says. "It *is* that great."

Bick nods. "It is."

They continue watching the action below. Joy Division's "Love Will Tear Us Apart" follows the sixties song. A few feet away the deejay with his headphones on puts a record back into its sleeve and pulls another from the milk-carton crate.

"Good segue," Willie tells the deejay, who doesn't hear.

"From fantasy to realism," Bick says to Willie.

"Forget realism, Bick," Willie says. "Remember? Sci-fi."

"What," Oscar says.

"Nothing," Bick says. "Any sign of the White Girl?"

Oscar shakes his head.

"What white girl," Willie asks.

Oscar explains. Willie is intrigued by Oscar's reasoning but thinks it's a shame. He's more successful than Oscar and he'll fuck almost anyone who will have him. "You guys have a similar problem," Willie says.

"*We* have a problem?"

"You've both watched too many movies. You're too strung out on this mythical movie-man idea, the Bogart character, the guy who sacrifices the girl to preserve his manhood, the American rogue ennobled by loneliness."

"Oscar has that problem," Bick says. "I'm perfectly well adjusted."

"You're threatening to run away to Alaska," Oscar says.

"Washington."

"What are the girls like there," Willie asks.

"Generalization?"

"Of course."

"Clean, bright-eyed, fresh scrubbed."

"Girls who don't look like some producer just shot come all over their face?"

"Right."

"I should go there. I've never even been to Europe. What are the girls like there?"

"Foreign."

"Sounds ideal," Willie says. "European men have done something right. Maybe it's that they've made fucking their top priority. Thousands of years of civilization has led them back to sex as number one."

"We're a young country."

"An immature country."

"True."

"I love Isabelle Adjani."

"But at least our women speak English," Oscar contributes.

"Not necessarily a plus," Bick says.

Bick and Oscar start bantering about girls. "You two can talk about your manly desires," Willie says. "I'm going to get laid."

"Anyone in particular," Bick asks.

"No."

Again they don't question him, but he feels the compulsion to explain. "Merri's got our business manager quickly closing a deal on this goddamn dream house. I'm weeks away from domesticity."

"Sounds good to me," Bick says.

"You serious," Willie asks.

"A couple years ago the idea of a calm homey life would have bored and scared me, now it thrills me."

"Just getting laid on a regular basis sounds thrilling to me," Oscar says.

Willie asks Bick what he's been doing. Bick tells him about *Till Death Do Us Part* and Jayne. Bick speaks of her in an almost reverential tone.

"You two are both bumming me out," Willie says. "I'm going to venture forth." He points to the crowd below. "Flesh, anyone?" Bick and Oscar look at each other and shake their heads. Willie thinks they should check each other's pulses. "Let's do something tonight that will make us ashamed to be human," he suggests.

"I'm already ashamed," Bick says.

"And I'm ashamed to be your friend," Oscar says to Bick.

"You're not going to help me find trouble," Willie asks.

Bick and Oscar both shake their heads.

"Do you think I'm too result oriented," Willie asks.

"Yes," Bick says.

"I don't mean as a person," Willie says. "I mean as a *professional,* as a *thespian.*"

"Yes," Bick says.

"I'm asking Oscar."

"Yes," Oscar says.

"No. Seriously?"

"Yes," Oscar says. "Sometimes you make lazy choices, but you're good so you get away with it. And your directors let you get away with it. Natural talent can only get you so far, you have to develop character as you get older." He smiles. "Or your career flounders. One or the other."

Springsteen's *Tunnel of Love* comes on and Willie gestures to the closest speaker. "Who didn't know the man's marriage was doomed when they heard this album?"

"Good album," Bick says.

"Yeah," Willie agrees, "but so fucking what. Think about it. What's going to happen to it in twenty years? Assuming the missiles don't fly first. It'll be history, but there'll be too much history for anyone to care. And what about 'M*A*S*H'? Great TV and it's going to be gone *before* the missiles hit. Temporary times we're living in. Radar, we hardly knew ya!" Willie laughs. "I don't know, I'm going to do something."

Willie wanders off with no destination in mind. If Oscar and Bick want to go home alone and moon about what they don't have instead of taking what they could have, no problem. Willie can find trouble without their help.

T hey're barely out the door into the relative cool and quiet when Poppy intercepts them with a screech. She is Willie and Merri's manager and Bick and Oscar like her for reasons neither can explain. She blocks their escape by stepping in front of them and putting one hand on each of their chests.

"Who's in there tonight," she asks, "any celebs?"

"Nobody," Bick says.

"We were," Oscar says.

"You losers don't count."

"And Julian Lennon."

"Really!" She drops her hands to her hips.

"No."

"Is it *boring?*"

"Yes."

"I don't want to go in," Poppy says. "Not if nobody's there. I have a reputation."

"You certainly do."

She laughs. "Where are you two going?"

"Nowhere."

"I love that billboard," Bick says, looking across the street. The billboard is an illustration of a morgue full of sheet-covered corpses on gurneys.

WELCOME TO THE GLAMOROUS WORLD OF COCAINE

"Looks pretty glamorous to me," Oscar says, "after the way I've spent the last few hours."

Poppy reaches into her purse and offers a vial of coke with a built-in spoon. Oscar passes. "I don't know why you don't do it," Poppy says, helping herself. "Everyone *thinks* you do." She hands the vial to Bick.

"I don't do this shit anymore," Bick says, taking the vial, "but that billboard is so inspiring."

"She looks like the White Girl," Oscar says.

"Who," Bick asks, saluting the billboard after a quick blast. He hands the vial back to Poppy. "One of them on a gurney?"

"The other billboard. The girl with the straw in her mouth. I want her."

"She's an illustration, I think."

"I still want her."

"You're going to have a hard time making contact with an illustration."

"I heard about you and Jayne Sky." Poppy smirks at Bick.

Bick says nothing.

"I don't see the attraction," Poppy says, "the girl's skinnier than an anorexic and she's got the complexion of a corpse. And she's not going to last."

Bick does not expect Poppy to see the attraction and he just shrugs.

"Let's *do* something," Poppy says, taking another blast.

Bick knows that Poppy has been hot for Oscar for a long time—ever since Oscar directed his first feature film at twenty-five.

"What's there to do," Oscar asks.

"Bick?" Poppy says, handing him the vial.

"I don't know."

They look at each other. Bick does a couple more blasts. Another herd of cars drives by on Sunset.

"What's there to do?"

"What do you want to do?"

"I don't know, what do you want to do?"

"This is starting to sound like *Marty*," Bick says, handing the vial back to Poppy.

Oscar laughs.

"What?" Poppy says.

"Old movie," Oscar explains.

A gust of cold wind blows over them and Bick looks up and can see a few stars beyond the street lights.

"It's *so* clear tonight," Poppy says. "We could go to Blue Jay Way."

"What's there," Oscar asks.

"Just a view," she says. "It's something to do. We'll buy some beer and park and get drunk with a view."

After buying beer at the Pink Dot, they drive up into the hills. Poppy leads the way in her VW Rabbit to an abandoned knoll on a ridge, a location used in many movies. Oscar tries to avoid running over any of the empty bottles as they pull off the road.

Wind bends the grass and the palm trees and the city sparkles unusually brightly in the clear air. Oscar sits on the hood of his car and stares out. Bick and Poppy, with a six-pack, join him. Bick hands Oscar a beer.

"This is really beautiful," Oscar says. "I've never been up here before. I can't believe I've never been up here before."

Oscar sits to one side of the car's hood and Poppy practically plops on his lap. "We need *music*," she says.

Bick turns on the car radio and an old Aerosmith song is playing. This is followed by an old Springsteen song that reminds Oscar he doesn't have a girlfriend. He chugs his beer. Springsteen is followed by The Doors.

As they start on the third six-pack Poppy announces, "We need *photos*, to validate the experience!"

Oscar knows too well the feeling that something hasn't truly happened unless it's recorded on celluloid. "I'd prefer to keep this experience invalid," he says.

Poppy produces a Polaroid camera from her car and says, "OK, boys," and points the camera.

Bick and Oscar are caught in the white flash.

"Nuclear blast," Oscar says, rubbing his eyes. He gets up, feeling the drunkenness, and takes the camera from Poppy and commands her to lie on the hood with Bick. She does, posing provocatively with the still-developing shot in her hand. Oscar looks through the viewfinder.

"Good, good," Oscar says. "But there's something not quite right." He looks up from the viewfinder. "What color bra are you wearing, Poppy?"

"Black."

"Good. Take off your shirt and sweater."

"I'll take off my sweater," she says, laughing, and whips it off to reveal a T-shirt with a stencil of a weeping woman above the caption NUCLEAR WAR?! . . . THERE GOES MY CAREER!

Bick and Oscar laugh. Oscar snaps a shot. He peels off the film and hands the developing exposure to Bick and sets up another shot. "Nope," he says. "This just isn't working."

"What?" Poppy says.

"The T-shirt isn't working."

She laughs.

"What's funny?" Oscar says. "I'm trying to do a job here. And this shot needs some flesh."

"Artistically speaking," Bick throws in.

"Yes," Oscar says. "Artistically, aesthetically, absolutely, all that shit." He looks through the viewfinder again. "Take it off."

"It's *cold* out," she says.

"Don't listen to your nipples."

She laughs and hands Bick the other developing photo. He looks at it for a second and then tosses both of the photos through the open top of his car into his passenger seat.

"What seems to be the delay here," Oscar asks.

"You really want me to take off my T-shirt? What if someone else drives up here?"

"Listen, if we're not going to do this right, let's not do it at all," Oscar says. "I can't work with people who aren't dedicated."

Poppy laughs and takes off her T-shirt and screams, "Angeleyne rocks!"

"Good, good," Oscar says. "Now lean back a bit."

The white flash pops.

Oscar takes the developing photo and puts it in the side pocket of his blazer. "OK," he says, "let's keep rolling here." He looks through the view-finder. "There's still too much clothing in this shot."

"Have Bick strip," Poppy says.

"No, he's probably wearing white boxers and the bounce would wash out the shot," Oscar says. "What color panties are you wearing, Poppy?"

"Black," she says and laughs.

"Perfect."

"No way," she says.

"Talent is so temperamental," Oscar says to Bick.

"Not unless you get in this shot with me," Poppy says.

Oscar smiles at Bick. Bick rises and takes the camera from him. Poppy pulls off her jeans and the panties are black as promised, but with little red whales. She giggles as she exposes these.

Bick watches from behind the viewfinder.

"It's freezing," she says and hugs Oscar tightly, one of her hands apparently seeking warmth through proximity to his crotch.

Bick snaps a shot and hands the result to Oscar. "Test photo."

Oscar removes the photo he took from his pocket and he and Poppy look at the one while they wait for the other to develop. "I look *bestial*," Poppy says.

Bick snaps another shot.

"*Bestial*," Poppy repeats. "Let's do this inside. It's too cold out here." She skips over to her convertible and gets in the passenger seat. "Get in here, Oscar." She starts the car and turns on the heat.

Oscar looks at Bick. They both shrug. Oscar does not want to think about this. He climbs in the driver's side. Poppy laughs and throws back the convertible top.

"How's this?" Poppy says, laying herself over Oscar.

"Good," Bick says and stands on the front bumper for a shot.

"Can you see this," Poppy asks, moving her hand.

"Yes."

She reaches over with her other hand and undoes Oscar's belt and opens the top button of his Levi's.

"How's that look," she asks.

"Like an R rating."

"I'm not sure I want a photo of this," Oscar says.

Bick snaps the shot.

"Thanks," Oscar says.

Poppy laughs and doesn't pull her hands back. In fact, she undoes another button. Bick hands Oscar the camera.

"Good night."

"Good night."

"Bye-bye," Poppy says without looking up.

This is not the kind of girl Oscar wants for a girlfriend and he doesn't need this kind of reminder. He should have stayed home and worked, or watched a movie, or slept, something. This is not making contact. This is not even honing his desires.

Oscar waves good-bye, or maybe he waves for help, but Bick walks back to his car, where the radio is playing another seventies song, and he takes a last look out at the lights of the city, the palms in the foreground blown by the cold wind. With Oscar and Poppy behind him making out against the riffs of the old song, the whole scene reminds Bick of his own palm-tree-less adolescence and makes him feel too old.

He starts the engine, turns on the lights, which make the swirling dust shine, and turns around and drives back down into the city, hoping Jayne has bought a new phone.

That dire late-night yearning to be holding a warm body makes his hands feel shaky on the wheel and he holds it tighter with his left and moves his right hand to the stick and shifts up into third, thinking that Sarah would probably let him sleep over and her sheets would be clean and warm and she'd say things that would make him feel less alone. Still, he decides it will be better to be alone than go there not knowing what he wants.

There are nine messages on Bick's machine. He hits play in hope one is from Jayne.

Beep.

"Bick, James Jankman, I just spoke with Mel and you should be advised

that your contract includes a two-hundred-and-ten-thousand production bonus for sole credit and half that for shared. So rewrite the shit out of that script." Bick is glad at least one thief in this town is on his side, but he won't over-rewrite just for a shot at screen credit.

Beep.

"Bick, pick up." It's Lee. That makes it two thieves. "Where are you? Did you decide to go to a club? You fuckers. Call me when you get home."

Beep.

"Hi, Bick, it's Liz. I'll call back. I'd leave you a number but my phone's been disconnected. Bye."

Beep.

"Bick, I want you to be the first to know. My search is over. Poppy and I eloped." Then Oscar gets serious. "Jesus, what is wrong with that woman? And why did I spend my night with her that way?" He pauses. "I'm in the editing room now, but I'll call you tomorrow."

Beep.

"I didn't call you just to tell you what a great time I had with Poppy, and it *was* a great time at the time, I called to tell you to take the chance with Jayne. If you think about it too much—like you're probably doing now—you won't do it. So don't think about it, do it. One of us should have a life."

Beep.

"And when you *do*, remember the key. When dealing with dangerous women, and all actresses are dangerous and all women are actresses, the key is don't let them know how much you like them. They need you to like them. It's the one edge you have. Relationships are about emotions, but dates are about ego."

Beep.

"Talk about *her*. Find something that bothers her, she's probably typecast, she probably wants people to look at her in a new way, find this out and talk to her about it. Go after it like a shark. Like *Jaws*. Because then she goes home and says, 'Gee, what an important conversation we had.' It's important because you talked about what's important to her—herself."

Beep.

"The chances of two people falling in love are like the chances of two people standing a hundred yards apart and shooting high-powered rifles at each other and the bullets meeting in midair." Oscar laughs. "Not likely, huh."

Beep.

"And keep in mind, when you consider my advice . . . I haven't been laid since Elaine dumped me."

Beep.

When Bick finishes laughing, he dials Jayne's number. It rings and rings. He's tired, but he turns on the computer to make himself work. Nothing

happens. He paces around, smokes some cigarettes, drinks water, then tries Jayne again. No answer.

When he's exhausted, after one Halcion and three Sominexes, just staring at the computer screen, when he's sure he's tired enough that thoughts of her won't keep him up, he goes to bed.

Thoughts of her keep him up.

He wishes to God he weren't alone.

When the phone rings, he answers before the machine picks up. "Hello?"

"Hi," Sarah says.

"What are you doing up?"

"I can't sleep."

"Yeah."

"You want to meet? For coffee or something?"

Willie wishes to God he were alone.

His vision isn't very clear, but he knows the girl in bed with him is not someone he wants to be with in the light. Fortunately the room is still dark. He wants to see how bad he's been and ready for the worst he cranks his head around to see her face. He's shocked. She's beautiful. He smiles. He pulls the covers slowly down her body—she makes hmmmmm noises—it's a young long beautiful body and tan all over. She wakes up and smiles and reaches her arms out around his neck and pulls him down.

He's going harder and faster and is just about there when she grabs his hips to slow him down. "Shhhh," she gasps. "No noise. Parents."

"Parents?" he gasps back.

"Next room."

He stops and stares at her.

"It's OK," she says, moving her hips slowly, moving his. "They're asleep."

He frantically glances from wall to wall, trying to imagine which one her parents lurk behind, and notices three-ring notebooks, a geometry book, pom-poms, all disturbing cues, and then he freezes. He's looking at himself in a poster for a movie starring WILLIE JOHN PAUL. In smaller print is MERRI SHELTON.

"I've gotta go home." He pulls out and rolls over.

"What's wrong?" she yells.

"Shhh," he says.

"What's wrong," she whispers, grabbing his shoulder as he reaches for his pants on the floor.

"What's wrong?" he repeats. "I obviously don't know, because if I did, I wouldn't be here."

After buttoning his Levi's, he turns to look at her. She seems hurt or confused, naturally. He considers a familiar dialogue: make her admit she fucked him for the stupidest and most superficial of reasons. Tell her she's been used. Call her a star-fucker, call her pathetic. Then tell her *you* feel used.

But he's done this before and it only makes it worse and it's not very funny. "Sorry," he says. "I've just gotta go home."

Merri's undoubtedly noticed his absence by now.

"Thanks for last night," she says. "It was great."

He hopes to make it out the door without being sick.

Bick orders his usual BLT and it's too late or too early to serve beer legally so he orders a vanilla milkshake. Sarah orders a Zucky's burger and more coffee. The middle-aged waitress with an accent of some kind makes Bick repeat the order. She seems very tired and unhappy but not angry.

"Me in ten years," Sarah says when the waitress walks away.

Bick and Sarah are the only two in their section of the coffee shop, the chain-smoking section. The window beside them dimly reflects the well-lighted orangy plastic interior.

"I'll eat here all the time if they hire you," Bick says.

"Thanks." She stares at him. "Why don't you look like shit?"

"What?"

"You drink and smoke like a madman and you never sleep, but you still have your looks. It's not fair, you're like Brick in *Cat on a Hot Tin Roof.*"

"Paul Newman's part."

"Right."

"Torn up about mendacity and his, uh, friendship with Skipper."

"Right."

"I'm not like Brick."

She laughs. "I heard the worst story today. Do you know Bret Taylor? He said he was a friend of yours."

"I only see him occasionally, but he's a good guy. Funny as hell."

"He's the most appalling person I've ever met."

"He's Libby's friend."

"He pitched me an idea called *Amputee Mom.*"

"Uh-huh."

"I won't bore you with the whole formulaic story. Suffice it to say this woman, Amputee Mom, is an amputee with a handicapped child. The town she lives in is populated with people so mean and ignorant it would make Charles Dickens blush. The townsfolk call the handicapped child Gumby. But in the end their ignorance is conquered when the child shows them all a happy-face stick-figure drawing. Taylor said he pictured Valerie Bertinelli as the amputee mom and Eddie Van Halen as her love interest."

Bick smiles.

"Your friend was *laughing* by the end of this pitch."

"Quit calling him my friend, I haven't seen him in weeks."

"He was smiling and laughing and he called the idea Emmy-bait."

"Probably would be."

"But how can someone be that goddamn *cynical?* How can someone laugh while pitching that idea," she asks. "Does this town make people that way, so that everything becomes a joke?"

"I don't think it's unique to this town."

"It's *worse* here. And I don't want to become like that."

"You're not going to become like that."

"How do you know? You say this guy is a good guy and he's *laughing* while he pitches this tragic idea about birth defects and ignorance and evil."

"He was laughing because he's smart enough to know you can't conquer ignorance and evil with a happy-faced stick drawing."

"Of course not, but . . ."

A young man with tattooed forearms moves by, sweeping.

"Sarah, I know you and you're not a jellyfish. Living and working in this town won't change you." She looks blank. "You're a strong person," he continues, thinking this is what she needs to hear, "you'll be fine."

She smiles slightly. "You don't think I can be ruined and dehumanized?"

"No."

"No?"

"No."

"You're not just saying this?"

"Of course, but I mean it."

"I am supposed to be in the office in about three hours."

"I'll sleep in till noon."

"You know what I'd like? I'd like a writer to come in tomorrow—today—and pitch me a character piece, a story that says something smart and interest-

ing and real about why and how we survive with each other, why and how we love or don't love. That's about ninety percent of what makes us happy or miserable, don't you think?"

"Assuming we've got enough to eat."

"But it's more likely I'll be pitched an idea about an alien robot babysitter," Sarah says, sipping her coffee, "which has actually happened."

"And it didn't make you insane," Bick points out.

"Not yet."

There's a commotion and they turn. Willie, in sunglasses, stumbles toward them. A waitress clutching four glasses of water is staring at him. He collapses in the seat next to Bick.

"I'm really glad you're here. I've just been wandering around. Merri's going to murder me with a fork. Everything's so shitty. Have you ordered yet? I hate everything. But I love this place. I need a cheeseburger."

"When he comes in the door, you hit him in the balls with a baseball bat." Libby and Merri are sitting in Merri's kitchen smoking cigarettes and not really watching "Donahue." Merri has been waiting since dawn for Willie to come home. Unusually upset, she called Libby and asked her to come over. "When he's doubled over," Libby continues, "that's when you use the scissors. Grab his hair and cut it off in handfuls."

"Why," Merri asks.

"To let him know you're drawing a line."

"I mean why his hair specifically?"

"I don't know. Just stab him if you want."

On "Donahue" drugs are the issue. A kid in the audience says, *"It's very simple: people do drugs because they want to get high."*

"There's always the chance he has a good reason for not coming home," Merri says.

Merri's naïveté really embarrasses Libby.

"Listen," Libby says, *"of course* he's going to have a good reason for not coming home last night. He'll have a good lie."

"Why are you assuming he'll lie?"

"He's an actor. He lies for a living."

"You're too cynical."

Phil scrambles up an aisle and shoves the microphone to the mouth of a middle-aged woman. She asks Phil how she can tell if her kids are doing drugs.

Phil turns and asks one of the three experts on stage to answer. One asks the mother if her kids seem dazed and confused.

"Willie's going to calm down soon," Merri says.

"What makes you think that?"

"Someday he's going to calm down and he's going to be a great husband and father and everything. Believe me, I know him. He has a great soul and a good heart. It's going to be OK."

"Nothing's going to be OK until you tell him he can't conduct himself like Caligula."

"I've told him that."

"But what do you *do* about it?"

"What can I do?"

"He fucks a *lot* of other girls, Merri!"

Libby expects Merri to react with tears or denial or anger. Merri just says simply, "I know."

"Why do you let him do this?"

"He only does it when he's been drinking or doing drugs."

"Which he does the way other people breathe."

"He's cutting down."

"No he isn't. And he probably won't until something drastic happens. Like you walk and leave him alone."

"I can't."

"Why not?"

"I know you're going to think this sounds sentimental or something—"

"But he needs you."

"No, I need him."

Libby grits her teeth. "Doesn't it hurt you? What he does?"

"You know."

"Does he know?"

"He knows."

"Then why does he still do it, for Christ's sake?"

"I guess he needs to."

"He's fucked up."

"Of course he's fucked up. He's an American male."

"That sounds like a line of his."

"It is."

Libby rises and walks to the window above the sink. She puts her cigarette out in the planter, which contains nothing but dirt.

"Drugs are getting a bad rap," a kid in the audience tells Phil.

"So what do you think I should do," Merri asks.

Libby twirls and screams, "I've been telling you what I think you should do! Tell him to fucking grow up or exit stage left!"

Merri puts out her cigarette and lights another. "You're pretty angry about Bick and Jayne Sky?"

"I guess everyone knows about it by now, huh?"

"My maid told me. She reads *The Star.*"

They both laugh.

"It could be worse," Merri says. "Willie could be having sex with men."

Libby can't tell Merri about Willie's experiment last year with a bisexual novelist.

"The problem with men," Merri says, "is they think with their dicks—and they have small dicks."

"And the ones who don't have small dicks *think* they have small dicks," Libby adds.

"That's the problem," Merri says.

"In a nutshell," Libby says, which makes Merri giggle.

"And the problem with women," Libby says, "is when we just want to not be alone, we convince ourselves we're in love."

Merri doesn't giggle this time. "Maybe that's true for some," she agrees seriously.

"I didn't mean you," Libby says, unsure if she did or not.

"Willie's going to be OK once we settle into the new house," Merri says. "He needs order in his life."

Libby shakes her head.

"I know you think I'm a fool," Merri says.

"No shit."

"But fuck you."

"Huh?" Libby is almost speechless to hear this from Merri.

"All of you think I'm a fool or whatever, but I know what I'm doing, I'm not lying to myself, I know what he does, but I love him so much I can't tell you how much or why but I do and because I love him the way I do, that's all that matters." Merri's mouth continues to move, but no sound comes out for a moment. "I mean, what else do I have?"

Libby is torn between admiration and scorn.

One of the women on stage is talking about Nancy Reagan and "just say no" and the black man next to her scoffs loudly. *"You can't address the drug problem,"* he says, *"without addressing the economic and psychological poverty of our country, particularly* within *the black community itself,* perpetuated *by the values of the white media, all of which Nancy Reagan is ignorant of."* Some kids in the audience cheer. The director cuts to a close shot of a kid with a Guns 'n' Roses T-shirt who looks dazed and confused.

"I'm almost thirty," Merry says, tightening her face into a look of fright. "Closer to forty than eighteen."

"Scary," Libby agrees.

* * *

Libby and Merri are still in the kitchen, now watching a soap opera, when they hear Willie drive up. "OK," Libby says. "This is it. You gotta be cold. If you love him, you gotta be cold to help him."

"I know," Merri says, lighting a cigarette.

"Want me to leave?"

"No, stay and send me silent support. If I'm not being cold enough, open the refrigerator to cue me."

Libby laughs. "I know how charming and winning Willie can be, but no matter what he tries—"

"I know. I know."

Willie opens the side door and comes straight into the kitchen. He is still wearing sunglasses and to Libby he looks clearly guilty of alcohol abuse and drug abuse and infidelity. *Guilty, guilty, guilty.* He stops and holds up his hands in surrender.

"Merri, I'm sorry, I'm so sorry."

"Where have you been?"

Libby anticipates some creative and entertaining fibbing.

"I started drinking and I went to this club where I hooked up with Bick and Oscar. They split, but I kept on drinking and I ended up with this girl. . . . After, I went to Zucky's for food and ran into Bick and Sarah. I didn't tell them about the girl." His rush of anguish even Libby almost believes, but she is wondering about Bick and Sarah. Next thing she knows Willie is saying, "I'm sorry, I'm so sorry." He takes off his sunglasses and throws them in the sink for some reason. His eyes remind Libby of wet red beach balls. "I'm so sorry. . . ." He collapses against the door, slamming it shut.

Nine points for the martyr pose, Libby almost says.

Merri rises from her chair. "Willie," she says, grabbing his face. "You're such a fuck-up."

"I'm so sorry," he repeats.

She hugs him. He hugs her back and notices Libby. "Hi, Libby," he says. Libby is too appalled to speak.

"Come on," Merri says, taking his hand and leading him away. "You need to get in bed and sleep. Come on." She mouths "I'm sorry," to Libby as they pass out of the kitchen.

"Good night, Libby," Willie yells from down the hall.

"Good night, Libby," Merri also yells. "Thanks."

So, this is love. Libby thinks it would be better if Bick were here, so they could laugh about Willie and Merri together, because it's hard alone.

W hen Bick wakes up, around noon, he calls Jayne. There's no answer. After a glass of orange juice and a shower he drives over to her place where he parks and looks around for signs of anything wrong. He knocks on the door, no answer.

Feeling like he's being watched, he turns to his right. She is looking at him through a window. She smiles and waves and disappears, opening the door a few seconds later.

"Good morning," he says. "I just wanted to be sure you're OK."

"Good morning?" She laughs and invites him inside.

"I take it you haven't bought a new phone."

"No, I was going to do that today."

"Let's do it now."

"Now?" she says.

"It's important to keep the lines of communication open."

A box of cereal, Cheerios, honey coated, stands next to a bowl on the kitchen counter. She slurps down the milk. "OK, let's buy a phone." She pauses. "Where do you buy phones?"

During the drive to the GTE Phone Mart in the marina he's thinking of how to suggest they get together soon in a nonprofessional nonfriend romantic manner. At the Phone Mart she picks out a phone shaped like Wonder Woman. During the drive back he's still thinking of how to best make this suggestion.

After they plug Wonder Woman in and test her by calling Bick's answering machine, Bick tells her he should go back to his place and work.

"I love knowing you're hard at work while I'm lollygagging." She walks him to the door.

"Everything's OK with this old boyfriend of yours?" he says.

"Yeah."

"You don't think he needs to be locked up or anything?"

"No more than most people I've worked with."

"That isn't reassuring."

"Everything's cool," she says. "Call me when you get home. We'll test Wonder Woman from the other direction."

He drives home, wishing he had said something.

As soon as he gets back to his apartment, he calls her.

"Hello," she says, sort of warily.

"Hello."

"It works!" she yells happily.

"Would you like to go out on a, uh, date?"

There's a pause as they both try to realize what he's just said.

"A *date?*"

"It's almost the nineties. People are doing that sort of thing again."

"A date."

"Yeah."

"Yeah, that sounds nice."

Nice, he thinks. It's been years since he's heard the word delivered without sarcasm, but he can't be sure there wasn't a slight touch there.

"How are you tomorrow night," he asks, remembering that you don't ask a girl for a date on the same day you're calling.

"No, I've got this meeting with a director tomorrow night."

"How about tonight?" *What the hell.*

"No, I'm busy tonight too."

He thinks maybe she knows how to play this game too.

"How about Saturday?" she says.

"Saturday, fine." He'll miss the screening and party he's supposed to go to that night. *Fuck it.* "I'll call you that afternoon and we'll make plans."

"OK."

"Talk to you then."

"Bye-bye."

He hangs up. His rush of youthful excitement amazes him. *This is good,* he thinks, and paces around and puts on music, choosing an old Wishbone Ash tape from high-school days, a guilty pleasure. He fast forwards to the only song on the album he truly likes. *"I thought I had a girl . . ."* The song works for him as it always has, but somewhere in the midst of this joy it occurs to him

that his life has regressed to a point where he's listening to a pop song by Wishbone Ash and enjoying it far too much to call himself well. If nothing else, he can call it research for his work . . . but, he suddenly realizes, what the fuck is his work if not a valentine for her?

"No," he says, sitting down at his desk, "you're not well."

Oscar feels as good as he imagines it's possible to feel. It's cloudy and cold outside, but he's in a high-school gym sipping coffee center court and hot white light is streaking through the windows from cherry-picker-mounted 10k HMIs and he's with his Panaflex gold camera and his Chapman Hustler dolly, surrounded by grips and gaffers and actors and actresses and high-school cheerleaders, all here for his movie. He's a reverend of high technology, captain of the cinematic ship. He will lead the wagon train to Art.

The director of photography, about twenty years older than Oscar, is setting up a tracking shot on a row of cheerleaders. The cheerleaders, except Oscar's leading actress, are all real cheerleaders. Ten years ago Oscar felt fortunate if a cheerleader deigned to acknowledge his existence. At twenty-seven he's sporting a crew cut and bags under his eyes and skin broken out from stress, yet they're offering him private pep rallies. He refrains. He's a high-school loser who's become a hip spokesman for the youth audience and the irony is enough for him.

The starlet sidles up to Oscar in full cheerleader costume, including pom-poms. "Hi, Oscar," she says with a smile. She has her script in hand, a bad sign.

"What's up?"

"Can I talk to you about Babette's last line?"

"Sure."

She sets down her pom-poms and opens the script.

The original writers offered to come for the reshoot but Oscar said no. If the hacks had written him a decent script in the first place, *nobody* would have to be here. He thinks they were bluffing anyway. *Why would they want to be here? They were paid, they're probably happy.*

She finds the page. "I think she has an opportunity here that's being lost, here when she says, '*You . . . ,*' and can't think of anything to say."

"Uh-huh."

"She's being rejected."

"Uh-huh."

"She should say something snappy after being rejected. She's a proud girl."

"What sort of snappy did you have in mind?"

She adjusts her sweater, pulling it tighter so the school name stretches across her chest. "Something like, 'You're the loser, geek.'"

Oscar can't believe he cast such an awful actress. Never again will he cast by breast size.

"I think Babette, at this point, is too shocked to reply with such spontaneous wit," he says. "She's just been rejected for possibly the first time in her life."

"This geek is rejecting her just to be a jerk."

Amazing how the cast has regressed into their roles so fully, he thinks. "No," he says. "In this new ending Wally's come to a realization. He realizes that he wanted her for the wrong reason—because everybody else wanted her and he wanted to impress everybody. Suddenly that doesn't matter to him anymore. He realizes it's the other girl he really loves."

"The geeky girl."

"Right." He sips his coffee, hoping he sounds convincing.

"I'll swallow that, but I still think Babette needs a snappy exit line. I'm sure Babette would say *some*thing. She's hurt. Or at least pissed off really badly."

"Let's try it the way it's written," he says. "I think you can capture every nuance of Babette's reaction without saying a word. You can kill the audience with a look. You can do that." Fact is, he'll have to use music to wrench any kind of emotion out of the audience.

"I'll try," she says, apparently willing to settle for the flattery.

"Maybe Babette has a realization here also, maybe she sees that Wally is growing up here."

"Yeah," she nods. "Yeah. Maybe she sees that."

"It's going to be a great last moment for you," Oscar says, picking up her pom-poms and handing them to her and hoping this will make her go away.

"Thanks," she says.

He nods, smiling encouragement.

She walks out of the gym rehearsing her cheerleader moves, butt out, pom-poms up.

He realizes he hasn't thought about the White Girl at all here on the territory where he's most comfortable. Unfortunately this makes him think about her. What would she think if she saw him here now? Would she be impressed? He'd want her to be, and think less of her if she were. He likes to imagine she'd have the good taste to tell him he's wasting his talent. His first was a hit and he should have left high school behind then, but his agent and his father and his father's friend told him he should do this so he'd have *two* hits under his belt and now he's reshooting the ending so he doesn't have a career-crippling disaster under his belt. He's supposed to be the fearless leader on this set and he's scared shitless.

Mona comes running over, out of breath. "Oscar, I've gotta go, it's an emergency, I'll call you later."

"Emergency? What?"

"Don't worry, it has to do with the real world," she says on the run.

Oscar has no idea what this could be about and no time to care.

Outside the hospital Mona is looking for parking when she spots Joy just sitting in the sun at the entrance. She wheels her Honda Civic around. Joy's eyes are closed and she appears to be tanning, something Mona has never known her to do. Her eyes open when Mona's brakes screech. She rises and walks slowly to the car, a little shakily. When she reaches for the passenger door handle the clean bandages wrapped around her wrist seem very white in the sunlight.

"Thanks," Joy says, strapping on her seat belt. "They wouldn't drive me back home." There are bandages on both wrists.

Mona doesn't know what to say. She's furious. She's furious with Joy for doing it, furious at herself for not seeing it coming. She takes some comfort in the certainty that Joy didn't actually mean to *kill* herself.

"You slit your wrists?" she finally says. "How lame. Why didn't you slit your ankles? Or your throat?"

"I didn't think of that."

A car behind them honks.

"Fuck you," Mona yells.

"Let's go home," Joy says.

"Don't I have to sign you out or anything?"

"No. Do you think I'm too pale?"

"They just bandaged you up and turned you loose?"

"After they made sure I had health insurance."

"How do they know you won't just do it again?"

"They don't care. What can they do? I told them I wouldn't do it again." The car behind honks again.

Mona puts her head out the window and screams, "Fuck you!" and then notices it's an old couple and feels bad.

"Come on," Joy says, "let's go home. I've had a big day."

Mona drives. Joy turns on the radio. She skips past several songs and stops on a commercial for The Gap and turns it up until it distorts.

Mona takes this to mean Joy doesn't want to chat.

It's just starting to get dark outside. Joy is lying in bed. Mona comes in carrying a tray with chicken soup and a Halcion pill.

"Are you going back to the set," Joy asks as Mona sets the tray in her lap.

"No," Mona says, sitting at the foot of Joy's bed. "I'll stay here."

"You don't have to." She picks up the bowl of soup with both hands and raises it to her mouth. "I'm fine. Really."

"Prove it. Use a spoon."

"Go back to the set."

Mona intends to stay and doesn't mind. She's just not sure if she should ask why questions. "I'm not needed on the set," she says. "Oscar probably feels more free to act like a little Hitler without his friends around."

"Is he just crazed on the set," Joy asks with a smile.

Mona nods.

"Don't tell anyone about this," Joy says.

"OK."

"Seriously. It was just like this impulsive thing and everyone thinks I'm disturbed enough as it is."

"No one thinks you're disturbed," Mona lies.

"Yes they do."

"Only people who know you well."

Joy laughs. She seems to be in a good mood, considering. As she sips from her soup bowl the bandages on her wrists suddenly strike Mona as comical.

"You look like Smokey the Bear," Mona says.

"What?"

"Didn't Mommy or Daddy ever read you that story? About Smokey the Bear being caught in the forest fire and how some good forest-ranger couple found him in a tree and bandaged his burns and everything?"

Joy starts to cry.

"It's not *that* touching a story," Mona says, surprised, confused.

Joy quits crying. "The soup's too hot," she says. "Daddy's still fucking young actresses."

"That's news to no one," Mona says, thinking it best to downplay anything about Joy's dad, a genuine pervert. He has won three Academy Awards for producing motion pictures that elevated the art form and humanity and he's friends with the Reagans.

"He's fucking a friend of mine's roommate."

"Who?" Mona finds herself saying.

"October."

"He's fucking October?"

"No, October's roommate."

"Oh."

"You know what he does?"

Mona shakes her head. She's not sure she wants to know.

"He makes this bimbo dress up in a girls'-school uniform and then he puts her over his knee and pulls up her skirt and spanks her."

Mona does not find this particularly shocking.

"And you know what he says when he's spanked her?"

She knows immediately but doesn't want to say anything.

"'*Joy*,'" Joy says. "He says, 'You've been a very naughty girl, Joy.'"

Mona tries to mask her repulsion. "When did you find this out?"

"A long time ago."

"Oh."

Maybe this doesn't explain as much as Mona originally thought. Or maybe it does.

"Daddy and Tim hated each other," Joy says grimly.

"Another tribute to Tim's good taste."

"Yeah." Joy sighs and swallows the Halcion with the last of her soup.

III

Saturday Bick has date stomach. Shaving, he almost expects the mirror to show he's suddenly sprouted pimples.

He dresses in Levi's, white button-down, rep tie, blue blazer and penny loafers, the same thing he wore on first dates many years ago. He considers chewing a Tums but pours himself some bourbon instead. He sips the bourbon and smokes a cigarette and looks out the open window at the boardwalk lights and the incoming planes over the ocean, trying to relax. From the northeast a Santa Ana is blowing strong and dry and its warmth seems weird to Bick.

Around eleven this morning, when he woke up uncharacteristically early, he called her and made plans for a movie and dinner. He told her he'd pick her up at seven thirty. About that time he leaves his apartment.

Driving down Pacific, the bourbon and nervous acids blend in his stomach. He doesn't like his inability to control his emotions, but as long as he can't he figures to revel in them, to appreciate the buzz. He needs to shift into the left lane, and a jeep makes room for him. He accepts this as a good omen. Entertaining the idea that maybe the jeep driver could somehow sense an important mission, he feels he's fortune's favorite for being the only one in the world who has a date tonight with Jayne.

She opens the front door and she's wearing a black scarf to hold back her hair, a thin white blouse, and a long black skirt that contrasts sharply with her pale legs and swirls around her knees in the warm wind. He's glad she's definitely dressed for a date. To him nobody could be more beautiful.

"Hi," she says.

"Hello."

"What do we do now?" she says, smiling. "Do you come in for like some Harvey's Bristol Cream?"

They both laugh. She seems as anxious as he feels.

"We should probably go if we're going to make the movie," he says.

"I'll get my overcoat."

He waits outside for a moment and checks his hands—dry. She reemerges wearing a long black ragamuffin overcoat.

As they walk to the car, he glances at her, looks ahead, glances at her, looks ahead. He wonders where her sense of style comes from.

"What?" she says and smiles as he glances at her again.

"Nothing," he says.

He opens the car door for her and she says, "Thank you." *This is* really *like a date,* he says to himself.

"Do you mind keeping the top down," he asks.

"No, not at all. I love convertibles."

Driving to Westwood, Bick puts on one of his own compilation cassettes. Jayne casually ejects the tape during the opening Replacements song and tosses it into the glove box. Bick glances from the road to her as she rummages through her overcoat and pulls out her own tape, which she puts on and turns up.

"Thank you," he says.

"For what?"

"For putting my tape back in its case."

After a pause she says, "I didn't."

"I'm anticipating your politeness."

She glares at him. He knows tonight's date could easily end prematurely. The last time he suggested to a young actress that the world didn't revolve around her, she replied that the world *she* lived in did, in fact, revolve around her. He can still feel Jayne's glare. He turns toward her. She turns the glare up a notch. He remains impassive.

"Watch the road," she says.

He smiles and turns.

With his peripheral vision he can vaguely see her return the tape to its case. Bick has read somewhere about how the Santa Ana winds demonstrably rearrange the air's molecular structure and affect the brain's nervous center, causing edginess and impatience, but he doesn't remember this well and it sounds too crazily southern California to say to Jayne now.

When they merge from the 10 to the 405, other drivers politely make room and Bick points this out to Jayne. He tells her it's a good omen.

Jayne smiles and Bick thinks things are OK, for the moment.

"Take the Santa Monica exit," she tells him.

"Why?"

"Just do. Please."

"Why," he asks, changing lanes.

"You'll see. Take Little Santa Monica."

The car bumps on asphalt piles as he maneuvers past the orange cones and striped barriers of construction work. "There," she says. "My favorite billboard in the world."

Scoreboard neon lights read:

SMOKING DEATHS THIS YEAR
105,304 AND COUNTING

"Pull over," she says.

"You don't want to sit and wait for the numbers to change, do you," he asks.

"Yep." She's suddenly joyous.

He stops on the dirt parking strip, facing the billboard. They both light cigarettes. "That can't be true," he says. "A hundred and five thousand this year?"

"Could be."

"Yeah, I guess it could. How long is this going to take?"

"I don't know. I've never done this before."

"We don't have that much time."

"We can wait."

They wait and smoke in the open car with the warm wind blowing and headlights of cars passing from both directions, listening to her Dramarama tape.

After a while Bick says, "Nothing like a hot cigarette on a hot night underneath a body-count billboard."

She laughs. "Just wait."

Suddenly all the lights brighten for an instant and the four changes to a six.

"*Two,*" Jayne says, excited. "Two deaths just then."

"And just in time for us to make the movie," he says.

"Two," she says.

"Yes."

"Two," she says, socking his shoulder.

"Yes." He doesn't know what else to say, but this doesn't matter because she turns up her tape.

By the time they find parking, the eight o'clock movie is sold out. They have two and a half hours to kill in Westwood if they want to catch the next

show. Bick does not have a contingency plan. "Should we buy tickets to the ten-thirty," he asks her.

"Yeah, I really want to see this. Everyone thinks a couple of the performances are going to win awards."

He buys two tickets to the ten-thirty showing from a girl about Jayne's age.

"We could eat now," Jayne says.

The collegiate hostess at Strattons tells Bick they can have a table in about half an hour.

"Should we have a couple of drinks," he asks Jayne, then remembers the age problem. "Or we could go to a record store or something. Or a bookstore, Butler/Gabriel is good."

"Let's do that. Go to a record store."

They stroll down the sidewalks past the cars and the shops. They're surrounded by roaming college kids, high-school kids, respectable-looking adults.

"There was a gang-shooting here last week," he says.

"Yeah," Jayne says. "I heard about that. The girl died. Didn't she?"

"Yeah."

"Someone should do a movie about the gangs, something like *The God-father* that shows how these gangs are like family in a sick way."

"Someone did. *Colors.*"

"No, that was an 'Adam-12' thing about an old cop and a young cop, I mean a real movie."

"'Real movies' is sort of an oxymoron."

"'An oxymoron,'" she laughs. "What kind of word is that?"

"It means a contradiction."

"Good word."

In Penny Lane, Jayne bops around picking out records and CDs and handing them to Bick. He already has much of what she recommends and she seems both disappointed and glad. Despite the age difference, they have similar musical tastes, hers extending back to vintage Dylan. They enthusiastically quote songs, not something Bick often does in public. Heads turn. She is definitely the store's top attraction for the moment, but he isn't sure if it's because she's recognizable, or because she's being such a spectacle, or if it's simply that she's so attractive. In any case Bick is sure they are annoying cooler customers but doesn't care. Jayne pushes a twelve-inch single in front of his face with her finger pointed to the lyrics on the back: *No one in the world ever gets what they want and that is beautiful.*

She adds it to his load.

"Well," he says as they walk out of Penny Lane, "so far this is a four-hundred-dollar date."

They have dinner in a booth, Thai pizza, and he drinks beer and she drinks Coke. The easy conversation about music helped and now they're relaxed

enough to talk about themselves. The first thing she wants him to understand is that unlike certain other actresses, "being on the cover of *People* is not my be-all." She won't say anything much about her parents except that they're sixties casualties.

Because of her resistance, Bick persists. "Do you think this gives you an edge as an actress," he asks, "having hippie parents?"

"Why?"

"Well, you probably started life with a skewed sense of reality. You didn't even have to work at it."

She doesn't smile. He smiles to let her know he intends this with humor.

"I have as good a sense of reality as anybody," she says, still not smiling.

"You really think so?"

"Yes and why are we just talking about me?"

"I'm just trying to even things out."

"What do you mean?"

"I feel like you have the advantage here," Bick says. "You've read my work and I've only seen you playing someone else in a movie."

"Who are you playing in your writing?"

"No one in particular."

"You mean God. I know about writers." She smiles and looks down at her food and plays with her knife, then asks, "Do you believe in love?"

"What? Yeah, yes I do."

He lights a cigarette, wondering if he really does.

"You're a romantic," she says. "Aren't you?"

"It generally works to come across that way on dates."

"You didn't answer the question."

"These aren't very romantic times."

"You still didn't answer the question."

"I don't want to get into a big conversation about what is romance and all, not now."

"Why not?"

"It's too hot out."

"Do you believe in love at first sight?" He looks away from his cigarette to her eyes. They seem very clear and intent. There's a moment of contact he can feel vibrate through his line of vision into his spine. She blushes a bit, he thinks, as she looks down at the table and picks up her own cigarettes. "You should," she says.

He lights her cigarette. "Thanks for the tip."

"I don't want to tell you how to do your work or anything," she says, "I believe writers just have to write, but there is one thing I wanted to say about *Till Death Do Us Part.* OK?"

"OK."

"Don't be afraid of romance."

Finishing his beer, he starts on his water.

"Do you think people are afraid of romance," she asks and before he can answer she says, "Why?" He is again slow with an answer and she continues. "Name me one good romantic movie from the eighties. And not an art film. A mainstream major-studio release."

Bick names the best and most recent he can think of, *Tequila Sunrise.*

"Very stylish and sexy love story," she agrees, "but it's between the two men."

He laughs.

"It *is*," she says. "Michelle Pfeiffer is beautiful, but she's *just* beautiful, so when Mel Gibson has to declare his love and all he can do is call her the most beautiful *thing* he's ever seen, it's too true. There's miles more depth to the men's roles."

"It's from a male point of view."

"No kidding. Raul Julia says, 'Women, you can always get another, friends are what count,' or something like that."

"Yes, but in the end Gibson kills a friend and risks his life for love. It's a very romantic movie."

Jayne thinks for a moment. "Did you buy it when Gibson and Pfeiffer were frolicking in the ocean through a zoom lens?"

"Worked for me."

"OK, name another."

"*An Officer and a Gentleman,*" he says, "big box-office romance."

"Great tattoo, Richard. Name another."

He knows there are others, but is blanking. "*Splash,*" he finally tries.

"A love story between a man and a *fish.*"

"Things are desperate. I'll give you that."

"*Why?*"

"And don't forget *Scarface.*"

"What?"

"Tony Montana sums up relationships. 'First you get the money, then you get the power, then you get the woman.' Or maybe he says 'pussy.' We should rent the video."

She laughs, "That's horrible."

"Why? You think it's true?"

"He writes the *worst* women characters. You better not Oliver Stone my character."

He laughs. "Writes great male characters though," he says. "And ballsy stories."

"With no romance."

"At least not in the boy-girl sense."

"That's the best kind of romance. Why do we run from it?"

She seems to sincerely want to know and he would like to tell her. "I don't know."

She stares back, wanting more.

He tries. "I think it has something to do with our natural reluctance to embrace the stupidity of the past." She seems to be listening closely. He finishes his water, tries to remember how many beers he's had. "The problem, I think, is that in trying to be smart and cool and all, we tossed the old rules but haven't found new ones, we lost something but haven't found anything, yet. I don't know. Could I have a sip of your water?"

She nods.

Her glass is full and he drinks most of it.

"You need another beer or something?" she says, smiling.

The crowd hisses and boos and tosses popcorn at the screen and then laughs and hisses and boos louder at the commercial for a Japanese car shown between the previews of coming attractions and the feature.

"I want my money back," a woman yells and people in the audience yell and laugh in a chorus of support. "This is a *movie palace*," the woman screams. "This is a fucking house of worship and celebration of the human condition and we will not stand for commercial desecration, at least not so blatantly!"

As people laugh and clap, Bick, sitting in a dark corner in back with Jayne, realizes it's Mona leading the facetious revolt.

"Friend of mine," he says to Jayne.

"She's loud."

"And angry."

"I'm mad as hell and I'm not going to take it anymore," Mona yells.

"I'm mad as hell and I'm not going to take it anymore," the audience repeats.

They repeat this litany from *Network* with escalating volume and humor until the commercial ends. Bick is surprised and glad about all the indignation.

During the feature Bick and Jayne comment quietly to each other about the lighting, the camera moves, the actors and actresses and Jayne tells the true story of the liaisons on the set, a story far more interesting and decadent than the one on the screen, and with no redemptive ending.

Jayne's legs are a constant distraction. Her skirt has hiked up and she keeps crossing and uncrossing and crossing the white flesh. She touches his arm a couple times when the movie is particularly bad or good.

She is pleased when Malkovich dies.

The lights come up and they exit ahead of the crowd. "What did you think," she asks.

"It's gotten to a point where I like a movie as long as I don't hate it."

He enjoyed the movie, as he usually does, because he enjoys the communal experience of moviegoing, but he's ready for a drink and is thinking of where to go.

"Yeah," she says, "I know what you mean. What I hate is when a movie is like *begging* you to like it."

Out in the light of the street they walk behind a couple who have their arms around each other.

"Uma Thurman was real good," he says as they pass the movie stills in the glass showcases.

"Huh?"

"You didn't think so?"

"All she had to do was look dumb and show off her tits."

He should know better than to compliment one actress to another. Of course, he does many things when he should know better.

She pokes him. "Is that Willie Paul?"

Willie had sex with Jayne in The Llasa Club bathroom the night of her sixteenth birthday party. Later her mother came on to him, but she was too old and wearing leather and it was too sad. He'd forgotten this until just now. Though Jayne hasn't really become the lyrical beauty reported by Bick, she has acquired a certain style. Willie thinks she's flirting with him, and he would go for her, but he does have some rules and one is don't fuck a friend's love interest.

"We're going to get something to eat," Merri says. "Join us."

"No thanks," Bick says, "we already ate."

"Drinks then," Willie suggests.

Bick again quickly declines and it's obvious he wants to be alone with this girl, or maybe he just wants to get to his car with the huge bag from Penny Lane.

After they split up, Merri asks Willie what he thought of Jayne.

"Seemed cool enough."

"Is she a good actress?"

"Haven't you seen her work?"

"Well, I guess I must have."

Willie thinks she's real good. "She's OK."

"Why's Bick writing the script for her?"

"Money."

"Money?"

"OK," Willie says, "it's probably something more, but I don't know what."

"Are they having sex?"

"I don't know."

Merri elbows him.

"Honestly, I don't know."

To avoid encouraging contact they walk fast and with eyes straight on the sidewalk ahead or on each other, but Willie glances up at two high-school-age girls in skirts and sweaters staring at him from across the street. He's accustomed to this but always vaguely aware of it, sometimes unsettled by it. Merri seems more comfortable with the constant surveillance.

Most of the actresses Willie knows have a serious case of self-love, but Merri is one of the only ones he knows who actually *likes* herself, but of course she also likes him so her taste is open to doubt.

"Willie John Paul," some girl shouts.

Willie smiles and looks over as he keeps walking. This girl is with a boy who is also looking over at Willie, but in a different way than the girl, not with awe or jealousy, but a sort of covetousness.

"She likes you," Merri says. "Her boyfriend doesn't."

He doesn't read his fan mail anymore, because it depressed him so much. Plus, there was something disturbing in innocent but incredibly boring letters from people who wanted to tell him about their weekend as though he were a friend or someone who actually cared. It was funny at first and then not.

"Bick is really into that girl, isn't he?"

"For now."

"What do you think's going to happen?"

"I don't know."

"He's not thinking of *marrying* her, is he?"

"Jesus, I don't think so."

Willie remembers one time he was unusually fucked up and watching Carson and a girl came on whose beauty riveted his whole being. The instant he saw her he wanted her. A couple seconds later he realized it was Merri. They'd already been going out almost two years.

"I want to find a role where I can play a decent human being," Willie says. "If I can't be one in life, I might as well be one in a movie."

"You need to find a good script," she says.

"I know."

"So do I," she says. "Something without a nude scene."

"I don't see why. You've got a fantastic body and you're totally at ease with it."

"Yeah, but my parents aren't."

He laughs. He likes her parents.

"I'm looking for roles for both of us," she says, "but you should be helping."

"Poppy reads better. And it's her job to find roles."

"You can't always depend on Poppy."

"But I can depend on *you.*"

"I haven't read anything decent in weeks. Everything I've been reading lately is for *ordinary* parts. It seems to be the hot new trend. What's the copy line on the new Meryl Streep movie, 'an ordinary woman under extraordinary pressures'?"

"What the fuck does any of us know about ordinary lives," Willie says.

"Basic motivations are pretty universal," Merri says.

Merri is the most grounded person Willie knows. It must have come from having that ordinary life her first eighteen years, until she got the series. Then she had a surrogate family, the people she worked with every week.

"You need to be thinking about what you want to do next," Merri says. She's obviously anxious for him to get back to work.

"I've been thinking about it." *Sure.*

Willie suddenly realizes he's about to bump into a guy who's walking quickly and blindly and sidesteps to avoid him. Then he realizes the guy is an actor he worked with a couple months ago. Willie calls out the actor's name. The actor pretends not to hear.

"He didn't realize it was you," Merri says, pulling Willie along.

"Rimjobber."

"He didn't know it was you. He was probably stoned."

"No, he doesn't do drugs. He doesn't drink. Though he probably would if he thought it would advance his career. He's the kind of guy who was *touched* by Dustin Hoffman's seriousness at the fuckin' Golden Globes. He's the kind of guy who comments on his own comments in an interview." He switches into the actor's voice. "Gee, I guess that gives you an interesting quote, huh?" Back in his own voice he says, "Would you like me better if I were a smug dumbfuck like him?"

She laughs and kisses him on the cheek. "Yes."

"Bick probably *is* having sex with her."

"Jayne? *Really,* you sure?"

"I'm sure he'd like to be."

"He should be with Libby."

"Libby is not his dream girl."

"Is Jayne?"

Willie doesn't answer.

"Bick should be with someone like Libby."

Willie knows the implications of arguing this, and doesn't.

Now that Merri's series has been axed, she's giving Willie more attention

than ever and it makes him uneasy. She needs more than he thinks he has. They cross the street against the DON'T WALK sign.

"I think I want to play a politician," he says.

"I thought you said you wanted to play someone decent."

"A *good* politician."

"I hardly ever see good scripts about politicians. But I'm sure something good will come along. Maybe I can find a script for both of us, we can play somebody *married* or something."

"Fuck it," Willie suddenly says. "I could *be* a politician. Why couldn't I run for the U.S. Senate or something and then be president?" He's joking, but then he thinks about it and it seems realistic enough.

Photos of movie stars and dead animals decorate the walls of The Forelite. Bick and Jayne sit in a booth beneath eight-by-tens of Gary Cooper, Tippi Hedren and a hunter with a handful of dead ducks. Jayne orders gin on the rocks with a twist and Bick orders straight bourbon. The older waitress with glasses hanging on a librarian's chain doesn't ask for ID. Jayne knows about Willie's wayward ways and asks why Merri puts up with it. "It's a mysterious and masochistic thing," Bick answers. Their conversation about actresses steers to Jayne after the drinks arrive. True to Oscar's prediction, she says she's tired of being cast as a teenage femme fatale and wants to play roles that show she's more.

"Even though *Till Death Do Us Part* is basically a femme fatale," she notes.

"I was going to mention that."

"But I'm sure you'll make her more complex, more real."

"More complex and real than what?"

"*Other* femmes fatales," she laughs. "I don't know. You think I'm too old for the part?"

"No, not at all."

"Too young?"

"No."

"I feel like maybe I should start playing adult roles."

"Don't rush it. You're going to have a long career."

She stares at her drink for a moment, touching a tear of condensation with the tip of her finger. Something has affected her and Bick doesn't know what. He understands why actresses are insecure about the length of their careers, but he doesn't see how he could have overwhelmed her with that small compliment.

"An old boyfriend of mine once told me something weird," she says.

OK, he thinks, *the cocktails are on the table—let's talk old boyfriends.*

"Was this the same one who trashed your parents' house," he asks.

"No, a different one. He said he spent a lot of time trying to figure out what about me fascinated him and he finally figured it out."

"Yeah?"

"He said I had this aura about me like I wasn't going to last. As a person. Like I was going to be dead within a couple years, he said."

Bick doesn't respond immediately. For a moment he imagines he sees this quality in her.

"Don't you think that's a weird thing to say," she asks.

"Yes, I do."

"Why do you think he said something like that?"

"I don't know."

"To freak me out?"

"Possibly. Do you have a history of these types of boyfriends?"

"Yeah, and they all fall in love with me right away."

"You mean in the first couple weeks?"

"I mean in the first couple hours."

"Uh-huh."

"And they never fall *out* of love. One guy I broke up with used to sit outside this one apartment I was living in, just to catch glimpses of me in the windows. I didn't know it at the time. I heard about it later from another boyfriend who was a friend of his. After I broke up with that one, they probably both sat out there." She smiles, looks down, sips her gin. "Don't you think that's weird?"

"Yes."

"I hate it when guys fall in love like that. I mean, before they really even know you. 'Cause what can it mean?"

Bick realizes he might have grossly misinterpreted the earlier love-at-first-sight question. "What about love at first sight," he asks.

"I believe in that, but it has to be mutual, don't you think?"

"No, not necessarily. Love is not at all necessarily a mutual thing."

"But then what good is it?" She laughs.

"There's something good in love, unrequited or not. It's good in itself, to be able to love is a good thing. If it's truly love we're talking about."

"Hmmm."

Bick excuses himself and walks over to the bar to order another round. While he waits, he looks at Alan Ladd next to a buck lying under the boot of a hunter with a crossbow. It reminds him of what he doesn't want to happen to him. When he brings the drinks back to the table, Jayne has her purse in hand.

"Time to exit," she says.

As Bick's about to turn from La Brea onto the Santa Monica Freeway west, she tells him to go east. He switches lanes.

"Where are we going?"

"To the Harbor Freeway north."

"Then?"

"We'll get on another freeway."

This turns out to be the Pasadena Freeway. As he speeds through the curves, he wonders where she's taking the night and allows his imagination to hope for the best.

"You drive well" is all she says.

"It's the car," he says, downshifting.

Somewhere in Pasadena they turn off the freeway. Bick has never been here. There are elm trees and oak trees and blown foliage in the street and it feels suburban, anywhere U.S.A. She directs him through an upper-middle-class residential area, past an English Tudor near a Spanish stucco near a French Normandy near a Colonial.

"Pull in here," she says, pointing. "Next one."

He turns, then stops in front of a closed gate. Through thick metal bars the broken beams of the BMW's headlights brighten a fountain at the top of the driveway.

"Park."

"Here?"

"Yep," she says.

He turns off the car, wondering. She smiles at him and gets out. He follows. No lights are on in the big house. She steps over to where the gate meets a seven-foot brick wall and reaches her hand out for his shoulder. He finds himself picking her up with one hand under her arm and the other under her knees and swinging her onto the brick wall. After tight-roping down the wall a few feet, she jumps off.

"Did you break anything?"

She laughs. "Come on."

He scales the brick wall relatively easily. By the time he is over, she is in front of a picture window, her hand inside a bush. As he catches up to her, he notices that the *Ordinary People*-style house is old, the white paint peeling, the windows clouded. The water in the cupid fountain is stagnant and green-brown and the marble statue is cracked in several places.

She pulls a key out from the bush and skips up the steps to the front door. "This," she says, swinging open the door, "is my house."

He follows her inside.

"My living room," she says, flicking on the lights, waving her hand out toward the mess of ladders and protective sheets and rolls of wallpaper. "I'll give you the grand tour."

She rubs her hands together, excited. Old smells of wood and fireplace fires and spilled wine mix with new smells of wax and glue and paint. The floors are dark hardwood. Paint is half-sanded off the wooden moldings. The fireplace is about the size of his first apartment. She leads him through the living room and an empty dining room into a kitchen with no sink or appliances. "I don't like cooking anyway," she says.

They walk past a bathroom with a brand-new toilet lying disconnected in the middle of the tile floor. "My business manager tells me that when *Till Death Do Us Part* goes into production, I'll have the cash to finish everything."

"Don't make me feel so responsible," Bick says.

She leads down a hall into a medium-sized bedroom. "All the closets are cedar-lined. It keeps clothes from getting moldy and stuff."

"I know," he says. "My mother once found my *Penthouse* magazines when she was putting cedar blocks in the drawers at the summer place."

She lets this slide and turns on a switch and they follow the light up a set of shaky wooden stairs.

"The game room," she says at the first door at the top. The room is unlighted and half-carpeted. "I'm going to have a Ping-Pong table and a pool table and one of those oversized TVs." They proceed back down the hall past a small room. "My office."

He wonders what the hell she will do with an office but doesn't ask.

She opens a door and they enter a large room with refinished hardwood floors and French doors that lead out to a deck. "My room. And walk-in closet." The walk-in closet is a room unto itself. They enter and she closes the door behind them and turns on a light. The door is thick steel with a bolt lock. "This room is totally secure." She picks up a portable phone from a wall mount with blinking red and green lights. "And I can call the police or whoever if someone is breaking in."

"Do you have a bomb shelter also?"

"I thought about it," she says seriously, "but then I thought, you know, what the hell. Why bother?" She leads out of the secure closet into an equally large bathroom with a big gold bathtub built for two. "I love water," she says, and turns a faucet and when water gushes she's surprised and excited. "It works!" She turns it back off. The room smells of caulk and the toilet appears to be functional.

"Mind if I use this room," he asks.

"You're going to be the first," she says, smiling.

"How thrilling a thought."

She walks out and closes the door.

After, he finds her downstairs staring out the French doors into the dark backyard, holding a bottle of gin and a bottle of bourbon.

"No ice, no glasses," she says, turning.

"No problem." He takes the bottles from her. "Where to now?"

"There are other rooms," she says, "rooms I might show you later."

"Why not now," he asks.

"No, I can't show you all my rooms right away," she says, avoiding his eyes. "Can I?"

He understands and says nothing.

She suddenly faces him. "You grew up in a house like this."

Bick glances around. "Well," he says, "we had furniture."

"Seriously," she says. "You grew up in a big normal house like this, didn't you? With pictures of golden retrievers and sailboats and stuff, right?"

He laughs. "Yeah, I guess I did."

"That must have been nice." She means it.

He realizes what she sees as his roots, stability, his *normality*, appeals to her. "Where to now," he asks again.

She flips some switches and the backyard is suddenly ablaze. They step out through the French doors onto the patio. New red bricks run down steps to a white Jacuzzi and glowing blue pool and past the pool and overgrown grass a freshly whitewashed gazebo bears red and yellow paper lanterns that are blowing about in the dry breeze coming in between tall shaking trees that have left yellowing leaves in the gazebo and pool and Jacuzzi and on the patio all the way up to where the two of them stand. He can taste dust.

"I love water," she says again.

They step leisurely down the steps and around the Jacuzzi. She tosses a cigarette, which fizzes out in the pool right above one of the underwater lights. "I'm going to have the Jacuzzi painted blue," she says. "To match the pool."

"I kind of like it the way it is. The white."

"Do you? OK, I'll keep it that way. Just for you."

He can't tell if she's kidding.

She leads him past the pool to the gazebo. In the middle of the gazebo table is a weathered book and a white candle in a wine bottle. "Matches," she says.

She lights the candle and hands him back his matches and picks up the book, *Haircut and Other Stories* by Ring Lardner. Does she always leave books outside, he wonders, or was this trip plotted?

"This book has one of my favorite stories of all time," she says.

"Which one?"

"'I Can't Breathe.'"

"Haven't read it."

"I'll read it to you. Sit down."

He likes the idea and hops on the table, since there's no place else to sit. She sits beside him and opens the book and then adjusts the candle for extra reading light.

She starts: "'July twelfth. I am ...'"

It's a girl's diary of her stay at a summer resort. The girl is a flapper who needs the attention of many boys and can't decide on any one in particular and Jayne reads it with great enthusiasm, making the character far more appealing than she ought to be, Bick feels.

"'He asked me if I still loved him and I tried to tell him no, but I knew that would mean an explanation and the connection was so bad that I could never make him understand so I said yes. ...'"

He can see smog-shrouded stars shining through the gazebo lattice. Her perfume is coming to him in puffs on the swirling warm wind. She licks her lips between sentences.

"'He asked me if I loved anybody else and I said yes and he asked if I didn't love him more than anybody else and I said yes, but only because I thought he had probably had too much to drink and wouldn't remember it anyway. ...'"

After a while he closes his eyes and just listens. He decides he would like to spend the rest of his life being read to by Jayne. This does not seem unreasonable at the moment.

The story ends with the girl choosing none of the boys she thought she was mad for but an old beau she suddenly remembers because of a song and is sure she is truly mad for. Jayne looks at him for a reaction.

"It worries me," he says, snapping out of it, "that this is your favorite story."

She laughs happily.

"But I really enjoyed it," he says. "Thank you."

She puts the book down and swings her legs and swigs her gin.

"I love your voice," he says.

"Thank you," she says, throatily, sucking in air to cool off the gin.

They are still sitting very near each other. He takes a hit off the bottle of bourbon. He wonders if she feels an amazing amount of sexual tension too.

She tosses her cigarette and it again fizzes out in the pool. "I love that," she says. "That sizzle sound."

He looks up at the unfinished house with the lights bouncing off the windows. After another hit of bourbon he looks at her profile, her lips. She turns her face to him. Her eyes come right to his as if in a camera zoom.

"I can't breathe," she says in her story-telling voice.

Her hand slowly rises up to his mouth and her very white finger touches his lower lip and a muscle in his leg slightly spasms and her finger pulls back and turns and touches her own lower lip and he feels her other hand on the leg closest to her and he has to kiss her and when his lips feel hers, the feeling shivers back to his neck and her hand is suddenly there to bounce the current back through his head to his lips and the feeling spreads.

When the kiss is over, his mouth is drier than ever and he feels like he just blacked out. He has no idea how long this went on or what he was thinking. Self-induced alcoholic ecstasy to be sure, but still. . . .

Lips like a remembered kiss.

She is staring at a yellow lantern above.

"I'm just a trashy girl who likes trashy lanterns," she says with a southern accent, lighting a cigarette.

Bick, still dazed, looks at her and then at the lantern.

"Zelda said something like that once, I think," she says, dropping the accent. "Fitzgerald said Zelda was the only god he had, but she was just a trashy girl who liked trashy lanterns." She points her cigarette up.

Suddenly she seems drunk to Bick. He can't figure out when she became drunk. *Was she drinking while she was reading, the lush?*

"Don't you think they had a pretty major problem?" she says.

"What?"

"Zelda and her husband."

He nods and takes a drink. He's not sure where to go with this.

She blows smoke. He watches the smoke fade to nothing in the yellow light.

His mouth is still dry. He imagines a naked swim in the cool pool would feel very good right now and just then she flicks another cigarette, which flies by and fizzes in the water.

"Let's get out of here," she says, rising, "before we get seriously smashed or something. I'm a lovely tipsy but an awful drunk."

He watches the back of her scissoring legs silhouetted by the glow of the pool.

Driving home they don't say much, but the pauses aren't uncomfortable and Bick has hopes of good things yet to come. As they pull up to Jayne's house, they notice a guy sitting in an old American convertible parked across the street. Bick instantly imagines the worst: psycho fan.

"Is this someone you know," he asks.

"I don't think so."

Maybe the guy is waiting for one of her neighbors, Bick tries to tell his paranoid side, *maybe there's nothing weird about this.* The guy in the convertible opens his door.

Bick parks directly in front of the house. "I'll walk you in," he says, getting out of the car.

The guy in the convertible also gets out and he's scruffy and walking toward them like a drunk. Adrenaline kicks in and Bick feels violent and protective, unfamiliar emotions.

"Hi," the guy says when he's directly under the streetlight.

Bick maneuvers sideways toward the guy, cutting off a path to Jayne.

"Oh," Jayne says, "hello."

"I just came by to say hi," the guy says, sounding more embarrassed than drunk. "I was about to leave. Glad I caught you."

Jayne steps out from behind the BMW and the guy edges toward her, away from Bick.

"Bick," Jayne says, "this is Rolly, an old, uh, friend."

Bick automatically holds out his hand to shake. "Bick Smith," he says, amazed by his own sudden civility.

Rolly shakes Bick's hand, then turns to Jayne. "I'm in town for this gig, you know, for a few days. I really wanted to talk." He's scuffing his feet like a kid, which he appears to be. "In person. If that's all right."

Bick watches Jayne's reaction. She seems genuinely surprised. "Sure," she says to the guy. "OK. Just a sec."

Now Bick's the surprised one.

The guy kind of nods to Bick, "Good meeting you." He walks over toward the front door. Bick looks at Jayne.

She forces a smile—embarrassed or nervous or something, he can't tell what. "Thanks," she says. "For dinner and everything."

"My pleasure," Bick automatically replies.

She shrugs and he can't figure out at all what she's feeling or trying to say. "See ya," she says.

He nods slowly in reply.

She turns and walks toward the porch, where the scruffy guy is waiting.

Bick gets back in his car. He turns the ignition, but he doesn't push down the clutch and the car's in gear and lurches against the parking brake. He then puts it in neutral and starts over.

He wonders if he should wait around but can't think of any reason why. She had plenty of opportunity to say something, anything, and what she did was say good night and invite Rolly inside.

Why are you in bed alone, Bick asks himself, remembering the things he said wrong and right, not remembering very well. He hears a Smiths song in his mind—*If you're so very entertaining, why are you on your own tonight?*—and tells himself to fuck off.

He knows he picked up enough material tonight to finish the script, sen-

sations he has not felt in a long while and needed to feel again to write the script well.

This is a girl who demands a romantic gesture as lofty as death, but Bick wants to leave that territory to her other boyfriends. What he wants to do is take what he has about her and deliver the valentine of her young life. If he works hard and fast enough, he can do it on Valentine's Day. This is all he will do until the job is done. She can date other boys, they can watch her through closed windows, she can have them over to trash her parents' house, whatever, but all the time he will be winning her love with the letters on his computer keyboard. He wants to use what he has to make her happy. It ought to beat the hell out of dating.

Bored, Libby decides to have a party. At her New Year's Eve party she had walked into the kitchen and what she was sure had to be the most narcissistic self-absorbed conversation in modern history. A group of actors and actresses were talking about how sensitive to the human condition an actor must be. Nobody was listening to anyone else. It was particularly appalling because she knew that in another mood she could have easily joined them. She decides a small dinner party will be far less annoying than a bash.

Bick is busy working, but Merri, Willie, Mona, Joy, and Oscar come. Candles drip in the silver candelabra. White wine and a panaché of steamed shark and monkfish with Merri's homemade sauce is being enjoyed when the conversation strays to politics, a topic Libby considers inappropriate for the dinner table.

"Politicians," Willie sums up, shaking his head. "They can all blow me."

"If you think they're scumbags for not caring about the world going to shit or whatever," Oscar says, "then why don't *you* care?"

"It's not my job," Willie laughs. "It's *their* job."

"But they're not doing it."

"Some of them try," Merri says.

"Name one," Willie says.

"Cranston's not so bad," Merri says.

"He hangs out with Barbra Streisand."

Everyone laughs.

"He needs the money," Merri says. "He has to be reelected."

"Exactly."

"Dukakis wouldn't have been any better than Bush," Mona says. "And his eyebrows are scarier."

"How are you going to feel when the Republican-appointed Supreme Court overturns *Roe versus Wade* and states begin outlawing abortions?"

"It'll still be legal in Minnesota," Mona says, laughing. "We can all fly there for abortions. Visit Prince while we're in the neighborhood."

"Seriously, what about those that can't afford to jump state lines?"

"The moral," Oscar says, "is don't get a poor girl pregnant."

"Did you vote," Merri asks Oscar.

"Didn't have time."

"Less than thirty percent of people our age vote," Merri says.

"Which is considerably less than the percentage who drink and do drugs and own VCRs," Mona says.

"Where did you get those figures," Oscar asks.

"Which proves we're in the right business," Willie says.

"Dukakis could have been elected," Oscar says seriously. "*I* could have got him elected. And this is how." Oscar suddenly has his intense rant look. "When the Bush boys started running the revolving-prison-door spot—which was a brilliant piece of cinema—possibly the best short of the year—Dukakis's people should have responded with their own tour de force." Oscar pauses. "Fade in, grainy super-eight color, menacing music, a woman walking alone down a wet dirty alley." He talks lower and faster. "Cut to a rusty metal table with a rusty blood-stained set of tongs. The music rises, becomes more disturbing, a hairy hand—hairy *bare* hand—with what might be dried blood under the fingernails reaches into the frame and picks up the tongs. The camera follows the blood-stained tongs as they're raised over a pale young girl's leg. Cut to the girl's face, sweating and frightened and obviously not anesthetized. She grimaces and closes her eyes. Screen goes black. Then white print over a black screen, these words with a voice-over: 'George Bush says abortions should be illegal.' End with an eggbeater-grinding noise and a gut-wrenching feminine cry."

Everyone has stopped eating.

"Good piece of work," Mona finally says, "but, if you think it through, couldn't it be taken to mean that abortion is a horrible thing and *should* be illegal?"

"If voters thought things through," Oscar says, "they wouldn't have elected an actor president. Voters only know what they see. And what they see in this spot is an ugly image linked to George Bush. The image is all that matters."

The conversation about politics and religion continues glibly and amiably. It occurs to Libby that politics and religion couldn't be discussed at her parents' dinner table because their generation took politicians and God seriously. Those who grew up with Nixon and Reagan know politicians are lying scum at worst and a bad joke at best, fine material for dinner chat. As for God, he's like the Academy Awards, distant and creepy and important only to those with a peculiar sort of sad need.

After dinner they are sitting around drinking and talking while a TV special honoring Martin Luther King that Merri turned on plays in the background.

"Disneyland," Joy says, apparently out of nowhere.

The others look at her. She's looking at the TV. A commercial spot shows Disneyland. "Tim and I went there on mushrooms," Joy says.

"We should do mushrooms sometime, Merri," Willie says.

Merri makes a face.

"Mushrooms come from Mother Earth," Willie says.

"So does arsenic," Merri answers.

"Mushrooms are really pretty good," Joy says. "They just make you giggle."

"I giggle enough without mushrooms," Merri says.

"Mushrooms and giggling are important," Willie says. "But if you want to change your whole weltschmerz, if you want to see the absolute Technicolor glory of everything, try mescaline. You haven't seen God until you've driven to the desert in the winter on mescaline with the stereo cranking *The Rise and Fall of Ziggy Stardust.*"

"How about 'Horse with No Name' on acid?" Joy suggests.

An argument about how best to escape the material world ensues, but suddenly they all realize they're missing something and turn their attention back to the TV. The man himself is speaking.

"I have seen the promised land. I may not get there with you. . . . But we as a people will get to the promised land. So I'm happy tonight. I'm not worried. I'm not fearing any man. My eyes have seen the glory of the coming of the Lord."

They're silent when he finishes. A McDonald's commercial blares on and Libby turns off the TV and they're still silent.

"Oh Jesus," Joy finally says, "I have to come up with a New Year's resolution."

"**L**ook at that shadow."

"Has there been a plot point yet?"

"What is *this* angle," Mona says, "the penis POV?"

"Should have used a wide-angle here."

"Would also help if they focused the camera."

"Is that a zit on her ass?"

"Fire the make-up girl."

"What the hell's going on with the camera?"

"Cameraman has a woody."

"They can't even lay dolly tracks."

"Personally," Oscar says, "I think it's tastefully lit."

"It's better than *Mississippi Burning*," Mona says, "at least it doesn't rape history."

When they're bored of commenting on the porn film starring Traci Lords, they put Oscar's movie back on the Steenbeck and return to work.

Bick wakes with his pillow no longer under his head. Daylight is angling through his windows. He reaches for his cigarettes and after getting one lighted, he sets the pack down next to his watch and notices the time, almost four thirty. He takes a swallow of room-temperature water from a nearby bottle and then begins pacing.

When he started screen writing, Bick was interested in greatness. Cleverness proved more profitable. No matter how he tries to laugh off or drink off or sweat off the shame of doing less than his best, some of it sticks each time. He doesn't want this to be one of those times.

For days Bick has been at work, first thing in the morning and last thing at night, though for him morning is sometimes sunset and much of his night day. He hopes this immersion means some section of his brain has been working on the script regardless of distractions. He has listened to The Doors' first album approximately three hundred times. He has opened novels to random pages and read until he fell asleep. He has eavesdropped on conversations at Small World Books. He has admired TV commercials shot in shaky close-ups that remind him of the home movies he made in high school with a super-eight camera. Everything has gone into the work in one way or another, including himself. He has gotten drunk when he felt the need and intoxicated ideas fueled him and then passed and left him blank enough to sleep and when he woke he rewrote. He knows this is not normal. If he weren't alone, maybe he'd

not have to work this way and he'd like that someday. For now the work is what he has.

He has compressed the original two-hundred-and-four-page script—which would have been about three hours worth of movie—into one hundred and twelve, turning the story of a steady descent toward murder-suicide into a tighter tale of redemption. He believes he has been true to the characters because he believes it is possible for these characters to turn one way rather than another just as he believes the people he knows can turn one way rather than another. It's a matter of plot. Plot is just the circumstances that serve to force the action, revealing the characters, and Bick has written new circumstances.

In his hard disk is a finished draft, but he's not satisfied. The script isn't truly clicking yet. He stops pacing to open a window. A cold western wind off the ocean sweeps in with a rush. He breathes the fresh air and tries to stretch out various aches. The sun is going down over Point Dume in chemical orange glory. A few people on the boardwalk below have stopped to stand at attention while others stroll past. Suddenly it comes to him. He will begin again and do what he should have done in the first place: reveal to the audience that the two lovers-to-be are brother and sister.

When Bick gets out of bed about two and a half days later, he takes pages from the laser printer to the futon and begins line editing with a pencil. Most Hollywood producers and executives hold their jobs because of political skill, not their eye for true characterization or language or story, so Bick has learned to do his own editing. In the background the TV is on and tuned to a PBS special about John Lennon's assassination. Well into the script Bick starts to feel good and imagines he would love somebody to have written it for him. He strongly suspects the work will connect with audiences but doesn't think too hard about this because he knows movies are a mystery, there's no explaining how or whether people will respond. Understanding comes after the fact. He doesn't usually like his own rewrite work, but he pictures Jayne in the role and he likes this.

He's reworking dialogue for a gazebo seduction scene when from the TV the phrase *"We have to see ourselves in them"* catches his attention. He tunes in for a moment, unsure whether this was referring to assassinations or celebrities or what exactly, but then he decides to turn off the TV and return his focus to editing.

He types the penciled changes into the computer and then commands a new copy. He fixes himself a bourbon while the laser printer does its job.

* * *

The phone is ringing. It's dark and Bick's trying to figure out whether or not he woke before the phone started ringing and if so why. The machine answers the call. "Hello, please leave a message at the tone, thank you."

Beep.

"Bick—pick up—please be there!" Jayne is yelling and there are loud noises in the background and then the phone hits the floor or something and disconnects.

Bick is out of bed and out the door into the car. He does fifty in third down Pacific. The BMW is the only car on the road and this adds to his uneasiness. He skids around a couple corners, does a four-wheel stop in front of her house and runs up to her door. It's locked. He can hear her screaming so he steps back and side-kicks.

Jayne is in the kitchen with her back to Bick when he darts in. She's holding a knife, not a long one, high in the air, screaming, "Stay back," apparently unaware that someone has just entered.

A tall guy looks over Jayne at Bick. He is armed with a corkscrew. "Who the fuck are you?" he says, voice cracking with emotion or drugs. "Another fuckin' boyfriend?"

Jayne turns around and sees Bick. Bick keeps his eyes on the guy, stepping forward and gently edging Jayne behind him.

"Do you love her?" the guy screams. "*I* fuckin' love her!"

The guy is poking the corkscrew at Bick as though it is a dagger. Bick wishes he hadn't quit karate training.

"Put down the corkscrew," Bick says, and almost laughs.

"What's so fuckin' funny?" the guy screams, obviously not amused. "You ever had your heart spit on?" The guy snorts and spits on the floor.

Bick notices blood in the huge glob of phlegm, a coke problem he can commiserate with.

"Do you fuckin' love her?" the guy screams again. He takes a step toward Bick. Bick edges his left foot forward, his left hand out, prepared to move.

Bick can sense Jayne moving farther back behind him.

"Answer me, man," the guy says. "Do you fuckin' love her?"

"What do you want?" Bicks says, trying to sound bored, trying not to inflame the guy.

"I want her to love me, man."

"I don't think this is the best way to achieve that."

"Fuck off."

Fair answer, Bick thinks.

"I fuckin' love her," the guy screams. "What do you know about love?"

"Not a hell of a lot."

The guy looks past Bick. "Do you love *him?*" he screams at Jayne.

"Leave me the fuck alone!" Jayne screams back.

"I fuckin' love you!"

"You don't know what love is!"

"The fuck I don't!"

"The fuck you do!"

Bick does not like standing between two armed and screaming emotional types.

"Let's cool down here," Bick says.

"You," the guy says to Bick, "get the fuck out of here. Can't you see this is between us?"

"There's *nothing* between us," Jayne screams back at him.

"Let's try to cool off a bit," Bick says, more to Jayne than the guy.

"I fuckin' love her," the guy screams, now sounding tired and sad. He looks at Jayne. "You *have* to love me!"

"You can't make me love you!" Jayne screams back.

"Do you love *him?*" He points the corkscrew at Bick.

"Yes!"

Bick doesn't know if the heightened emotions of the moment have flushed out the truth or a desperate lie, but in any case he would have preferred to hear about her love for him under more romantic circumstances, the corkscrew in a bottle of wine perhaps, rather than pointing at his chest.

The other guy obviously would have preferred not to hear it at all. The blow seems to drain what's left of his rage. Bick relaxes. Then suddenly the guy screams and swings the corkscrew at Bick's face. Automatically Bick deflects the guy's right arm with a rising block and counters with a quick straight punch to the nose. Bone cartilage cracks.

The guy is out cold on the kitchen floor, blood bubbling from his nose and dripping to the dirty floor. Bick is standing over him, hand feeling fine, almost wanting more of a fight.

Jayne swoops in under Bick's left arm and hugs him. He holds her tight, her erratic breaths and sobs vibrating against his chest. It feels like she could shake apart.

She cries, "I don't want him to be mad at me."

After answering questions and filling out police reports, Jayne and Bick are back in his apartment as the blue light of dawn spreads. Bick closes the blinds.

Jayne sits on the bed smoking. "First he'd say how much he loves me," she says. "Then he'd say how he wanted to kill me."

Bick nods. He doesn't know what else to say, since he's heard this about a hundred times. He sits next to her and lights a cigarette.

"He's a very passionate person," she says.

"Passionate?" Bicks says. "The guy's a fucking psychopath."

"No, he always says he wants to kill people. He wouldn't really."

"Don't defend him—he threatened me with a corkscrew."

"I'm not defending him. I'm defending passion."

"Jesus."

"You have passion, but you control it too much."

"So I don't try to murder people, I'm a boring guy."

"He wants to kill you."

"I noticed."

"He wanted to kill you even before tonight."

"Why?"

"I told him I went out on a date with you."

"I hope you told him you had a shitty time."

She sort of laughs.

"I don't know what love is," Bicks says, "but it sure as hell isn't killing someone because they're not giving you what you want. It may be romantic but it sure as fuck isn't love."

"What brought that up?"

"I just sometimes get the idea that you think it's romantic or something that this poor fuck who wrote *Till Death Do Us Part* is in jail for killing his girlfriend."

"I think it would have been *more* romantic if he had the balls to kill himself, like in the original script," she snaps. "But I told you death was not my idea of romance."

"You *said* that, but I'm not convinced."

She inhales deeply on her cigarette, crushes it out, exhales. "Don't be, then." She heads for the bathroom.

"Do you think you *deserve* this shit?" he yells out.

She turns at the door, slowly, and she looks back at him.

"You deserve better," he says, more quietly.

She hesitates, plays with the shiny doorknob, her hand circling the wide-angle reflection of him alone on the bed in the near-empty room, then steps back and closes the door.

He turns down the sound on his answering machine. He doesn't know what he can do or say to convince her she deserves good things.

She vacates the bathroom and he enters. He washes his face and brushes his teeth. He's looking forward to sleep.

When he comes out of the bathroom she is in bed, sheets barely covering her bare breasts, reading the rewritten *Till Death Do Us Part*. She's wearing glasses.

"Oh God," he says.

"I'm going to read the whole thing right now," she says without looking up.

He hangs up his clothes. "I'm going to sleep," he says.

"I'll wake you when I'm finished."

"Please no."

She doesn't look up from the script.

"I like the glasses," he tells her.

"The better to read with," she says, the fight gone from her voice.

"Happy Valentine's Day," he mumbles, slipping into bed in his clean white boxers. "It's past midnight, isn't it?"

"Yeah," she says. "Happy Valentine's Day." She kisses him on the cheek and returns to reading.

Somehow his exhaustion and the comfort of having her near overcome the terror of what she's doing and he feels himself fade to sleep.

As Bick dreams of kissing her, his eyes touch right up against her glasses. Her own eyes are just on the other side of the glasses and though his eyes seem inside hers, there's a feeling of being separated by the glass. Then he wakes up. Her lips are inches from his. Suddenly he isn't sure if he woke up or just dreamed he woke up.

"I love it," the lips are saying.

What? he wonders, then realizes she must mean the script. Her glasses are gone.

"*Till Death Do Us Part*," she says.

"Right. Happy Valentine's Day."

"Thank you."

It looks like day outside the blinds and he's definitely awake. He wonders about his breath. He tastes Crest and cigarettes. He runs his tongue over his teeth.

"Good night," she says, and kisses him on the cheek and turns off the light and turns away.

He is suddenly stripped of purpose and hope.

Hold on, he says to himself. *What can you realistically expect? The girl has just been through what has to be one of the most traumatic nights of her life and then she reads the script, another traumatic event, no doubt. She says she likes it. Why not settle for that?*

"Excuse me," he says, tapping her on the shoulder.

She rolls over and looks at him. "Yes?"

"What do you mean, you like it?"

She laughs. "I *loved* it."

"Uh-huh."

"And I don't mean love in the Hollywood sense. I *really* loved it."

"Uh-huh."

"Do you want my notes now?"

"Notes?"

She laughs and rolls back over.

What kind of shit was that? he says to himself. She didn't look so tired. He taps her back again.

"Yes," she says without rolling over.

"It's not really how much you like the script I'm interested in, or your notes."

She rolls over. "What's wrong?"

"I need to know some things."

"Go to the library," she says and smiles.

"Don't do this now," he says.

"The library isn't so bad," she continues smiling.

"Don't play naive anymore, OK?" He is surprised by his own seriousness.

"Bick, what's wrong?"

Images of the psycho screaming "I love you" make Bick feel guilty. He does not want to picture himself as a variation on the psycho's story.

"Sorry," he says, "never mind. Go to sleep."

"Bick, what's *wrong?*"

He finds his cigarettes. "I don't know," he says as he lights one. "I haven't slept for a while, we've been through a lot, I don't know."

She's sitting up, looking at him curiously.

"I just want to know what the fuck is going on," he says. "That's all."

"What do you mean?"

He looks at her. "You know what I mean."

"You mean with us."

"Yes."

She looks away. "I don't know."

"Let's figure it out."

She looks at him.

"I just want to know if I'm having romantic delusions," he says. "I want to know."

"Romantic illusions? You're a little too safely cynical for that, don't you think?"

"No, I don't."

She turns her head after a moment.

"Now that you have what you want, are we finished," he asks. "Is the show over?"

"Bick, are you serious? Is that what you're thinking?"

He's not sure.

"I don't know if you're having romantic illusions," she says, "I don't know if *I'm* having romantic illusions, but I know I'm not *using* you. I couldn't do that."

"Yeah you could."

"No."

"Yes," he nods. "I'm not saying I'm sure you *are*, but I'm sure you *could*."

"No. I see so much emotional rape around me . . . I couldn't be like that."

It's almost impossible not to believe her. He thinks about it, then says without any real sting, "The psycho with the corkscrew probably doesn't have a bad self-image either."

She stares at him. "That was a shitty thing to say."

"Sorry, I'm just trying to figure out the truth here."

"What do I have to do to convince you?"

"Depends. What are you trying to convince me of?"

"What do you want me to convince you of?"

"I don't want you to just tell me what I want to hear."

"Don't you?"

"Fuck it," he says. "This is aggravating me."

"It's aggravating me too," she snaps back. "It's pissing me off. Why do we have to dissect it? Why can't we just *enjoy* it?"

"I don't enjoy torture. Call me a killjoy."

"What torture?"

"The not knowing."

"The not knowing what?"

"What's going on."

"With what?"

"What do you think!?"

"I don't know what you mean!"

"Don't suddenly act like a bimbo!"

"Don't suddenly act like a psycho!"

This cools him down. "OK," he says. "I just want to know what you're doing." He pauses. "Remember that night, that night with the books, when it seemed like something was building and you cut it?"

She nods.

"And you told me you were going to go to twenty-fucking-something the next night?"

She nods.

"What was going on?"

"You know."

"Tell me anyway."

She smiles. "I seduced you into wanting to seduce me."

"Did you have any intention of going to twentysomething?"

She shakes her head.

His look asks why.

"I wanted to make you spend the night thinking of me," she answers. "I

knew whatever happened that night, whatever girls you looked at or flirted with or whatever, you'd be wondering about me."

He nods. "It worked."

"I wanted you to like me," she says.

He rubs his eyes. "So where are we now," he asks.

"I don't know where we are—and I don't mind. I like the mystery."

"Mystery is a romantic word for confusion."

"Maybe I like confusion too."

"Maybe you're going to drive me to suicide."

She brightens, apparently flattered.

"I don't need this," he says. "I don't want this."

"Kiss me?" she says.

"What?"

"Why do you always say 'what' like that?"

"I went to too many rock concerts as a teenager."

"You heard me."

"Yes, I heard you," he says. "'Kiss me.' Are you fucking *kidding?*"

"Do I look like I'm kidding?"

She doesn't look like she's kidding.

He kisses her, telling himself he doesn't want this. He's spent years adjusting to the idea of modern loneliness and he doesn't want this. Her hands come around his back to his neck and her fingers intertwine on his spine and he tells himself he doesn't want this. Her tongue slips in behind his upper lip and his whole mouth tingles and he tells himself he doesn't want this. He pulls back—he still has a lighted cigarette in his right hand. He takes a long hit and the tip glows hot.

"Am I interfering with your smoking," she asks.

He puts out the cigarette, then lights a match to have another, but he glances up at her and the flame is reflected in her pale blue eyes. He freezes. She holds his gaze. It occurs to him his fingers will burn if he doesn't do something. She blows out the match. He lights another, doesn't look in her eyes, pulls the white string on the side of her bikini panties away from her skin and touches the flame to the cotton. This is a move from the script. Here in reality he finds the material is sort of melting rather than burning. The cotton glows orange for a moment and then turns brown and black and shrinks up, but the string does split. She blows out the match, kisses him. He tells himself he doesn't want this as he goes down.

VI

VI

O scar accidentally turns a switch. The reels start spinning and the film is racing by in reverse motion on the screen and this just urges Oscar on faster, further into the hot breath and sweat. He's standing and holding her hips, which are sliding wildly against the Steenbeck. Her ankles are pressing on the back of his thighs and she doesn't seem to care about the increased noise level.

This is her fault, he thinks, but thinks it to her credit. He closes his eyes and can almost imagine she's just an extension of the Steenbeck, he's fucking his movie, but this is too twisted and he opens his eyes and there are the characters in his movie doing everything backward, looking like will-less fools.

He wonders in a second moment if maybe they're doing this backward—she was starting to grow on him and maybe sex should have come later, when it could possibly be something more than an animal act, but he's not going to pull out now.

The film is almost all spun to one reel and he presses on still harder, trying to synchronize his orgasm with the last frame. The Steenbeck screen goes dark and he closes his eyes and when he comes, it's like the climactic shoot-out of an action movie, the blasts, shudders, gasps, sighs and the inevitable letdown when you realize a lot happened but it was nothing.

T here are only two cars left in the section of the parking lot they're walking through, both near the same lamp pole. His is German. Hers is Japanese. Both are lightly sprinkled with smog particles. Her ulcer is starting to react. When they are a few feet from her Honda, she quickly kisses him on the cheek, trying to spare them both whatever goodnight obligations he has in mind. Then she looks down and reaches into her purse and feels around for her keys.

"We've been bad, haven't we?" he says.

She knows he wants to hear that she hasn't assumed anything from his sudden slip of passion. He's a guy. She also realizes that she feels bad only because she could sense that he does. "You know what Marilyn Monroe said," she says, looking up with keys in hand.

"No," he says.

"What's a fuck between friends?"

"Her intellect was definitely underappreciated."

He seems relieved. She's glad. Still, she's curious about his feelings for her.

She simply wanted to fuck in the editing room because others in college had and she hadn't. She lied to him when she said she had. Anyway, it was not as good as she imagined it would be. *Nothing to complain about though.*

"Friends ought to be able to fuck each other these days," she says, "since strangers all have AIDS."

214

"Good point," he says, "but I should apologize."

"There's nothing to apologize for," she says. "It was a no-fault fuck."

He laughs, still uneasy.

"We worked hard," she says. "We were entitled to some recreation in that horrible room."

"I appreciate all you've done, Mona. On the movie, I mean."

"I know what you mean."

"I'm going to tell everyone you're a genius."

"And a great fuck."

"Yeah, you'll get more job offers than you can handle. In fact I've already talked to some people about you."

"Let's not talk about jobs right after sex," she says, unlocking her car door. "It dirties up sex."

"OK," he says. He kisses her on the cheek. "Good night."

"Good night."

She opens her door and turns, "I just remembered," she says, "tomorrow's Valentine's Day, and it's already tomorrow."

"I know."

"Big fucking deal, huh?" she says and laughs.

He laughs also, but it looks like a strain.

"What was your New Year's resolution," she asks.

"A girlfriend."

"Right."

"What was yours?"

"A job."

"Right."

"But I don't believe in resolutions."

"But you got a job."

"And you're still alone as hell, huh?"

"Thanks."

"Everyone else probably fucked up too."

"There's still time."

"For what?"

"There's still time until Merri's birthday."

She laughs and says, "I hate fucking holidays, good night."

He taps on the car window. She opens her door.

"Window doesn't work," she explains.

"You're coming to the test screening, right?"

"Of course."

"We'll meet here."

"And take separate cars."

"Of course."

Merri wakes up to the sound of fire-crackers, but it's not firecrackers but gunshots and Willie is not in bed with her. The shots are coming from the backyard. She jumps over to the window and opens the shades and there's Willie in the backyard shooting at cans in the early morning light. She bangs on the window. He turns, smiles and waves, then returns to shooting. She grabs her robe.

The grass is cold and wet on her feet when she dashes out the back door. Willie is putting new bullets into the gun.

"Happy Valentine's Day," he says.

"You could kill someone with that!" she screams.

"Who?" he says. "There aren't any golfers at this hour. And even if there were—"

"What the hell are you doing!?"

"Huntin' down food for our dog."

Merri realizes the cans at the foot of the fence are cans of puppy food. Brown drops are dribbling from jagged bullet holes.

"Where is she?"

"Hiding in the new house there, waiting for me to hunt down her food." Willie blasts another can.

"Stop it!" This is it. His lips are chapped and gross. He must have snuck out of bed after they went to sleep.

"Who were you doing drugs with," she asks.

"Nobody," he says. "Myself. And not drugs. Just tequila. Are you wearing anything under that?"

"You got up to drink tequila?"

"No, I drank tequila as long as I was up. I got up because of the earthquake."

"What earthquake?"

"There was an earthquake. It woke me up."

Merri involuntarily groans.

"Swear to God," he says. "And I couldn't get back to sleep."

"There was an earthquake?"

"Swear to God."

"How did I sleep through it?"

"You're a heavy sleeper. Me, I'm sensitive to these fluctuations in the earth's stability."

The puppy pokes a little face out of the doghouse.

"Oh, look, you scared Madonna."

"I'm huntin' down food for the bitch."

"Come here, Madonna, good girl." Merri gets down and makes kissy sounds. "Come on, Madonna, come on."

The puppy, a mutt with the look of a bleached blond, warily puts two paws out of the doghouse.

"Come here, good girl."

Madonna decides to dart across the lawn under the swing set to Merri.

"Good dog, good dog." Merri stands with Madonna in her arms. "Did that big mean asshole Willie scare you with his dumb gun?"

"It's an ugly dog," Willie says, not unaffectionately.

"But ours."

Once Merri talked Willie into wanting a dog, she further insisted on one from the dog pound. When she saw Madonna in the cage, filthy and full of energy, she knew the pup needed them. If she leaves him, she's taking Madonna.

"As long as we're up, you want to go get breakfast?" he says. "The movers are coming in a couple of hours."

Merri doesn't answer.

Willie raises the gun. "Better feed Madonna now."

"Don't shoot again!"

"I'm just trying to shoot open one of these goddamn cans."

"Give me the gun, please."

"You want to take a couple of shots?"

He knows she hates guns. She'd like to berate him for being so senseless and waking her and the whole neighborhood, but she knows what she really wants.

"That gun does not move with us to the new house."

"What? What do you want me to do with it?"

"Give it to me. I'll get rid of it." She sets down Madonna and holds out her hand.

"You're going to shoot me," he says.

She keeps her hand out. He removes the bullets and hands her the gun. She holds it by the butt with her thumb and forefinger.

"What are you going to do with it," he asks.

"Madonna, no!"

Madonna is licking the dripping cans.

"No!" Merri yells again.

Madonna looks back at her, then resumes licking.

"She's hungry," Willie says.

"She could swallow a bullet or cut her tongue or something," Merri says, quickly moving the cans out of the dog's reach onto the fence. "No more guns or late-night craziness at the new house." She comes back to Willie still holding the gun like a soiled diaper. "I'm serious," she says.

"I know," he says, "I'm really sorry. The earthquake set me off or something. And this moving thing is so stressful."

"You haven't had to do anything!"

"The *idea* of it stresses me out." He lights a cigarette. "Never mind. I'm sorry."

Madonna jumps on his leg and he gets down on his knees and starts playing with her. "Are you burning up for my love?" He kisses the dog.

Merri hears a car pulling into the driveway. She walks around to the side gate of the fence and through a gap she can see the emblem on the side of the Westec private security car.

"Someone here to see you, Willie," she says.

He stands up, looks around frantically and digs into his pocket and tosses a rectangle of white paper toward the shrubbery. The puppy chases it and gobbles it up.

"Was that your coke?" Merri yells.

"Shh," Willie says. "There was hardly anything left."

"You just poisoned Madonna!" Merri drops the gun and pounces on the animal, prying open its jaws and pulling the paper out with a handful of saliva. She wads it up and throws it back to Willie. "It's just Westec! Now get out of here! Get in the house and I'll handle this. Take the dog and feed her. Use a can opener."

"Good plan," he says, grabbing the dog and disappearing through the back door. She hears it lock.

Merri picks the gun back up and puts it in her pocket, tightens her robe and walks through the gate around the side of the house to the driveway. One of the Westec men is just stepping out of the car and adjusting his holster. He is tall and handsome, *probably an aspiring actor.*

"Good morning," she says.

"Good morning," he responds. "We received a complaint from one of your neighbors."

"Did the gunfire disturb them?"

"Yes, I'm afraid it did."

Another Westec man watches from inside the car. He is wearing sunglasses even though the sun is barely up.

"I'm really sorry," she says. "But I was awakened by the earthquake and . . . I'm sorry." She doesn't know what to say. "It'll never happen again."

"Was there an earthquake?"

"Yes, didn't you feel it?"

"No, I guess not. But in any case, I'm afraid it's illegal to discharge firearms here."

"Really?"

"Yes."

"Well, here, why don't you take this, then?" She reaches into her pocket and pulls out the gun. She's holding it upside down by the butt, but he still seems startled. "Take it," she says. "It's yours."

"Uh, well, um, I'm not here to take your gun. I'm just—"

"I know, but I don't want it. Take it."

He seems confused by this request.

"Please," she says. "You'd be doing me a favor. My boyfriend gave it to me and I don't want it. I don't know how to get rid of it. I was only shooting it to get rid of the bullets. I can't just put bullets or a gun into the trash compactor, now can I?"

"I suppose not."

"So I'm giving it to you."

"Hold on," he says, and signals for his partner to join them. The other Westec man says something into the radio and then comes out of the car. He is not as handsome as the first but just as laid back.

"I really like your show," he says.

"Oh, thank you," she says.

"I'm sorry it was canceled."

"It's OK. I didn't really want to do any more TV anyway."

"I never watch TV," the handsome cop says.

"Neither do I," Merri admits.

"What are you doing now," the cop who does watch TV asks.

"Movies." She doesn't want to discuss her career right now. "And trying to get rid of this gun."

"She says she doesn't want this gun anymore and would like us to take it and dispose of it," the handsome one explains.

"We can't just *take* it from you," the other one says.

"What would you do if you saw it just lying in the street?"

"Pick it up. Take it back to the station."

Merri strolls out into the street and sets the gun down. "Look," she says, "a gun in the street."

The Westec men chuckle and the one who watches TV comes over and picks it up. "Guess we'll have to turn it in," he says.

"Thank you."

"No problem."

"Thanks a lot," Merri says directly to the handsome cop.

"Just doing our job."

They say good-bye and Merri goes back to the house, but the front door is locked. She knocks. The Westec men are watching her, so she waves good-bye. They wave back and drive off.

"Who's there?" Willie says through the closed door.

"Open up," Merri says. "You owe me *so* much."

Her life would be a lot simpler if she didn't love him she thinks as he fiddles with the lock. *This is what life with Willie is going to be like, always.* Nonetheless she is happy to be rid of the gun. He finally gets the door open. "Can I help you," he asks.

She needs boys like you need booze.
Bick writes in his journal while Jayne is in the shower. Now that he isn't working on the script he makes a point of writing in his journal, a black-and-white composition book.

She had made suggestions on the script, mostly specific dialogue changes to suit her delivery, but using her strong instinct for how people deceive each other and themselves she also found moments where the characters were too honest, and they worked on the scenes, burying the characters' wants. Bick was glad to have her help. Then he gave the script to Lee. Lee swore he loved it, of course, had no notes and turned it in to the studio to see what they thought. Now they wait.

In the mornings there she would be and if the sun was shining through the blinds they would rise and drive somewhere for a good breakfast, sometimes on the Pacific Coast Highway toward Santa Barbara, but if the sun wasn't out, if it was gray outside or—even better—raining, they would stay in bed and make love not fully awake and feeling still in a semidream. After, they would shower together and there would often be vodka with orange juice for her and a bloody Mary for him, and then back to bed wide awake.

He hardly talked to his friends, wouldn't answer the phone and she, he discovered, didn't have any friends to speak of, besides a gay actor who was working on a play in New York and a wardrobe guy on a Bertolucci film in Morocco. Alone together small things became great. Watching her choose the

redness of her lipstick or rustle her hair or tug at a stocking could be an ecstatic experience. They did things he had always wanted to do but didn't have anyone to do them with. They visited the Getty Museum, drove up to the Griffith Observatory, rode the brightly lighted rides of the Santa Monica Pier amusement park, sat in multiplex theaters and watched three movies in a day, even spent hours at the UCLA research library looking up old articles about dead authors and dead movie stars and anything else they were curious about.

They were usually together, but if he drove into town to buy something at Tower Records or Book Soup, or just to be alone, the drive back was the best part. He would speed home on the freeway with anticipation and then he would be with her.

Jayne insisted they celebrate their one month anniversary. That night she cooked pasta and they ate by candlelight and he thought the pasta was delicious even while knowing it probably wasn't. For dessert they drank brandy, which was a different drunk for him. Warm with the burned wine he rose from the table and returned with her present, a book of poetry. She sat cross-legged in thigh-high tights on the futon and read aloud. Bick knew the poems would, for him, forever resonate with the memory of Jayne's voice. Maybe the alcohol opened him to this, but it was her he heard. After reading, she started rummaging through the many shopping bags around the futon, bags that seemed to serve as her luggage and her closet. She pulled out a white package wrapped with a red bow and handed it to him, not quite smiling. He read the note, *Some ties bind and some bonds tie, love Jayne.* She laughed and lay prone, putting her little fist under her chin to watch him unwrap. He removed the red bow. She took the ribbon from him and made a choker of it. He ripped shiny paper off a blue Tiffany's box.

"What do you think it is," she asked.

"I don't know. I don't shop at Tiffany's."

"I didn't really get it at Tiffany's."

"Want to give me another hint?"

"I already did." She laughed and her eyes held his.

There was something so mischievous and suggestive in her smile he was lost for a moment. Then he opened the box. Inside were two pairs of black handcuffs, a black scarf and a small bottle of Johnson's baby oil. "Just what I always wanted," he said without looking up.

"Do you prefer S or M," she asked. "*S-ing* or *M-ing?*"

He stared at the heavy cuffs until he realized what she meant. Then, meeting her eyes, he said. "Depends. You?"

"I like both."

"Uh-huh."

"But I *prefer* M-ing."

"I guess I can S."

"You guess."

"I can S."

"Should I take off my clothes," she asked, standing.

"If you want."

She dropped her shoulders and rolled her eyes.

He laughed. "Yes."

"Yes what?" She stood straight.

"Yes please?"

She rolled her eyes again.

"Take off your clothes," he said, smiling.

She moved her hands around behind her and he heard the zipper of her skirt. When the black skirt dropped to her ankles and she stepped out of it, his eyes were level with the few inches of white skin between the top of her black tights and the bottom of her panties. Her eyes drew his up to hers while her fingers unbuttoned her blouse, but soon she let her eyes look down at her hands and he looked down too. Her fingers seemed to move slowly and awkwardly on the buttons, which made his own fingers twitch. The blouse fell off her shoulders and her bra was plain. It undid in the front. Her nipples pointed over his head. She placed her thumbs inside the elastic of her panties. "OK," she said throatily.

"OK," he said, clearing his own throat.

The panties slid down. Naked except for the homemade red choker, her body seemed even more white and more wonderful than usual and she seemed to be smiling, but her mouth wasn't shaped in a smile. "Now what," she asked.

"Now what?"

He was still wearing his blazer and a tie, only his shoes were off. He picked up a key and a pair of handcuffs, which was still sheathed in protective oil of some kind, and opened it wide.

She lifted a skinny leg and pointed her foot at his lap, her painted toenails aimed at the tight buttons of his Levi's. The steel circle easily closed above her ankle bone. He let go and she lay herself down on her belly and raised the ankle so that the free half of the cuff dangled just above where her leg curved into her pretty bottom. She reached her hand around and placed it on the small of her back. He gently closed the free half of the cuff on her wrist. She spread her legs slightly and raised the other ankle and met it with her other wrist. He could hear her breathing as he reached into the box and took out the other pair of handcuffs and the key.

He flips back in his journal to see what he had written about that night. *Happy Anniversary.*

Soon he discovered how needy she truly was. At times he liked to read or listen to music or just think, but he could rarely do this with her in the room because she demanded constant attention. She liked to play a game he called

Destruct and Heal, not an unusual game, but she played ferociously. She would start a fight, didn't matter about what—once it was over whether the moon was full or almost full—just so they could ride the dramatic roller coaster to reconciliation. He learned not be sucked in. Often he just sat silently and drank and smoked while she emoted. This didn't slow her down. She would play the scene out in a self-fueled monologue.

One gray morning after a particularly exhausting episode, Jayne decided they should go on the Graveline Tour. Neither of them had ever taken the sight-seeing excursion past the places of death of famous Hollywood people. She booked a hearse for just the two of them.

The driver, clearly Australian, possibly drunk, narrated in an amusingly macabre monotone. It was, Jayne said, like having one of the guys from INXS as a tour guide. With "Piece of My Heart" on the stereo they rolled past the nondescript motel where Janis Joplin OD'd. The driver described her last trip to the lobby for cigarettes and her convulsions. They passed the parking garage where Sal Mineo was stabbed to death, the hairpin turn where Montgomery Clift crashed and mangled his face, the house where George Reeves, the original Superman, either killed himself or was murdered for having an affair with a studio executive's wife, the mansion where Errol Flynn indulged his taste for young men while women waited outside for a glimpse of him.

Jayne sometimes laughed, but she reacted less as the trip went on and toward the end was quiet, not sullen but subdued. The repetition of "heavy alcoholism" and "rampant promiscuity" and "tragic death" became numbing. Bick was both pained and perversely proud to be reminded he was a part of something so ugly and so historically evil. He was slowly swirling into a morbid fog and imagined she was too.

Jayne seemed most moved when they drove by the small apartment Marilyn Monroe lived in after her break with Joe DiMaggio. The driver told the stories of Monroe's affairs with the Kennedys and how Jack had allegedly promised Marilyn he would dump his Catholic wife and make the actress his wife and the country's first lady. The driver didn't see how Marilyn could have been so stupid as to believe him.

The driver stopped the hearse outside Robert Wagner's house to tell about Natalie Wood's fall from a yacht in a Catalina Island harbor and how she drowned while Wagner and Christopher Walken were both on board. Loud debauched parties raged on boats all around and Wood's screams went unheard, the driver said, and he seemed to be teasing toward an explanation of why exactly Wagner and Walken didn't come to the rescue when a new BMW pulled into the driveway. Jayne dived below her seat. "She didn't see me, did she," Jayne asked from the floor.

Bick watched as a wild-haired Katie Wagner bolted out of the BMW and held high a middle finger. The driver merged the hearse back into traffic.

"Shit, she didn't see me, did she," Jayne asked again, still on the floor.

"Naw," the driver said. "The windows are tinted. Was that his daughter?"

"Yes," Bick said and helped Jayne back up.

"Did she see *you*," she asked Bick.

"She doesn't know me."

"She doesn't know me either, but she might have recognized me. She'd really think I'm sick or something."

"She couldn't see you two," the driver assured them, and he took a long look at Jayne in the rearview mirror. His face seemed to react as though he'd seen her in a movie or two but all he said was, "This is where Jean Harlow died at twenty-six. Another tragedy that might have been avoided. . . ."

In bed that night, as they were reading their separate books, Jayne fidgeted. Finally she spoke. "Remember what I told you about what one of my old boyfriends said about being fascinated with me," she asked.

"Which," he joked, knowing exactly what was on her mind.

"The one who said there was something about me that made him think I was *doomed* or something."

"Oh, yeah."

"You didn't say if you thought he was right," she asked, smoking and smiling.

"Maybe that's what he saw," Bick said.

"What does *that* mean?"

"Other people will see something different."

"What do you see?"

"I'm not sure."

"Doomed," she had said. He thought the word right. Doomed, desperate, secretly tormented, for some reason he found these perfectly appealing qualities. The girl he wants has always been the girl whose beauty was misunderstood, the schoolgirl hated by bony blond cheerleaders who see what most boys don't, the girl whose distinctive style makes more moving her desire not to be so different, the girl longing for and weeping about something wildly vague that the boy suffering beside her will never truly understand.

These were the girls Jayne must have read about in his scripts and now he wondered where these girls ended and Jayne began.

She said something, but he didn't answer.

"Yoo-hoo," she said.

"Sorry," he said. "I was just thinking it's a good time to listen to the new album."

"Oh, yeah." She nodded. "The Replacements. Good."

He was so hopeful it would be good he hadn't played it yet. He didn't want to suffer the usual massive disappointment that follows such hope.

The first song was good, not great, and the two of them quietly listened all the way through without speaking. By the third song he was not concealing his pleasure and she seemed to echo his emotions. During the fourth song,

"Aching to Be," her eyes turned moist. It was almost as if she were taking his emotions and expressing them for him—she'd weep because he wouldn't—and this made him a little uncomfortable at first but was still affecting. By the eighth song he was not uncomfortable anymore and was thinking he hadn't enjoyed the first listening of an album so much since he was a teenager, totally stoned. They made love with the CD player programmed for constant repeat of "Aching to Be."

"Thought about, not understood, she's . . ."

He once thought he'd be happy if he had her and this has certainly proved true in moments, but he's not sure if it's true in the bigger sense, because every time he's happy he senses its fragility.

What he dislikes most is this ability of hers to affect him. She can make him very happy and she can depress the hell out of him. This is what he's always heard love is like, but he doesn't like not having control over his emotions. On the other hand, he likes some of the places she takes him and he can't go there on his own.

Still, he wonders if the emotions might be modeled after these rumors of love rather than something true. *You have seen too many friends fuck themselves into a lie they call love because they're bored and lonely and desperate for some emotion.*

He taps the razor-point felt pen on the page over and over until he's made hundreds of dots, then writes, *Fact is you feel it.* And he wonders when it will end.

He needs to know who he's in love with. Though she's no more a mass of contradictions than most of his friends, she seems more tangled up. She is afraid of letting herself be known too well, as if she fears she won't be liked. Though true of many people, in Jayne the fear seems magnified, as many of her qualities are.

He remembers a girlfriend in high school told him the only person he loved was himself and he said he thought that was a good start. At the age when most kids are developing a sense of self, Jayne was becoming an actress. Her sense of self was partially shaped by some of the sickest and most manipulative people in the country. Still, she survived, she developed secret strengths, she learned the art of emotional combat, but somehow a piece of her he cannot name is missing. If she becomes the star she is supposed to, she will have more money given her and lies told her and leeches on her than a hundred Hollywood screenwriters and it could all end almost instantly and the horror is if it does end, she might want it back.

She steps out of the bathroom, towel on from her breasts to her thighs, skin seeming whiter than usual, black hair showing a red tint. He wonders for the first time if black hair and blue eyes are an impossible biological combination.

"What are you writing," she asks.

"Just making notes in my journal."

"About what? Anything about me?"

"Yeah."

"Can I read it?" She comes closer.

"No."

He puts down the journal, intending to hide it somewhere later. She reaches for it. He quickly slips it into a desk drawer.

"Why can't I read it," she asks. "What kind of things are you writing in there?"

She tries to open the drawer. He holds it shut.

"Just observations," he says.

"Lemme read."

"You want to read it because you want to read about you."

"Yeah, so?"

She tugs at the drawer. He resists.

"Must be something important if you won't tell me," she says and sits in his lap. She kisses him. He returns her kiss, keeping one hand on the closed drawer. She smells very clean. Her hand tries to pull his hand away from the drawer.

The phone rings. "Hello, please leave a message at the tone, thank you." Beep.

"Bick, James Jankman, pick up."

"He sounds so serious," Jayne says.

James doesn't call just to chat, so Bick picks up.

"Hello, James."

"We're at battle," James says, as pleased as he is serious. "Wanda hated your draft. She said it was 'too visual.'"

Bick laughs.

"Those were her words. She said the script was too visual and too ambiguous but that's not what's important. What's important is the politics."

"Uh-huh."

"She wants you off. They've offered to just pay off your contract and hire someone else for revisions."

"And what did you respond?"

"I told them to suck my big white dick. But we've got a couple of problems. First problem is Jayne. The only reason you were on in the first place is her and they've lost their, uh, eagerness to have her."

"What? Why?"

"Her next movie isn't previewing well and the rough cut of the one after that is rumored to be a disaster. She's not what she was when this project started. She's lost her sparkle for them."

"In two months?"

"I know, I know, but you know how short memories are. We've got another

problem. Your producer, your buddy Lee Chassler, he's panicked. When he found out that Wanda hated the script and had the support of a couple other executives, he sided with her. He was afraid they were going to dump him with you and Jayne. As we speak he's brownnosing so many butt holes over there if he scrubs himself every day until 2001, he still won't be clean." James laughs, enjoying this. "Lee's so slimy it shocks even me. The best part is Wanda and Lee hate each other and now they're on the same side and it's the *wrong* side. We have no legal way to beat them, of course, because they can just pay you both off, but I know you two have invested a lot in this project emotionally and I think I have a solution."

"Yes?"

"Now, nobody at this studio has an opinion of his own. They only know what they're told, and right now they're being told by Wanda and Lee and Wanda's allies that the script is uncommercial and Jayne's career is history. We'll give them a *different* opinion. Myself and Amanda and Lynn are already working their ranks. We're swearing the script is one of the best any of us has ever read and Jayne's career is just *beginning* to take off and every hot director in town wants it and so on, but the key is going to be Jayne herself."

Bick looks at her. She's on the bed painting her toenails black.

"I've got a good relationship with the big guy over there, I've gotten him laid a few times," James continues. "I know he hasn't read the script. He doesn't read. The only reason he's listening to Wanda is he doesn't know any better *and,* more importantly, because the last time he met Jayne she was, I'm quoting here, 'bratty.' Benji was ignored by girls like Jayne all his life. He may be president of a studio now, but he's still a pushover for a girl of Jayne's natural, uh, talents. I strongly believe that if we can get Jayne to have a powwow with Benji, we'll win."

Bick says "Hmmm."

"Don't worry, I'm not saying she should stick her twat in his face, I'm only suggesting she talk to the man and treat him with some of the pseudorespect he expects. That's all."

Smart as James is, Bick is still disturbed to find himself in a battle with this man as his tactician. "What exactly went wrong here," he asks.

"Doesn't matter," James says. "Wanda doesn't like you or Jayne and it's easy to fuck something up, any cunt can do it. And Lee, he's expendable, he's unimportant in the equation. Anyway the battle's on. It doesn't matter what started it, just who wins."

"You haven't already talked to Hobel about setting up a meeting, have you?"

Jayne looks up.

"Here's the plan," James says. "Benji knows your friend Willie Paul's dad and he's going to be at the birthday party for Merri Shelton. You and Jayne work him there. Just be friendly, introduce him to the younger set, have Jayne

ask him about his spread in Palm Springs. You know my motto," James laughs. "Sleazy solutions for sleazy problems."

"I'll talk to her about it."

"I know this crap disgusts you, Bick, but it's necessary if you want to get the movie made. Jayne's been in this business a long time. She understands."

"I'll talk to her."

"'Onward Christian soldiers, marching as to war. . . .'" James sings with glee and Bick thinks this is a man who would have been a valuable warrior in a darker era. Then it hits him that maybe this *is* a darker era. "Good-bye and good luck."

Bick says, "Thanks," and hangs up. He sits down on the mattress next to Jayne and explains the situation without hiding his lack of enthusiasm for James's plan.

"The only weird thing," she says, "is I thought Lee worshiped you."

"I thought he worshiped *you.*"

They both laugh.

"Oh well, he's nothing," she says. "It's Benji who counts and I can show ol' Benji the light."

"No, fuck it, I didn't think they'd really want to make this movie—"

"They don't know *what* they want to do. We have to tell them."

"You've been talking to James." Bick laughs.

"Yeah," she says. "I have been."

Bick takes a moment. "What do you mean," he slowly asks.

"I knew about this yesterday," she confesses. "But I didn't know what to tell you. And James asked me not to talk about it with you until he had."

Bick doesn't say anything.

"Don't look at me like that. It's not like a conspiracy or anything."

"What is it like?"

Jayne looks genuinely remorseful. "I'm sorry," she says. "It's hard, what's happened, with you and me. I have these feelings for you and I didn't want to complicate it with this other stuff."

"Uh-huh."

"I don't want anything to interfere," she continues. "Honestly, what I wish most is that we could just be alone together, somewhere away from all this shit." She reaches over and holds his hand. "Bick, don't be mad, I wasn't holding anything back from you. It's just that I didn't think I should be the one to talk about all this with you."

He pulls his hand away, knowing he can't touch her and talk to her reasonably at the same time. Particularly while she's wearing only a towel. "You knew," he says, "that we were going to have to talk about it eventually."

She's looking into his eyes and it's killing him. "Bick, what's going on here? What are we fighting about?"

"Are we fighting?"

"We're about to. And we shouldn't. We don't want to let this other shit affect us. So there's some bitch at the studio who doesn't like us. Fuck her. And fuck Lee, we don't need that ball-less leech anymore. Fuck 'em.'"

Bick walks over to a cabinet and pulls out a bottle of Jim Beam and a glass. He pours generously.

"This is not a time to be cool," Jayne says, rising and following him, demanding his full attention. "You're thinking that if we just let the project die, somehow it will prove that we're above it, that we're too cool, but we both want to do this movie, we've put a lot of ourselves into it, so let's fight for it. I *want* to fight for it, it's important to me."

"I'm not thinking we're above it. I am above it."

"No, no we're not. This is how business is done and you can't escape it. You can pull your Zen screenwriter act and make it not matter, but that's not going to get our movie made. That's what Lee calls you, by the way."

"He calls me a lot of things."

"He probably abandoned us because he was afraid you wouldn't fight."

"Maybe he's right."

"No, we're gonna fight. I *know* this is important to you." She adjusts her voice. "And it's important to me."

Bick doesn't say anything. The bourbon burns without ice. It's hard for him not to consider some of the more unappealing possibilities. This is a girl who gets what she wants. *What does she want?* She has been playing the game in this town a long time, knows and plays it well, and maybe she hates herself for playing at all, maybe this is why she thinks she deserves whatever her self-destructiveness invites, but she doesn't know anything else but this game and she isn't going to quit.

"I hope you know though," she adds, "that it's not as important to me as you are."

He admires her delivery and timing and even wants to believe it.

"The script is our baby," she says.

The baby analogy makes him light-headed.

There is, he tells himself, *nothing I can do here.* "I hope it's a good party."

She reaches out again and holds both his hands. He reciprocates. Her look promises glorious triumph and her towel threatens indecency.

"Where did the name Bick come from?"

Total self-concern to sincere curiosity, her moves have him reeling.

"High school," he says. "Why are you asking that now?"

"I was thinking 'baby' and then I thought about names and I wondered where yours came from."

"I've already told you."

"No you didn't."

"I totaled my parents' Volvo when I graduated from high school." His

voice is flat. "For the rest of that summer, until I inherited the BMW from a dead uncle, the only car my parents would let me drive was an old Buick station wagon. It was pretty beat up and on the hood where it's supposed to say Buick, the *u* was missing, so the car was called Bick. And somehow so was I."

"You became your car?"

"Only on weekends."

"That's it? Now you're Bick?"

"That's it."

"I've never done that," she says. "I've never had sex in a car." She tugs the towel up. "Sort of un-American, huh?"

"You're still young."

"But aren't you supposed to do that when you're like seventeen? After the prom or something?"

He nods. He's not in the mood for this conversation.

"I missed it," she says sadly.

At first he thinks she's joking, but she's not. She's sad. Her emotion is sucking him in once again.

"There'll be other things in your life," he says, "better than proms and car sex."

"We'll pretend," she says, brightening. "We'll dress up and pretend we're skipping the prom and buy a bottle of something like Black Velvet and go Bicking! And after, we'll throw up from the cheap whiskey and everything."

He laughs despite himself and pulls his pillow farther under his head. "I'm going back to sleep, where I'm safe," he says, muffled.

"But one of these nights we'll go Bicking?"

"Mmmm." He closes his eyes.

"Promise?"

"Mmmm."

"Now," she says.

Drunk out of their minds they fuck in his BMW on the Pacific Coast Highway while the cars whiz by and the waves crash. He desperately tries to freeze-frame the images: her white breasts taut in the cool wind coming through the window, her belly and his angling into each other and curving into a V of darkness, her eyes closed and her mouth barely open and those light blue eyes opening and letting him in and then closing again.

"**Y**uck!" a boy in the audience yells.
A chorus of laughter and applause follows.
"What a loser!"
"Go for the cheerleader!"
"Geek!"
Oscar's worst nightmare is coming true and the only thing that surprises him is how well he's taking it. Here he is at a test screening for his movie with a real live adolescent audience in a real theater in a real town outside LA and they hate the most important part. They are literally booing the ending he reshot. The boy forsakes the cheerleader, whose superficial favor he was dumb enough to want, and in his moment of triumph finds the strength to turn to the pure-hearted girl he suddenly realizes he truly loves and they hate him for it *and are booing,* but Oscar can't see cause for much concern.

The studio executives down the row do not seem to share Oscar's new-found calm.

Afterward, in a back room of the theater, with the producer, three executives and his agent, Oscar doesn't feel like reading the preview cards the audience filled out. The executives, however, do.

"Fifty-six percent said Wally should have ended up with Babette," one executive says, looking at a sheet.

"Yes," another says.

"Fifty-one percent said they liked Wally less in the end than they did in the beginning," another says. "Almost sixty percent said it should have ended differently."

"Yes."

Oscar stares at an autographed picture of Marlon Brando on the wall and wonders if the signature is real.

"They simply didn't respond well to your new ending," Wanda Dillady summarizes.

"No shit?" Oscar says.

His agent laughs. No one else does.

Oscar wishes his father's friend were here but knows it wouldn't matter because the studio is going to recut the ending again. Wally is going to end up with the cheerleader. Oscar's going to end up drunk.

His second quick martini blurs the memory. He doesn't remember what the theater looked like, what the executives said. He could almost convince himself it hadn't even happened if it weren't for the memory of the kid's cry at the screen, "What a loser!"

So this is how failure feels: you're alone in a cocktail lounge sitting on a maroon bar stool leaning on a bar trimmed with maroon vinyl, surrounded by maroon booths and maroon wallpaper, Frank Sinatra on the jukebox, *"When I was twenty-one, it was a very good year. . . ."*

The bartender, who's not much older than Oscar and is backed by a hundred bottles of booze and a mirror and neon beer slogans, looks like an alcoholic. The men down the bar from Oscar look like mid-level executives who came by for a quick one and forgot to leave. They also look like potential alcoholics. On the other side of Oscar are two older guys who look like they woke up here and never intend to leave. They look like full-fledged alcoholics.

Nobody is joking and laughing and having a good time.

"Another," the bartender asks.

Oscar nods. He was looking for the freeway back to LA and he saw the universal sign for cocktails—the blinking martini glass—and it seemed like the right move. This is what a guy in a movie would do after a career setback. Oscar can't help but think of his life as a movie edited by a lunatic. This appallingly lighted bar is a set, the drinkers and the bartender are actors and Frank Sinatra is on the sound track. Now would be a good time to take up smoking. His drink appears inches from his hand. He sips it. The martini, at least, is real.

"When I was thirty-five, it was a very good year. . . ."

The bartender waits for a reaction as he does every time he delivers a

mixed drink. *It's a good touch,* Oscar thinks as he nods approvingly. The bartender seems pleased. A man who takes pride in his work. If Oscar told him the martini had a shitty ending, would it destroy the man psychologically? Would he start thinking of himself as a failure?

"Yes?" the bartender says.

Oscar holds up his glass. "Not quite dry enough. Now that I really taste it."

"Was the first one better?"

"Now that you mention it," Oscar answers, "the others were a little too wet also. Not dry enough." Oscar has no idea what he's talking about. He's never had a martini before.

The bartender shakes up a new martini without any accusatory frown. The other men in the bar pay no attention. Oscar wonders if the young guys with loosened ties have ever been told their hard work is bad and useless. Of course they have, they must go through the same sort of setbacks and pains and doubts. But they probably have girlfriends.

Oscar wonders if he's better matched to the White Girl now that he's a failure. She'll hate his movie. No, worse, she'll never see it. He wishes Mona were here.

Another Frank Sinatra tune comes on as the bartender slides a martini into Oscar's open hand. "Excellent," Oscar says, sipping. "Excellent." He wants the man to feel good about his work. "Really excellent."

"I've been, uh, experimenting with my martinis," the bartender explains. "Working on them."

"Sounds like a good thing to do."

"The thing is, it's personal taste."

Oscar nods.

"One guy likes a drier martini than the next guy."

Oscar wonders if this was intended as a metaphor.

"I haven't found the perfect formula yet," the bartender admits.

"Neither have I."

"You bartend?"

"No." Oscar smiles. "I drink though."

"Right." The bartender chuckles. "What do you do professionally?"

If this were LA the bartender would be an actor or a writer and want a favor after learning of Oscar's trade, but this is—Oscar forgets the name of the town—somewhere about a hundred miles from LA.

"I work," Oscar says.

"Bad day?"

"I have failure written all over me, huh?"

"No, you just look a little beat up."

"Yeah." He laughs to prove he doesn't take it too seriously.

"Nobody said it would be a cakewalk," the bartender says, sounding as

though this is something he says often, then turns to help one of the other drinkers.

Oscar avoided talking to Mona at the theater, which was probably a mistake. Now he wishes he had a friend or two to drink with, Bick or Willie would be worth a few laughs. Bick would romanticize the situation and then Willie would make a mess out of it. He hadn't invited them to the preview because he was afraid what happened might happen, but now that it's happened it doesn't seem such a big deal. Maybe if he were trying to do something more than a high-school comedy, his failure would seem more important. It's easy not to care when you're not doing anything important. Problem is, he wants to care.

He's here because he happened to make a competent short movie at a time when hiring feverish young directors was in fashion. He had a career before he knew what it meant. *What the hell went wrong,* he asks himself but knows *he's* what went wrong. He hadn't been prepared for the success of his first movie and the monstrous shit that came with it and he let them get to him. On his first movie he had been an underdog, full of faith and not afraid of trying anything. After its success he was suddenly an overdog, afraid of trying anything too new. Worse, he found a way to pervert his faith—he used it to sell himself. There was an actress he didn't cast in his second movie though she had been innocent and fresh in his first, because in the meantime she had learned to manipulate that innocence and freshness and so it had rotted. He was unusually disturbed by what had happened to her and now he realizes why.

He directed his righteous anger at Mr. Steele for not having anything to be true to, but now he knows *he* is worse because he *had* something to be true to and wasn't. His effort to save the movie was too little too late, too lame. *Fuck,* he thinks, *they got you. No, that's bullshit. You got you.* He slams his martini on the bar and it splashes over.

"Another," the bartender asks.

"No. I'm fine, thanks." He lifts his half-full glass as the bartender mops the overflow with a graceful sweep of a white towel.

The next movie he'll push like a man possessed and if he fails, *fuck it,* it will be in a big way and he'll invite his friends to share in the potentially epic disaster.

He's never really thought about getting old, but it's going to happen anyway and he'll have to look back on the life he's living now. He promises himself he'll try from now on to make his older self proud, give himself something to smile stupidly about when he's drunk on the porch swing boring the kids. Kids? He's shocked he's thinking things like this. He can't even find a girlfriend.

"Excellent martini," he says to the bartender on the way out. "A bargain. Best I've ever had."

"**H**ello, please leave a message at the tone, thank you."

Beep.

"Bick, pick up. It's an emergency."

Bick recognizes Merri's voice and hears the word "emergency."

"Old girlfriend," Jayne asks, sounding more awake than Bick feels.

"No," he says, "friend's girlfriend."

"Bick, pick up." Libby's voice now. "I realize it's only noon and you're still sleeping but we need to talk to you. We're going to keep calling until you pick up."

Bick fumbles for the phone. "Hello," he says, turning off the machine.

"Merri needs to talk to you," Libby says.

"What time is it," Bick asks.

Merri comes on the phone. "Thanks, I don't want to bother you, but Willie ... he's on another binge."

"You sure?"

"We were moving into the new house last night and he went out for cigarettes and never came back and I heard he wound up acting crazy with those slut sisters at twentysomething."

"I didn't see him. I wasn't there."

"Bick, you know where he goes when this happens."

"He could be anywhere."

"Do you know the slut sisters?"

"What slut sisters are we talking about?"

"Marcia and Jan, I think."

"Marcia and Jan were the girls on 'The Brady Bunch.'"

"Marcia and whatever her slut sister's name is!" Merri screams. "I don't know their names!"

Jayne covers her ears.

Libby comes on the phone. "You don't have to protect him, Bick. Merri doesn't want you to tell her where he is, she just wants you to find him and tell him to come home. You know the girls we mean."

He does.

Merri comes back on crying. "You know how people are. Willie's so talented and great, they *want* to see him fuck up. You know how they are."

Bick spots Willie's convertible parked where he expects to, in the parking lot of an ugly postwar motel that has been converted into apartments.

He and Jayne walk through a broken gate into the courtyard of the two-story building. All the rooms face the pool. Bick knocks on a first-floor door. The Stones' "Gimme Shelter" is vibrating the windows.

Bick knocks again, loudly.

A young girl's head appears from behind the curtains over the barred picture window. It pulls back quickly. Then Willie's head peeks out. He smiles.

The door opens a second later.

"Enter," Willie says, sweaty and green, grinning madly.

Bick and Jayne enter where the two slut sisters are waiting. Bick imagines they were probably very pretty several hours ago. He notices eight-by-ten glossies of them around the room. *Actresses, naturally.*

The thick air smells smoky and sweet, the multicolored shag rug is dirty, dishes and pizza boxes are littered all over. Willie's freebasing paraphernalia—glass pipe, eye-dropper, brown bottle of ether, distilled water, beaker, razor blade, cub torch—and a healthy supply of cocaine are spread over a framed movie poster on the floor.

Bick tilts his head to read the poster.

THE CORPSE GRINDERS

THEY WENT IN PEOPLE

AND THEY CAME OUT HAMBURGER

A girl's legs with stiletto heels stick out of the business end of a meat grinder.

"Jayne," Bick says, "this is Willie Paul."

"Hi," Willie says, shaking her hand. "Good to see you again."

"You too," Jayne says.

"The pleasure's all mine." Willie laughs. "Sit down. Make yourselves at home. The girls and I were just saying to ourselves, Wouldn't it be nice to have company?" Willie may look like shit, but his debauched sparkle's intact. "Wouldn't it be nice if a bright boy like Bick Smith dropped by with his latest lover for some bridge and a little freebasing?" He turns to one of the sisters. "Do you have any cards. Playing cards?"

She shakes her head.

"Oh well, what the hell?" he says. "We still have drugs."

He and the young actresses sit down on the floor next to *The Corpse Grinders* poster. Bick does the same and lights a cigarette. Jayne sits on the dirty white couch. Bick is surprised she seems horrified. Maybe she hasn't seen as much as he imagines she has or maybe she just doesn't like to see self-destruction practiced so crudely.

Above her is the black-and-white poster of Marilyn Monroe standing in heels on a subway grill with her white dress about to blow over her head. The poster is torn at the edges.

"Oh," Willie says. "Bick, do you know Marcia and Judy? Marcia and Judy, Bick and Jayne." Hellos are said all around. "Judy, tell Bick your baby story. Bick likes stories."

"I don't see why you like that story so much," she says.

"Tell it."

"It's not really a story or anything."

"Fuck it. I'll tell it. A couple months ago Judy decided her career wasn't going very well."

"It wasn't," Judy confirms.

"So she decided she'd get pregnant. She thought having a baby would be fun." He turns to Judy. "Isn't that what you thought?"

"I just sort of thought it seemed like what everyone was doing, like *both* Don Johnson's girlfriends and everyone, you know, I got carried away, I admit it."

"So," Willie says. "She fucked this bitchin' young actor who's the son of a famous actor and who shall remain nameless because he has enough problems and she's pregnant with his baby without even telling him."

"I would have told him eventually," she says.

"But she doesn't have to because when she's into her third month of pregnancy—almost to the point of no return—something wonderful happens. . . ." Willie is having a great time. "She gets a TV commercial for a 976-LIVE!" Willie laughs crazily and for some reason the sisters both laugh with him. "So she aborts," Willie says. "The career is back!"

"I don't see why you like that story so much," Judy says. "It's like you're making fun of me."

"Not you personally," Willie says. "It's just that this is the only story that makes me believe in God. How about you, Bick?"

"Willie . . ." He doesn't know what to say.

"Avail yourself, dude," Willie says, gesturing to the coke.

As a gesture of camaraderie Bick takes out his car key and helps himself to a couple small blasts. Bick can feel Jayne watching but doesn't look at her.

Willie meanwhile pours the distilled water into the beaker. He adds coke. Then he adds ether. He puts a black cap on the beaker and shakes it. The sisters watch every move hungrily.

The Stones cassette plays out and no one seems to care.

As Willie shakes, he speaks in a broken rhythm, "AA meetings are the worst—I ran into my manager at one. My manager doesn't even have a drug or alcohol problem! She's there fucking *networking*."

One of the sisters looks up, like maybe she should check one of these meetings out.

"But it was worse than networking," Willie continues, "because—this will kill you—at the end everyone held hands and recited the fucking Lord's Prayer and then started chanting, 'It works. Keep coming back.' I felt like we were doing a TV commercial. *Keep coming back.* Wild rhinos couldn't drag me back." He quits shaking the beaker. "People are no fucking good, Bick. Cold fact." Willie's smiling, but his jaw is too tight to pull it off. "Dostoyevsky said something about how a conscious man can't possibly live with himself in this world, so I'm making an effort, you know, to be *un*conscious. I think you're the one who told me that."

"What?" Bick says.

"The Dostoyevsky thing. I think you told me that."

"Probably on drugs. I probably made it up."

"Doesn't matter. None of that shit matters. With any luck at all we're the last generation anyway. Mankind's been fucking up for centuries, but we're the ones who've finally figured out how to totally snuff the planet. You know what I think the biggest moral issue of our time is?"

Oh Jesus, Bick thinks, *incoming coke rap.* In defense he helps himself to another keyful.

"Whether to be a sick pig and be ignorant about the fact that you're a sick pig and contributing to the general sickness or whether to be self-conscious about the fact that you're a sick pig and contributing to the general sick pigness and laugh about it." Willie runs out of breath. "There are possibly other choices, but I don't think so. I mean, I can't think of 'em."

"Think harder," Bick suggests, "but not right now."

Willie takes the cap off the beaker. With the eye-dropper he sucks up liquid from the top layer. As he squeezes out drops onto the glass of *The Corpse Grinders* poster, he blows on them and the drops dry instantly into shiny white

powder. He scrapes up the powder with the razor blade and deposits it into the bowl of the glass pipe. The cub torch clicks on and Willie turns the flame on the bowl and sucks.

The sisters are practically drooling.

When Willie's finished with his hit he smiles and scrapes more coke into the bowl and holds the pipe and torch out to Bick.

"No thanks," Bick says. "I already had my heart attack this week." He lights another cigarette instead.

Willie gestures to Jayne.

"No thanks," she says, sitting with her legs crossed, smoking. When she stares back at Bick, he shrugs and turns.

Willie passes the pipe and torch to a sister, who is far more grateful than either Bick or Jayne.

"Music," Willie says, "what happened to the music?" He hops up and turns the tape over. The riffs of "Jumping Jack Flash" come blasting out and Willie cranks it up and starts pacing. "Rock and roll used to be about sex or rebellion or whatever," he says, careening around the apartment. "Not anymore. Now it's about *surviving.*" Sweat drips off his face. "Madonna is the Andrew Carnegie of our generation. She's not a singer or an artist or a sex symbol—she's the greatest businessman of our time! The industry of today is imagery and she is selling hers for *top fucking dollar.* Publicity firms are taking over the world. You must've noticed this."

Bick laughs and this seems to keep Willie going.

"Here we are," he says, waving hands wildly in the air, "with all our knowledge and supposed understanding and we do all this evil shit 'cause we don't know anything that connects us to fuckin' anything!" He laughs, a discomforting cocaine laugh. "Listen to this song—it's fuckin' Nietzschean, it's about being beyond good and evil, looking the debauchery and the brutality and the horror in the eye and saying 'yeah, so?' Saving yourself from evil by fuckin' embracing it."

"How long have you been bingeing?"

Willie starts singing along manically, *"I was crowned with a spike right through my head,"* but suddenly stops and seems to switch characters. "What are you doing here?"

"I'm doing a feature article for *Teen Beat,* your young fans want to know about the real you."

"Here I am," he thrusts his arms out.

"Merri wants you to come home."

Willie goes to the refrigerator. "Anybody want anything to drink?"

"No thanks," Bick says.

"No thanks," Jayne says.

The sisters are too busy with the blow to answer.

Willie opens an Amstel Light. "Less filling," he says. "More expensive. What do you think, Bick?"

"I think cocaine's history. Alcohol and marijuana are better for you and heroin's a less sweaty way to kill yourself." Bick gets up. "I'm going back to my place. I'll tell Merri you're ... I don't know." He turns to the young actresses and says good night.

"Nice meeting you," one says.

Jayne looks relieved as she joins Bick in rising.

Willie goes to the door and turns. "Thanks for coming, kids." He touches Jayne's shoulder. "I hope we meet again in, uh, a better light." Then he slaps Bick on the back and says, "Thanks."

As they walk back to the car, Jayne shakes her head. "He gets what, a million dollars a film?"

"A million five."

They both almost laugh.

"What's he so afraid of?"

"Same shit as everyone." Bick shrugs. "I'm the last one to know."

"He'll get AIDS if he fucks those sluts."

"He's not going to fuck them. He's just going to watch."

"Watch?"

"Yeah, they'll do each other and he'll watch. He's into that."

"That's weird."

"He'll probably fuck them afterward though."

"*Oh,* I guess *that* makes him normal."

Bick realizes what he's just said and laughs.

"What's wrong with his girlfriend? Why does she put up with this shit?"

"I don't know," Bick says. "She loves him, I guess. She thinks there's hope for him."

"She must be crazy too."

"No."

"No? He's *way* out there."

"No."

"No?"

"No, I think he's probably just like everyone else—just more so."

Jayne looks at him.

"And a little more fucked up," he admits.

"How does he function? How does he work?"

"He cleans up when he's working. He only binges in between movies. Unfortunately he's made so much goddamn money he never has to work again."

"Doesn't it piss you off?"

"Piss me off?"

"Seeing him totally fuck himself up? How can't you be angry?"

"You can't get angry at everything there is to be angry about."

"Isn't he a friend of yours?"

"Yeah."

Jayne mumbles something.

"What," Bick asks.

"Nothing."

They walk out through the gate.

"You know," she says, "you're taller and heavier and you can see straight."

Bick stops. "I don't want to do this."

"Yeah you do."

"No I don't." He reaches into his pocket and hands her his keys. "Bring the car around."

The sister who lets Bick back inside doesn't seem pleased to see him. Willie is at the stereo holding up an album and when he turns to face Bick, the disk falls out of the sleeve to the floor. "Whoops." He shrugs and tosses the cover over his shoulder.

"Get the fuck out of here," Bick says.

"What?"

"We're getting the fuck out of here. You're going home to a girl just ignorant enough to love you." Bick looks at the sisters, who wholeheartedly have returned to their coke intake. They're cutting lines on *The Corpse Grinders* poster that stretch all the way from PEOPLE to HAMBURGER. "These two are brain-dead. They're nothing but starfucking coke whores."

"Of course," Willie says. "That's their *charm.*"

Bick puts his arm around Willie and leads him out the door. Willie drags his feet but not very hard. The sisters don't even bother to get up. "Hey," one finally says as Bick slams the door.

"We're not well," Willie says. "Are we?" He laughs. "Wow it's bright out here—could I borrow your sunglasses?"

They twist up into Bel Air with the top down and Willie is in the rear seat leaning between Bick and Jayne, moaning "Oh God," between giving Bick directions. Then "Oh my God, *stop.*"

Bick pulls to the curb along the shaded residential street. "What?"

"Did you see that license plate?"

"What?"

"It says," Willie clenches his jaw, "'I DO TV.' And I don't think it means 'I do transvestites.' I'm tossing a brick through the fucker's window."

Willie jumps out and stumbles over toward the Saab with the offending license plate.

Jayne looks at Bick as if he should do something.

"He won't find any bricks around here," Bick says.

Willie scans the smooth road, the flawless sidewalks, the well-groomed grass. "Does either of you have a brick?" he yells to Bick and Jayne.

"Get in, Willie," Bick says calmly.

"What's wrong with you anyway," Willie asks the mute Saab. "Don't worry," he says in an airy voice, "be happy." Then he rips the car-phone antenna off and lets it fly toward the sun. "At least he won't be doing TV in his car for a while."

Bick laughs but tries to sound serious, "Come on."

Willie raises his fist, cranks up his whole body and lets out a scream as he punches the rear side window with a hollow crunch.

Bick and Jayne run over to him, but Willie seems fine except for mild bleeding of the hand he proudly holds forth. The safety glass is shattered, with jagged lines stretching out from the slightly indented point of impact.

"I would've knocked him out easy if he weren't an import," he says as Jayne takes his hand and begins picking out the shiny bits of glass.

"This is it, kids," Willie says, pointing his hand wrapped in white oxford cloth ripped from Bick's shirttail. The object of his gesture is a pinkish Italian villa with dwarf palm trees scattered through the yard. Bick turns down the long horseshoe driveway. "Scary," Willie says, "isn't it?"

"It's very large," Jayne says.

"Somebody famous had it built in the thirties," Willie says. "I forget who."

"Mussolini," Bick suggests.

"Mussolini?" Jayne says.

"President of Warner Brothers way back when," Willie explains.

Jayne looks skeptical, or at least Bick hopes she does.

"Wanna come in for croquet or anything?" Willie continues. "Help me postpone a severe bout of self-loathing?"

"No thanks," Bick says. "We'll see you at the party."

"Oh shit. Is that tonight?"

"It's a few nights away."

"I have to get Merri something good for her birthday," he says, "since I pretty much fucked up my New Year's resolution." He tries to hop out of the car and instead falls onto his hands and knees as the sunglasses skitter across the cement. "Fuck!" He bounces back up and then bends to pick up the sunglasses. "Sorry, Bick," he says, examining them with a squint. "I'm really sorry." He wipes the shades on his shirttail and hands them back to Bick.

Both of the lenses are scarred, but Bick puts them on anyway. "No problem."

"Everything's going to be in softer focus now. I did you a favor."

"Don't think I'm not grateful."

"Drive safely, kids."

"Sweet dreams," Jayne says.

"Thanks for the ride." He turns and bounds toward the front door. "I'm home, honey!"

Libby drives her jeep down Hollywood Boulevard with the top up and turns off onto a side street and parks in a yellow zone not far from the Angels' Flight entrance. She'd rather have a ticket than walk around this area. As soon as she steps out of the car and clicks on the alarm a man she didn't see is almost on top of her.

"Got twenty bucks?" he says.

"Sorry," she says and walks away.

"Nice outfit," a bag lady calls from a doorway.

"Thank you," Libby answers.

The next building has a plate-glass door with ANGELS' HOME written in chipped paint. Libby opens the door and immediately notices the incredibly tacky linoleum and the cheap desks. In the corner, sitting on cots, are two scraggly kids talking with a girl around Libby's age wearing ripped jeans and a Princeton sweatshirt. In a business-like blue skirt and blue blazer, Libby's already very uncomfortable.

"Can I help you?" says a young girl behind a desk that has none of the usual secretarial clutter.

"I'm here to see Brother Chris," Libby says.

"Brother Chris!"

Libby is a little surprised when she notices the girl is reading a very tattered copy of *Town and Country*.

A door just to the right opens and a thirtyish man in traditional Catholic garb appears. "Hello," he says, looking right at Libby. "You must be Miss Bridgham."

"Yes."

He comes over and takes her hand. "It's good to meet you." He's warm and disarming in the way she always imagined priests to be and she hopes the stories Bick told her about sodomized altar boys are exaggerated.

"My pleasure," she says as he finally releases her hand.

"Come in, please."

He leads her into his pale green office, where there's only a desk and two chairs and a crucifix on the wall. He sits behind his desk under the crucifix. She sits in front of him and crosses her legs.

"I should have advised you to dress more casually," he chuckles.

"It should've occurred to me," she says.

"Well," he says, folding his hands on the desk. "This may be a relatively novel situation for you."

"Janet gave me some warning—or information, rather."

"And how is it you and Janet know each other?"

"We were in acting class together."

"Oh, you're an actress?"

Though he's still smiling, Libby knows this is a no-no. "Not any more," she says definitely.

"Your references spoke very highly of you."

"They're friends of my mother's. They'd better have." She returns his smile.

"What do your parents do?"

"My father died when I was young and my mother doesn't really do much of anything anymore."

"I guess that's good work if you can get it," he says and chuckles.

She politely laughs.

"Let me tell you about Angels' Flight. We have essentially three steps of operation. Sort of a trinity. Outreach, Intake and Referral. I'll tell you about each." He pulls an ashtray and a pack of Merits from a desk drawer and taps a cigarette out of the pack toward her.

"Thank you," she says.

He lights their cigarettes with a Zippo and continues. "Outreach. That's the first job of the counselors. This means going out into the streets, walking Hollywood Boulevard down there and reaching out to the new runaways. There's a community of sorts among the street kids and we make ourselves available to them by just being a presence in their community. We particularly try to spot the baby runaways—the new ones, that is—and contact them with our flier, which explains who we are and what we do."

He stares at his cigarette.

"Uh-huh," Libby says to indicate she's listening.

"The ones who are ready for help come here. That's what we call Intake. You take down their information and assess their case. If the kid is a situational runaway—that is, a runaway who left home because of a particular situation, say bad grades, loud music, Dad doesn't like her boyfriend, that sort of thing—we try to put him or her back in contact with the parents so they can work it out. If the situation isn't a rectifiable one—like physical abuse, sexual abuse, pregnancy, drug problems, whether the kid's or the parents'—we turn to Referral, which means we refer the kid to an agency that has the proper resources. Shelters, maternity homes, drug rehab centers, the job corps, those sorts of places."

He inhales deeply on the cigarette.

"We're just a crisis center. Kids in a crisis want to go home. If we can help them get home, we do. If we can't, we refer them to where they can get the specific help they need. If they want it."

Libby nods.

"We also offer Band-Aids, food, temporary shelter, clothes, showers and just somebody to talk to."

Finished with his cigarette, he folds his hands. Libby's cigarette is less than halfway finished. She's about to speak when he resumes.

"You ever read Mark Twain?"

"Mark Twain? Sure, *Tom Sawyer, Huckleberry Finn.*"

"Let me tell you something Mark Twain said: 'The best way to cheer up yourself is to bring cheer to someone else.'"

"Didn't he have a cocaine problem?" Libby has no idea why she said this, but instantly blames Bick.

"I don't know," Brother Chris answers, "but I've heard that said, yes. Anyway. You'll find that observation true here. And not true. Last year Georgia, aged fourteen, came knocking on the door. She had hitchhiked out here from the South to become an actress. New idea, huh? But she wouldn't go back home because her dad liked to beat her with two-by-fours."

Libby isn't sure but suspects that two-by-fours are pieces of lumber.

"She soon picked up a heroin habit. One of the counselors referred her to drug rehab. A couple months later we heard she was back on the streets. Many runaways are functionally illiterate and without any job skills, plus they don't have ID or regular addresses or anything else you need to get a job. About the only way for them to make money is prostitution. This is what Georgia was doing. Her counselor explained the obvious dangers of this and referred Georgia to job agencies and generally did all she could. She also told Georgia if she was going to turn tricks, use condoms. This last bit of advice was the only bit Georgia took." He smiles slightly. "One day Georgia mentioned in passing to

this counselor that she thought condoms should be better designed. It seems Georgia was worried about the men's ejaculation's splitting the condoms, so she'd been poking pinholes in the tips."

Libby returns his slight smile.

"Georgia died recently of AIDS-related pneumonia." He stands up and reaches out to shake her hand. "If you want the job, it's yours. But think about it."

Libby thinks writing a few checks to the right charities would be more her style.

On her way out in the morning Mona checks the mail in the hall box. YOU MAY HAVE ALREADY WON $5,000,000, an oversized brown envelope screams in red. Mona wads it up and tosses it, leaving the other junk mail, mostly coupons to neighborhood stores, in the box to pick up later. There is also an embossed white envelope, which she knows must be an invitation to Merri's birthday party. She opens it.

We're saddened to invite you
to a wake
celebrating the death of Merri's youth.
The big three-o.
Dinner and cocktails. Please come dressed to mourn.

This reminds Mona of the last bash and her resolution—to find a job. She decides the invitation is a little grim for Joy and puts it in her purse.

T he valet takes the BMW at the street. Bick and Jayne walk up the red carpet to the front gate. A big woman is standing there with a clipboard, two security guards flanking her.

"Bick Smith."

The woman checks the list. "Yes, welcome."

They stroll up the driveway. As gaudy as the Mussolini villa was in the daylight, it is more of a visual menace by night. It's exactly the sort of Hollywood house Bick's parents warned him about.

"It doesn't feel like a hip party," Jayne says.

"No, but it's going to be a drunk party."

As always, Bick feels the preparty anticipatory buzz and he marvels at how he still hasn't shaken this unjustified sense of expectation.

They follow a pebbly bridged walkway over a small stream with a cement bed and on the other side is a huge wreath on an easellike stand.

FAREWELL TO MERRI'S YOUTH

The castle-sized wooden door is opened by a servant in tails. In the foyer is a big black and gold casket surrounded by more wreaths and flowers, in which the presents are stacked. Bick adds theirs, a book they picked up at The Bodhi Tree, *The Good Stuff Happens in Your Next Life*. It's wrapped in several sheets of typing paper taped together. He'll buy her a real present later.

People are lingering and grouping but nobody is present to offer official greetings. Bick snags a couple glasses of champagne from a passing tray. He hands one to Jayne and holds his up.

"To success with ol' Hobel," she says.

"What?"

"Hobel, *Benji*. To selling him *Till Death Do Us Part*."

"Oh yeah." This takes some of the festive wind out of his sails and knowing that tawdry motives are the case for most of the guests just makes him feel worse.

There is no furniture, just bare hardwood floors and bare walls with wreaths and flowers everywhere. There are ashtrays, however, laid out every few feet. They move farther into the party, where the interchanging groups mingle and recombine with each other, young and old, actors and actresses, writers and directors, executives and agents, rock and rollers and even a handful of people with real jobs. Bick exchanges greetings with many. He is hugged by pretty girls and doesn't mind Jayne's subtly possessive frown.

"I didn't realize you were so social," she says.

"I'm not anymore."

"My God," she says, "that's a Monkee, Mickey Dolenz. Talking to a Beastie Boy." She laughs and looks away.

"No."

"Yes. Behind on your left."

Next to Dolenz is Paul Anka and two pretty actresses, their daughters. The room is full of well-known Hollywood faces along with their not-quite-as-well-known offspring. Clock Girl is also here.

"Let's keep moving," Bick whispers to Jayne.

"Bick!"

Dunphy is wearing his "Brady Bunch" girls T-shirt and Bick introduces him to Jayne. "So which one is your favorite," Dunphy asks.

Jayne looks to Bick.

"I couldn't help but notice you were admiring my T-shirt," Dunphy continues, "and I was just wondering which is your favorite? Cindy?"

Jayne smiles back at Dunphy and says, "I've only seen 'The Brady Bunch' once or twice, in reruns. I didn't really get it."

"There's not that much to get," Dunphy says, good-naturedly. "It's not a Bergman film."

"Might as well have been," Jayne says.

Dunphy laughs. "Watch it again sometime. You'll like Cindy. Bick can explain the significance."

Jayne looks at Bick, who looks at Dunphy.

"I gotta get myself a drink," Dunphy says. "The bozos with the bottles of Cristal keep snubbing me for some reason. Nice meeting you, Jayne."

Bick tells Jayne about Dunphy's "Brady Bunch" personality test as they make for the patio, not mentioning the sad-life punch line.

"Bick Smith," a man with white hair says.

"Timothy," Bick says, stopping. "Hello."

"Have you left New York for good yet?"

Each time they see each other, Timothy asks Bick this question. Bick has given up explaining that he has never lived in New York.

"Not yet," Bick says and then introduces him to Jayne.

"This is where you want to be," Timothy says with great meaning. "This is where it's taking off from, the information runway." And he takes off himself.

Finally Bick and Jayne move through open doors onto the large patio, where there are dozens of white-linen-covered tables set with silver and crystal. It's all elegantly underscored by the large speakers blasting The Replacements' "Gary's Got a Boner." A lawn with croquet wickets and burning tiki torches stretches to the big brightly lit pool at the edge of the grounds, which slope off, leaving a high view of the sparkling city.

"Look at that pool," Jayne says. "It's twice the size of mine."

"And pinkish to boot."

They continue down the slight incline to the pool, lighting cigarettes off a tiki torch on the way. As they get closer, they can see pink lilies floating in the pool, glowing from the underwater lights. The diving board is ringed with wreaths. A pretty young girl at the edge is pointing out over the city at the darkness of the ocean while an older guy nods his head.

"These people your friends," Jayne asks.

"Who?"

"The people at this party. All the people you said hello to."

"No, just acquaintances."

"You don't have any friends here?"

"Hopefully. I just haven't seen them yet."

"What's Paul Anka doing here?"

"Willie's dad is an accountant for pop stars or anyone else who's filthy rich. Willie grew up, or didn't grow up, with a lot of these people."

"Is his girlfriend's family in the business too?"

"No, hers is real."

"That must help."

"Yeah."

"They here?"

"No, they live in a real state."

She nods, sips her champagne. "I like parties sometimes."

"The thing I like about parties is when they're over."

"Is this an example of your pleasure-is-just-what-happens-when-the-suf-fering-eases theory?"

She throwing German philosophy back at him *here?* The thought makes him guzzle his drink. She takes a hit of her cigarette and tosses it in the pool and instantly puts her hand to her mouth. "Ooops."

"Hey," Willie yells, skipping down the lawn. "I saw that! Now get up here. We're saving seats at our table for you." He's wearing a Matt Groening LIFE IN HELL T-shift under his dinner jacket.

Bick and Jayne walk toward him and he introduces himself to Jayne as though they've never met. She plays along. He seems in good spirits, neither drugged nor drunk, and briskly leads them up to the patio. A dog runs up to dance around them and Bick notices a crucifix on her chain.

"Madonna," Willie says, "quit whining for attention."

Jayne laughs. Madonna barks and then runs off to pester someone else.

"Bruce Willis and Demi Moore were in your seats," Willie says. "I threw 'em both out on their smug butts. Have you seen Lee Marvin? I invited him, but I think he's dead."

At the table are Merri, Libby, Joy, Oscar, Mona, and Anna, an impish singer in an all-girl pop group who is charming now that she's off drugs. Merri is wearing a new hat, black with a red rose.

"Happy birthday," Bick says.

"Thanks," Merri says, sniffling, wiping an imaginary tear from her rouged cheek.

"You're late," Libby says to Bick, "as usual."

"Love me anyway," he says and kisses her on the cheek.

Bick then introduces everyone to Jayne.

"I believe we've met," Libby says.

"Oh yes," Jayne says sweetly, "I hope you didn't get caught in morning traffic."

Bick pulls out a chair for Jayne and seats himself between Jayne and Anna, who immediately asks, "Did anyone see Paul Anka."

"I did," Jayne says.

"That *was* him!" Anna raises her champagne glass and sings into it, *"Having my baby . . ."* She takes a deep breath. *"I did it my way. . . ."* She sets her glass down when a man with a towel over his arm offers her a refill.

"Just leave the bottle, please," Willie says.

"What have you been up to," Bick asks Libby.

"I quit acting."

"I know."

"It seemed like a good first step."

"I'm sure it is."

"Mona has a new job," Merri announces.

"Yeah, it's true," Mona says, "Stallone offered me the female lead in *Rocky VI.*"

"She got a good job with a real producer," Merri says.

"He didn't really want to hire me," Mona says. "But Oscar badgered him into it behind the scenes."

Oscar confirms with a smirk.

"Yes," Mona says, "I'm a D-girl now, but if I'm going to be a D-girl, I'm going to be the *angriest* D-girl who ever lived."

Anna leans in to Bick, "I'm glad you're here."

Bick doesn't know what to say, since he can't imagine why.

"I have a question for you," she continues.

Bick leans toward her receptively.

"This is sort of a continuation of the conversation we had a while back."

He has no idea what they talked about and, in fact, can't even remember talking to her recently.

"You were saying how guys grow up with these one-dimensional masturbation fantasies about women, remember?" She smiles. "You were saying how guys love slutty fingernail polish because it subconsciously reminds them of the magazine girls holding open their labia."

Now he remembers the conversation. He was drunk out of his mind backstage at the Universal Amphitheatre.

"You never said whether you think guys can outgrow this. I mean, do guys have to keep sex and love separate or can they put both together? Can they love the person they're fucking? Or like if you're going down on a guy and you let him come all over your face, can he ever think of you as an equal?"

Everyone is following this conversation.

Noticing this, Anna laughs. "Uh-oh." She has a shamelessness Bick imagines only people with platinum records or such can acquire.

Libby's jaw has dropped almost into her lap.

"No," Mona says. "Men are hopeless."

"Men have plenty of hope," Bick says.

"Despite the fact that they're surrounded by belligerently neurotic women," Oscar adds.

"Fortunately," Mona says, "men are so mature."

"Men have this bizarre obsession with their come," Anna says. "It's like they think their come is the staff of life or something."

"Food's ready," Merri says.

They come back from the buffet, their plates decorated with stuffed mushrooms, poached salmon and dark green asparagus with hollandaise sauce.

"Excellent," Libby says as they sit down. "Well done."

"Thank you," Merri says, "but compliment Willie."

"No," Libby says.

"Yep," Willie says. "I'm the visionary behind all you see." He looks at Oscar. "It was much more demanding than directing a movie."

"And you didn't have to deal with actors or actresses," Oscar says.

"Yes I did, the chef once was a semiregular on a TV series."

"Now," Libby says as the group settles into their seats, "can we talk about what became of everyone's New Year's resolution?"

"Yes," Merri says and everyone else makes "oh yeah" sounds except Joy who says, "Oh shit" and gets a solid laugh.

Bick has a bite of the salmon and it's only fair but reminds him of Seattle. He wonders what Jayne would think about moving to the Northwest.

"Did you get a normal life yet," Libby asks him.

"Technically, no."

"Blown resolution number one," Mona says.

"My resolution was to get a part," Libby says. "But since I quit acting—"

"Blown resolution number two," Mona says.

"Blown resolution number three," Oscar says holding his hands up, palms out.

"Blown resolution number four," Willie throws in. "Spit on me."

"You're coming along," Merri says.

"I failed too," Joy says.

"What was yours?" Oscar says.

"To come up with one."

"Right. Well, come up with one now. Or join us boys in our failure if you'd rather."

"That's a hard decision." She seems serious. "I guess I failed."

"*I* succeeded," Mona laughs. "Thank you very much. Success story of the year. Thank you. The boys and Joy all failed, Libby dropped out, Merri was already grown-up so she doesn't count, but *me*, I'm a raging success story. Thank you."

During the laughter Libby turns to Jayne. "How about you," she says. "Did you have a New Year's resolution?" Libby times this so Jayne's mouth is full.

"Yes," Jayne says when she finishes chewing. "But I, uh, didn't quite keep it."

"Oh?"

"I was going to give up boys."

"That's a tough one."

"Maybe next year," Mona says to her.

"Merri!" A tall actress who spent last year poised for a stardom that didn't

happen stops on her way by. "This all looks so wonderful." She can't say enough good things about the party and the wonderful people and makes a point of smiling at everyone at the table. "It's good to see you all," she says, sounding perfectly sincere.

"Amazing what a little failure can do for a girl," Mona says when the would-be star walks away.

Everyone laughs but Merri. "She's getting better. Really."

"Isn't this just like a high-school party?" Mona says.

"Speaking of high school," Anna says, "I miss Quaaludes."

"Someone once said Hollywood is like high school with too much money," Willie says.

"Who?"

"I don't know. Someone funny."

"It's not Hollywood," Mona says. "It's us. Everybody. We're all just *geeks*. Look at us."

"So? Look at Lucas and Spielberg," Oscar says. "Total misfits. Cinema majors before it guaranteed a kiss-ass article in *Rolling Stone.*"

"I'm not talking about that. I'm talking about the fact that we're all geeks." She points with her knife. "We were geeks in high school and we're still geeks."

"But *cool* geeks," Willie says.

"We've learned to *act* cool but it's only because we know we're really just geeks."

There's a moment of silence as everyone considers the old Hollywood–high-school parallel and their geekiness and takes the opportunity to eat.

Poppy breaks the contemplative quiet when she drags over a chair while balancing a high-piled plate in the other hand. "This place is celebs galore," she declares as she pulls her chair between Merri and Anna and plops down her plate. "I wish I weren't so fat."

"You look great," Merri assures her.

"I'm *bestial.* I have to get my period during the *best* party of the year." She grabs at the skin under her jaw with both hands and pulls for effect. "My uterus feels like it's in my esophagus."

Those at the table who know Poppy laugh. Those who don't know her, such as Jayne, appear appalled. Bick smiles at Jayne. She doesn't smile back.

Poppy turns to Oscar and says, "I forgot the Polaroid." She smiles. "Fuck."

"Who are you here with," Oscar asks, ignoring the Polaroid comment.

"Stephen Fisch."

"The man who almost made me an anti-Semite."

"He's part Catholic."

"Oh."

Poppy turns to Bick. "Why doesn't Oscar like movie critics?"

Bick vaguely remembers when Oscar's first movie had been in successful release a couple months, Fisch had a fit clumsily disguised as a review. In the fuss about Oscar's youth and friends-slash-connections, Oscar's work was either misunderstood or just missed. Everyone at the table feels misunderstood by nature and being misunderstood in print just confirms their worst suspicions.

"If you're not pissing off people like Fisch," Bick says to Oscar, "you're not doing your job."

"It's not that I don't *like* movie critics," Oscar insists, "I like professionals. But people like Fisch, I don't know how they live with themselves. They're either bitching about your success or kissing your ass."

"Yeah, well, Stephen would have kissed *your* ass, Oscar," Poppy says, "if your arrogant producer hadn't ignored him at Cornelia's party."

"He can lick the sweat off my balls."

"If you'd just *told* him that, he would have given you a good review."

"Didn't Fisch win a Pulitzer," Mona asks, setting down her knife and fork over her uneaten food and lighting a cigarette.

"A Pulitzer for kiss-ass celebrity profiles?" Oscar says. "That's like giving an Academy Award for selling popcorn!"

"It was a joke. I'm on your side. The guy's a joke."

"All you have to do," Poppy says to Oscar, "is pretend you like him and he'll like you. *You're* the one being stupid. Ever hear of envy? Most people have it. It's totally understandable."

Bick and Oscar shake their heads.

Mona smiles. "*Of course* it's understandable," she says. "The poor fuck is surrounded by this," she waves her cigarette at the festivities, "and has to live his own life unaccomplished and underpaid and undersexed."

"Underpaid being the worst," Poppy nods.

"Under*sexed* being the worst," Willie says.

"Unaccomplished being the worst," Oscar says, "but fuck him. You know what *really* irritates me? Every time some jerk goes insane with a high-powered rifle, it's always at a McDonald's or a Bob's Big Boy, places normal people eat. Why doesn't it happen at a place like this? Where some random violence might benefit the world."

"Yeah," Mona says, "a madman with good aim could kill the root cause of dozens of bad movies."

"And TV shows."

"And records."

"'Why?'" Willie says, imitating the boy in *Blue Velvet.* "'Why are there people like Frank Booth? Why is there so much trouble in this world?'"

"'There's trouble until the robins come,'" Merri and Libby quote together and laugh.

"What the fuck does that line mean?" Oscar says.

"Don't you get it?" Mona laughs.

"No," Oscar says. "Do you?"

"Yes," Mona says. "And I'm not going to let you in on the secret."

"Fine," he says. "That's how my life is."

Mona laughs and pats Oscar's back, then hits his spine with her fist.

"Shit," he says, also laughing.

"Oscar," Willie says, "come on. You and Bick. I want to show you something." He bows to the rest of the table. "Excuse us."

"Excuse me," Bick asks Jayne.

"No problem," she answers, faking a smile and not trying to convince him.

"We'll be right back. I hope."

Bick and Oscar follow Willie through a side door into the pantry.

"All right Oscar," Willie says. "I see you're a little upset about your screening."

"Not anymore."

As they file through, a man in a white apron tosses something in the air and catches it.

"I hear the audience hissed and threw shit at the screen," Willie says.

"Just Mona. I'm OK about it now."

Oscar's face has lost the death pinch since the last time Bick saw him and his whole body seems more relaxed.

"You do your work," Bick says. "And you try to make it good."

"It *wasn't* good," Oscar says. "Or even entertaining. I tried to rip off my first movie and I fucked up. How sad—stealing from myself at this age."

They leave the kitchen through a door leading up a flight of narrow stairs.

"Reviews are forgotten in a week," Willie says. "Quicker if you drink."

"Hemingway, right?" Bick turns to Oscar. "You know, whether they love or hate your work it's probably for the wrong reasons."

"OK, OK, I'll buy you both dinner next week."

"Don't try too hard," Willie says as they climb the stairs. "Because success is just a fluke. You can't control it. It's luck and timing and all sorts of strange shit."

"With you it was a fluke," Oscar says. "With me it was blazing talent."

At the top of the stairs they turn down an empty hallway. Their shoes echo on the hardwood.

"What did you do about the White Girl," Willie asks.

"Nothing," Oscar says. "Maybe I'll see her again, maybe I won't. That's the tragedy of it."

"What did you do to keep Merri from castrating you," Bick asks.

"I made a promise," Willie answers. "It's sort of like my New Year's resolution but this time I'm serious."

"What?"

Willie leads them around a corner. "It's my new life policy: don't drink to excess, don't do drugs to excess, which in my case means don't drink or do drugs at all, and, lastly, don't fuck people you don't love."

"Good words," Bick says. "But I have a policy too: don't make promises you can't keep."

"I'll keep it. And I'll do it alone. By alone I mean I'll be calling you guys at three A.M. pretty frequently."

Bick and Oscar look at each other.

"He's serious?" Bick says.

"She won't ever marry me if I don't," Willie says.

"Can't be serious," Oscar answers.

"I think she might actually consider marrying me if I can keep that promise."

"Might?" Bick says.

"Now close your eyes," Willie says, stopping outside a door. "I should have saved this, but it's so happening I have to show you now. Close your eyes."

Bick watches Oscar close his eyes and then closes his own. Willie opens a door and steers them into a room. Bick can't imagine what Willie might be about to show them.

"Lie down," Willie says.

"Is this going to get sexual," Oscar asks.

"Lie down. Don't open your eyes."

Bick lies down on what feels like stucco and Oscar and Willie lie on either side of him.

"Open your eyes," Willie says.

Bick opens his eyes—he almost pukes up his whole stomach and he automatically lets go of his beer and tries to grab at the stucco he's lying on because above him is the floor—the wood floor with an oriental paisley-patterned rug and a couch and chairs and a table with a lamp.

Willie is laughing wildly. "Can you imagine passing out and waking up in this room? You'd throw up for days."

Bick sits up, as do Oscar and Willie.

"I almost threw up anyway," Oscar says.

Bick reaches for what's left of the beer he spilled.

"The guy who built the house specifically designed this room to throw drunk friends in after a party," Willie says.

"Wonderful friend," Oscar says.

"If I had any patience, one of you might have awakened tomorrow morning with a surprise."

Bick looks up again. He's regained his perspective and the effect of the room doesn't bother him too much. On the kidney-shaped table is a copy of

The Great Gatsby and a box of cigarettes and an ashtray complete with butts, all presumably glued in place.

"Is the book real," Bick asks.

"Probably. The guy used to party with all those people. You're very likely lying on the same floor Mr. Fitzgerald ralphed on."

"Touched with eternity."

J oy excuses herself from the table during a familiar conversation about celebrities and channeling and earthquakes and AIDS. She intends to go home and kill herself, but she wants to find the bathroom first. She wanders upstairs and opens a door and there are Willie, Bick and Oscar laughing and gesturing with their beer bottles, male-bonding crap. The boys say hi to her. Something's not quite right and she slowly realizes it's the furniture hanging from the ceiling.

"Why is the furniture hanging from the ceiling," she asks.

"Just a visual effect. What do you think?"

"Tasteful furniture."

"It's more effective if you're looking up from the floor, preferably first thing in the morning with a hangover."

"It's pretty funny," she says, even though it isn't.

"I'm taking the guys on a tour," Willie says. "Want to join us?"

"No, I'm just looking for the bathroom."

"Through that door." He points across the room.

"The toilet's on the ceiling," Oscar says. "But it still works."

The boys leave and she goes to the bathroom. The bathroom is perfectly normal except for the emptiness of the medicine cabinet.

She stops on her way back through the upside-down room and tries the view Willie suggested: lying on her back looking up. It doesn't really affect

her—everything's upside down, so what? She sits up. The floors and the wall are all white, very white, the way she imagines a nuthouse would be. She doesn't want to botch another suicide because they could then put her away. It occurs to her that home is a long way to go just to kill herself. Out of her purse she pulls her key chain with its attached rape-protection penknife. She opens the knife and without hesitation slashes it across her left wrist. The blood spurts high and powerful and she's happy, she thinks she must have struck the right vein, but then she's afraid it won't be enough so she reaches down and slashes at the big vein just forward of her ankle and this one spurts in a really beautiful red arc. She does the same to her left ankle but misses and though she isn't really feeling much pain, she knows she doesn't have much strength left and her last gesture is a desperate clumsy cut across her throat.

Her head falls back against the floor and she sees smeared colors and the bright white light of the GE lamp bulb.

Willie, Merri, Libby, Mona, Oscar, Bick and Jayne all sit on the edge of the swimming pool watching the cold blue predawn light spread. The postparty situation would not be unfamiliar to Libby if it weren't for Jayne. To Libby even the ambulance and emergency men and white sheets and all the blood seem less out of place than Jayne, who keeps tossing her cigarette butts into the pool.

The sun is in sight and yellowing the smog when someone finally clears her throat to speak. "How could we not see?" Merri says.

"We saw," Mona says. "We just didn't do anything about it."

Libby looks at Bick, who is drinking from a vodka bottle.

"I told her if she really wanted to kill herself she should slice up her ankles," Mona continues. "Or cut her throat."

"Mona . . ." Merri says.

"Don't try to hog all the guilt," Willie says.

"Fuck y'all," Libby finds herself shouting. "We wouldn't have fucking noticed if Joy had sliced open her chest and removed her beating heart at the goddamn dinner table . . . and what's it going to take to, to . . ."

Bick passes Willie the bottle and Willie takes a hit.

"Fuck you both," Libby says to them.

Merri opens her mouth.

"And you too, Merri. For letting this fuck," she points to Willie, "get away

with so much. And fuck me for letting this fuck," she points to Bick, "get away with just as much. Fuck y'all." She wants to say more but doesn't know the words to express her sense of excruciating disgust and shame and she thinks if they start talking, they'll talk it all out and feel better and nobody deserves to feel better now. She runs up the lawn past the burned-out tiki torches, then trips on a croquet wicket and falls face first into the damp grass. "Goddamn fuck!"

"Her language has certainly gotten salty," Willie says.

Merri slaps him, the sound seems to echo off the large empty house.

Bick is shivering in the morning air but he's flying on the freeway and doesn't want to pull over to put the top up. He can still hear Merri and Mona and Libby. *"We saw. We just didn't do anything, fuck y'all"* and the only thing good or warm he can think of is the girl next to him.

He looks at Jayne to see their shared pain in her eyes.

She says, "What are we going to do about Benji?"

Somewhere in the throes of a classically executed chronologically indeterminate bender, Bick finds himself in his apartment, waking up on the futon fully clothed as usual, still drunk and bruised and sore, deciding it's time to try and remember, if not understand.

Once, a long time ago, you were a budding genius, he thinks as he pulls a beer out of the refrigerator, *then you became a moron. You can't focus on people, you don't listen so well anymore. In the last few years you've drunk enough and done enough drugs—slaughtering so many brain cells—that now you feel you're catching up to the people who started out dumb.*

As he opens the Bud, he wonders about those who seem somehow naturally stupid to the torment of deep emotion, those who exist safely in the petty, and he almost wishes he could join them, but not really.

The cold beer is his idea of a step toward sobriety.

He sits down at his desk with the beer and picks up his journal and stares at the composition book's black-and-white Rorschach pattern. *So things don't make sense.* He has always known this, of course, but still he has spent his professional life pretending they did, forcing them to make sense, crafting chaos into semisensible stories with a moral order. *That, goddamn it, is the job.* Now he feels guilty because things make sense only in dreams and movies.

You will get what you want only in dreams and movies and then only if it's that kind of dream or movie. Religion, he knows, would come in awfully handy right now.

Instead, he picks up a pen and writes. *She has the mystery of a person who doesn't know herself. She's not alone there.*

He puts down the pen, lights another cigarette, drinks his beer and looks out the window at the ocean. The westerly wind is blowing the dark afternoon clouds and the ocean is a stormy green. As always planes are flying in and out of LAX. *And why the hell wouldn't they be?* Then he looks down—*the palm trees are burning*—but he thinks this unlikely and he reconsiders as he stares and realizes that it's just a ray of sun reflecting off the twisting wind-driven palm fronds, it's just his angle.

The cigarette between his lips spins smoke right into his sore eyes, so he adjusts his head slightly. He's not sure what to write. *Someday, maybe, she'll decide to be someone other than a movie star.* He knows the odds are against her. He remembers Oscar's words, *Kisses mean nothing to girls like that,* and remembers laughing and wonders if someday this will make him laugh again. *She was the only girl you know as thrilling and full of promise as girls of fiction because she was fiction.*

Packing is easy. A few shirts and boxers and pairs of pants and shoes stuffed into a duffel bag, a few books and his journal and toiletries and bottle of bourbon stuffed into his old leather satchel and he's done. The rest he can deal with later.

He's not maudlin enough to believe he can return to innocence by moving a thousand miles north, nor is he willing to totally reject the idea.

Into the back of his BMW he loads his duffel bag and satchel. The car stinks of bourbon. He tosses an empty bottle from the passenger seat out the window into the parking lot. It shatters among a variety of other bottles. He can't help but think how things would be different if he had just got on the road north on New Year's Day, but he knows this is now just something besides the late movie to keep him up nights.

He backs the BMW out into the alley. There's the squeal of brakes and the back right corner is smashed, the rear end shoved along in a sideways twist. "No." He rests his head on the steering wheel. The engine has died and the two cars are obviously locked.

He opens his door and steps out. The other driver is already out of his large American sedan and he's small and ugly and dangerous looking. He appears to be drunk, which makes Bick aware of his own lingering drunkenness.

"What the fuck is your problem?" the guy yells.

Bick thinks this could take a very long time to answer properly.

The guy is looking at the way his chrome bumper is humping the rear corner of the BMW. Bick joins him in staring at this. The bumper has scrunched his fender into the tire, which is now flattened.

"Oh God, no," Bick mutters.

"What the *fuck* is your problem?" the guy repeats.

"Listen," Bick says. "It was my fault—"

"No shit."

Bick musters the last of his energy into a plea for peace. "Your car looks fine. Let's just pull them apart and fucking forget it. OK?"

The guy tries to look difficult for a moment but apparently can find no good reason to argue.

"OK?" Bick repeats.

"OK," the guy says. "I'll try to back it off."

He gets back into his behemoth and slams it into reverse. It drags the BMW back a foot or two, but then there's a sound—*almost like sighing,* Bick thinks—and the two cars disengage.

Bick revs up his car and releases the clutch. The rear tire is obviously still dragging on metal, but he keeps the RPMs high and steers the crippled car back into a parking space.

In the trunk he finds a tire iron and begins prying the metal back from the tire so that he can put on the spare. Several minutes later his hands are bloody and the metal has not moved.

Back in his apartment he ties his duffel bag with spring cords onto the back of the dusty motorcycle. He bleeds on everything he touches.

It's been more than a couple months since he last started the Triumph, but there's still gas in the tank. He dons leather gloves and sunglasses. He has a strange confidence she will start now that he needs her. She doesn't, of course. He keeps kicking, adjusting the fuel mixture, kicking some more, praying, and she coughs to life. The carbon monoxide quickly clouds the apartment as he warms the engine. Sitting on the bike, he steps it to the front door and leans forward and noses the door open. Then he pops the clutch and rides down the hall with one foot skimming the old carpet. He turns down the wide stairs, not minding the bumping much, and up to the front door, which he opens, leaning forward, again without getting off the bike.

Suddenly he's out in the light going fast and it feels good to be moving. The air is cool and he doesn't have a helmet so his hair is blowing back and his ears are turning to ice. He drives north on Pacific Avenue until it becomes Neilson and then, just before it becomes Ocean Avenue, he turns onto Pico and heads east toward the Fox studio.

At a traffic light he stops in view of a billboard for a movie he thinks he might have performed a dialogue polish on. His name doesn't seem to be among the fifty or so in black letters at the bottom, but that doesn't mean anything. It must have been true hack work, he decides, if he's buried the memory and is done thinking about it by the time the light changes.

He turns onto the lot and shifts up. Ahead of him is the entrance with a bar gate and a guard hut that always puts him in mind of a Communist coun-

try's border checkpoint. He waves at the guard and drives around the gate, not waiting for the guard's reaction.

A blue line painted on the concrete traces his path past low buildings and huge sound stages and parking lots to a group of weathered trailers used as offices. He spots Sarah's old Volvo.

"Hi, Bick," her secretary says when he enters, but her smile stops short.

"I've been on a bike," he says helplessly.

"Sarah's in a meeting," she says.

"We'll just be a minute." With that he walks through the undersized doorway into her office.

"Oh no," Sarah says when he enters.

"Hello," he says in return.

She's sitting in front of her desk, which has the same awful wooden veneer as the walls, and in front of her is a young guy Bick assumes to be a screenwriter in search of a development deal. *Full of hope,* Bick thinks, *the dumb bastard.*

"Hello," Bick says to the guy.

"Howdy," he answers and Bick figures he's trying to gauge whether Bick is important or just crazy.

The secretary then appears in the doorway. "Sarah?" she says.

"Could I speak with you alone for a minute," Bick asks.

Sarah takes a moment, nods, then turns to her appointment, "Could you excuse us, please?"

As the secretary and the screenwriter clear out, Bick reminds himself that this is the woman he always retreated to in his loneliest worst moments and tells himself he's right to say what he's about to say.

"Are you OK?" Sarah says.

The door closes with a flimsy click.

"Fine, thanks," Bick says.

"Are you going to take off your sunglasses?"

"If you'd like."

"No, on second thought keep 'em on. Finally you look like you should, like shit."

"Thanks."

"I've been trying to get a hold of you," she says, "to check on you."

"I've been sort of indisposed."

"On a drunken binge?"

She knows me, he thinks, while saying, "I want you to leave with me."

"What do you mean?"

"You hate what you do. Every time you develop some project, *if* you do a good job, they end up taking it away. I think you once compared it to kidnapping."

"You're *supposed* to hate your job in your twenties."

"I'm serious. I'm leaving, I'm going back to the Northwest and I want you to come with me."

"Why? Why on earth would I do that?"

"I'm buying a house and—"

"So?"

"I'm buying a house and trying a normal, more religious life. And I thought you might want to try it with me."

"Are you totally insane?"

"No, maybe not totally."

"Bick," she says, "this doesn't sound like you. Think about what you're saying."

"I'm acting on impulse here. Operating on instinct, right. You're a woman, you should approve of that. I'm talking about passion."

"Passion?"

"Never mind, the joke's for someone else."

"You're drunk, aren't you?"

"No, I pretty much sobered up on the motorcycle."

"The motorcycle?"

"My car is sort of immobilized," he explains. "We'll need to take yours." She starts to laugh but stops.

"What?" he says.

"Go home," she says. "Go home and sleep. I'll come by after work and tuck you in."

"Don't come by," he says, "I'll be in a Motel 6 on I-5."

"Come on, Bick."

"I appreciate all the nights you let me in," he says.

"Bick?"

"It was a good thing and there aren't many of those these days." He wanted a better exit line but this may have to do. "Thanks."

Night has come quickly and the vastness of the lights of the San Fernando Valley startle him as always as he comes over the hill of 405 out of LA. Then flying past a turnoff he thinks the sign reads NO EXIT but attributes the sighting to his state of mind.

He rides until after midnight, past the point where I-5 becomes just two lanes cutting through farmland, past the point of exhaustion, past the point of thought and ready to continue on to another vague point, but it starts to rain. The raindrops spike his face like BBs and his sunglasses smear over. He has to slow back down to the point where he starts to think again and what he thinks is *Stop and rest, for Christ's sake.*

After a few minutes he can see the red and blue stripes of a white Chevron sign shining in the dark ahead. He shifts down on the turnoff and winds into the gas station, pulling the bike around to the side of the building with rest rooms.

Stock-still, he feels the cold country wind. He removes his sunglasses. The night is suddenly full of light—he's beside a well-waxed classic Buick Road-master with water beaded up on its phallic hood. He dismounts and stretches, taking a couple steps. The men's-room door is locked.

Bick walks over to the attendant's booth, where a short-haired teenager in a letterman's jacket is watching a miniature black-and-white TV. Bick asks for the key and the kid sends it through the cash tray under the window.

The stink of urine and cleaning fluid floats up from the rest-room floor. The mirror is cracked and a piece is missing from the lower corner. Bick steps into the stall for some toilet paper to blow his nose. Written or scratched on the walls are all the usual graffiti, semiliterate testament not unlike what he's seen in LA.

I'm bored, got no drugs, can't get laid
JOIN THE FUCKING ARMY

More noise, it seems to Bick, from a generation without war and nothing yet in its place.

Across the street is a Holiday Inn. A nice middle-aged couple is working at the desk and they look at Bick like he might not be crazy.

The motel room is smothered in earth tones and he finds this comforting as well. He takes a long hot shower, enjoying the little bar of individually wrapped soap. He brushes his teeth and drinks tap water from a sanitized glass, concentrating on all the little normal tasks, then crawls in between the stiff clean sheets. He reaches over the Gideon Bible on the nightstand and turns off the light.

He wonders about Jayne. Though he might again hear her voice reading or taste her on a dry Santa Ana wind, he knows it won't sound as mysterious or taste as intense. Still, he believes where there's something lost, there ought to be something gained, maybe just an experience that becomes a memory that's an experience in itself.

He wants to see the other rooms in her house.

You're going to be fine, is his last thought before sleep. *You're on your way home.*

Willie's bedroom is dead black. He's lying in bed, his eyes open and looking at nothing. He hasn't heard from Bick and wonders if he'll show at the funeral tomorrow. It would seem mandatory, but he has this weird intuition that Bick finally has left town and won't be coming back. He pictures one of those islands north of Seattle that Bick sometimes talks about when drunk, a huge freshly whitewashed house with rocketlike spires on the corners and windows all around and Bick standing behind one of the windows looking out on surrounding fields of wheat, rain falling in streaks. Willie wonders if he should migrate himself. He could bring a few friends, but Bick would probably throw them out.

There's a knock on the door.

"I'm sleeping," he says.

The door starts to open and there's light.

"Ahhh!" he yells, shutting his eyes. "Close the door!"

When the door closes he reopens his eyes, but the room is back to black and he can't tell who—or what— has entered. He can hear breathing other than his own, so maybe it's Madonna, but there seems to be a human-shaped shadow standing in front of him and Madonna probably couldn't have knocked. It can't be Merri because she wouldn't have closed the door, she would have let the light incinerate him. *What the hell*, he decides, *I'm ready for anything.*

"Hello out there," he says.

"Why," Bick says, "is this room so fucking dark?"

"I like it this way. And what are you doing here?"

"How'd you get it so dark?"

"I painted the windows black and I weather-stripped the door. I even out-did you. Pretty industrious, huh?"

"Have you got out of bed yet today?"

"Nope. Sleepy but proud, my man."

"Get up, then. We're going for a drive."

"What time is it? No—don't even answer!"

"It's about three. By the time we're finished driving, it'll be drink o'clock."

"A cocktail hour does sound good."

"You're still drinking?"

"Well . . ."

"What about your promise?"

"I haven't actually made it yet, I'm still *thinking* about it. After you and Jayne left, I couldn't sleep, obviously, so I went out and bought a car. That didn't seem to help, so I tried another AA meeting. Drunk. That didn't help much either, but there was this one gorgeous actress—"

"Oh, Jesus."

"Listen. I just talked to her. She told me that if I quit drinking, after I'd gotten past all the reasons I drink—need for stimulation, insecurity, fear of death, boredom, everything under the sun—in the end I'd be left with just me. *Horrifying.* It was like she was trying to talk me *into* drinking."

"You're not left with just you."

"What else?"

"Come on, let's go. Where's a light switch?"

"Please, sit and wind down. I just woke up. I need time. Sit."

"Where's a chair?"

"No chairs, but there's room on the bed. I won't molest you, promise."

"I know what your promises are worth."

"You sound like you could use some sleep yourself. Where are we driving to?" He talks so Bick can follow his voice. "You driving or me? Whose car do we take? I told you, I got another new one."

The king-sized mattress slumps when Bick sits.

"We're just driving," Bick says.

"Where to?"

Bick doesn't answer.

"Why? You want a dialogue?"

Bick doesn't answer.

"What about?"

Bick again doesn't answer, so Willie does. "Why I do the things I do?"

"No. Why *we* do the things we do. And don't say, 'why not?'"

"Why," Willie says. "Because we can."

Bick doesn't laugh, just sort of snorts.

"Self-destruction is a national passion," Willie continues. "And, hey, it's something we're good at."

"It's stupid."

"I know, I know and I know about the cost too."

Willie can hear Bick's breathing at the foot of the bed.

"I know you know more about the damage than I do," Bick says. "Decisions we make now we're going to be stuck with for a long, long time."

"I figured out a way around that. I'm not making any."

"Come on, let's go."

"Did you say something about cocktail hour?"

"Get out of bed. Rise and shine." Bick raps Willie's knee with his knuckles.

"Lucky shot," Willie says.

"Let's go."

"What about Merri?" Willie's desperately stalling. "She might have other plans in mind, you know."

"No, she's turned you over to me."

"What happened to Jayne?" he tries.

He can hear the crinkle of cellophane as Bick pulls out cigarettes. This makes Willie think about acting classes, because he sometimes misses the sensory exercises, because it would be something to do when he's not working.

"It's history," Bick finally says. "Already gone."

"Yeah?"

"Yesterday I left town."

Willie doesn't know what to say, so he lightens his voice, "Have a good trip?"

"Yes." Bick laughs a little. "I did. But it started a little shaky, my car was practically totaled."

"No. Fuck. Oh, man."

"It's just a car. I took my bike."

"Yeah, 'Get ya motor running. . . .'"

"And it started to rain."

"Rain's cool. Cleans everything."

"Yeah, but it doesn't make for a good driving experience. I pulled over and spent the night in some motel in this town I couldn't find again if my life depended on it. Anyway, I had this dream, this dream that you and Oscar and Merri and Mona and Libby, all of you showed up with beer and chips."

"I'd love that." Willie laughs. "If I have friends, I want proof."

"It's strange," Bick says. "Oscar said something about proof in the dream. He kept ranting about proof and action."

"Gotta love Oscar Mayer—full of his crazed will to greatness despite the obvious fact it doesn't matter."

Bick half-laughs. "I don't know."

"So what happened?"

"We came back to LA."

After a pause Willie says, "Yeah, is that it?"

"No, when we came back to LA, the six of us took five cars."

Willie laughs.

"Then I woke up. I don't know."

"I think," Willie says, "Oscar and Mona are doing it."

"Yeah?"

"Nobody else knows. Not even Oscar."

Bick laughs for real this time, whether at his line or the idea of Oscar and Mona having an affair, Willie doesn't know, but making someone laugh always wakes him up a bit. He reaches for his cigarettes. They're not there. Merri must have taken them again and he can't even be angry at her for this sort of thing anymore. "Did I hear the rustle of friendly cigarettes," he asks.

"You want one?"

"Thanks."

"We smoked a lot in the dream. You had a pickup full of Marlboro reds."

"Cool."

"I'm holding a Camel out for you right now."

"Gee, thanks." Willie reaches out and waves his hand around in the air until it hits Bick's.

"You just knocked it on the floor somewhere," Bick informs him.

"Shit. Try it again. Double or nothing." This time he reaches out more cautiously and finds Bick's hand and then the cigarette. "Got it. Light?"

Bick strikes a match and for a moment they're both clear, but then the flame eases them down into shadows. Willie leans in and lights his cigarette, then Bick lights his own and blows out the match.

"Throw it on the floor," Willie tells him.

Their outlines sharpen and fuzz as their cigarettes brighten and dim.

"The dream," Willie says.

"Never mind the dream. I woke up. And once I was up I was hungry, so I went to the local McDonald's."

"Jesus, you must've been starved."

"I was. It had one of those playlands—you know, Ronald McDonald."

"With the weird chairs and whirly things?"

"Right. So I'm out there—"

"Riding the rides?"

"No, just sitting on a cheeseburger."

"OK."

"And there's a girl, a woman, about our age, real normal looking, and she's got a kid who must be about seven. Wearing a Batman sweatshirt, naturally."

"Naturally."

"He asks me what I do. Simple enough question, but I'm in this strange mood. I feel like I'm on the edge of a religious experience, probably just because I'm exhausted. In any case I start thinking. What do I do? Mostly, I pretend to be a drunk and a hack."

"It's not much of a life," Willie laughs, "but it *is* yours."

"No. I'm a writer. Which is what I tell the kid. He asks me if I write about sports."

"Of course you do."

"He means for newspapers. So I tell him, 'No, I mostly write movies.' He asks me if I'm the guy who wrote the *Batman* movie and he's disappointed, of course. He asks if the movie is going to be as good as the comic book. 'It'll be about the same,' I tell him. Then the mother jumps in, telling me how *advanced* her child is and how difficult it is to raise him. Mothers have to worry about diseases you and I have never even heard of and the kid is so bored he interrupts her and asks what's wrong with me. Keep in mind I've been riding a motorcycle in the rain with a blue blazer and a tie—the very clothes you can't see ruined on me now—and my eyes must have been screamingly red."

Willie knocks his long ash off onto the floor. Bick hesitates, then does the same.

"So," Bick continues, "I tell him it's artificial stimulants, as though I'm blaming Ronald McDonald's coffee. And then I start telling this kid about stimulants, you know, the artificial versus the pure, the fleeting versus the healing. The old rap."

"You were losing it."

"I was borderline," Bick admits, "but the mother seemed to understand and she still wanted to talk, about her life and the kid. So I went back to listening and she starts making me think about how disconnected everything gets down here. Maybe this is why we're so obsessive. Death and self-destruction make us feel connected somehow, I don't know. But during all this my throat is hurting like hell."

"Throat cancer."

"Probably. Anyway, she does a riff on loneliness and you can tell she's lonely in ways she's not saying and I decide to tell her about Tim and Joy and everyone and I say we have to be alone sometimes and we have to be able to be alone and she says, 'Sure, but in the end we're in it together or we're alone with a loaded gun.'" Bick takes a long bright drag on his cigarette. "That was

pretty much it. So I got on the bike and drove back here, totally focused because I didn't want to die in a fiery accident with a car."

"Did you get her phone number?"

Bick laughs.

"But you'd made contact."

"Yeah," Bick says, still laughing.

"Then what?"

"That's it. Then I came home. I'm back and we're going for a drive."

"Well, welcome back."

"Thank you."

"I had kind of a dream," Willie says, "or maybe it wasn't a dream, since I was wide awake, but I've been lying here and I had an idea."

"That's usually a plus."

Willie tells him about his image of the house on the island.

"No wheat," Bick says. "There's no wheat there."

"We could all move there *anyway.*"

"Maybe for a summer."

Willie's cigarette is burned down to the butt, so he tosses it.

"Where's an ashtray?" Bick says.

"The floor. Can't miss it."

"I'm opening a window," Bick says, rising from the bed, "and the light's coming in and we're going out."

"I'll drive. The car I just bought, it's an old Corvette like the one in 'Route 66.' Convertible. It's not insured yet, but I think my insurance was canceled anyway."

Following the light of his cigarette to the window, Bick unlocks the hook latch. "Ready?"

"No, not really."

"The Bible assures us love is stronger even than death." The minister's miked voice echoes through the dark building and resonates off the giant stained-glass image of Jesus bleeding on the cross and glowing in the light from outside. "Love shall cover a multitude of sins. . . ."

Libby flicks away a tear while Mona rolls her eyes. Oscar is nodding along and Bick is gazing over the minister's head at the polished golden pipes of the organ. They're all together in a V-shaped line on the altar, girls in off-white silk, boys in basic black, the ceremoniously robed preacher at the point.

Merri's parents are sitting in the front row, holding hands. Her father is wearing a dark blue church suit, her mother is wearing a plain beige dress and a hat. They're not smiling but seem happy.

Willie's father is across the aisle in a black suit with a skinny tie, thin and shaking slightly.

"Amen," the minister ends.

"Amen," the audience murmurs.

"Please face each other," the minister says to Willie and Merri. She hands her long white roses to Libby and turns toward Willie, who glances over his shoulder at Bick and Oscar and opens his eyes wide in terror before relaxing and turning toward Merri.

"Will you William John Paul, take Merri Shelton to be your lawfully wed-

ded wife, in joy and sorrow, in sickness and in health, in plenty and in want, for as long as you both shall live?"

"I will."

As the minister repeats the litany to Merri, Oscar whispers to Bick. "Don't do it, Merri, he'll ruin the carpet."

"I do," Merri says.

"As symbols of this commitment you have chosen rings. William, do you have this ring?"

"I sure hope so," Willie says, and some of the guests laugh.

Bick passes the ring to Willie.

"William, please repeat after me, I give you this ring in token and in pledge of our constant faith and abiding love."

"I give this ring in token of our constant faith and abiding love."

After a long pause, "William, you may place the ring upon Merri's finger." Willie does.

The ritual is repeated and then the minister says, "Let us now bow our heads and pray together. Dear Lord, in sending us your only Son, Jesus Christ the Savior, you showed us love must be carnate, love is not just a thought, love is flesh, love is action. We humbly ask you now to nurture your love in the love of William and Merri so that their love may be nurtured in others. . . ."

Libby tunes out and prays Willie will grow up.

Bick wants to believe Willie will make this work because of Merri.

Oscar suspects the marriage is doomed but hopes it isn't and is happy for them in any case. He wonders if he will ever be married. First he has to find a girlfriend. He needs an idea for his next movie, something true for a change, and the story of a hellish marriage seems as good a starting point as any.

Mona hasn't been out of black since she was twelve and creamy silk is making her itch, but she doesn't scratch because Oscar is looking over.

"Amen," the minister says.

"Amen," they rejoin.

"Here before this community of friends, according to the laws of California and the ordinance of God, I now pronounce you man and wife. May God's joy, a joy this world cannot give and cannot take away, be with you forever. To signify this, you now may kiss."

For a moment everyone's eyes seem to converge on this kiss, faces reacting with smiles and questioning expressions and blank stares. Merri's mother discreetly weeps.

An unseen flute begins a vaguely familiar tune and the organ joins. The newlyweds turn and hold hands and cameras click and flash as they come down the aisle framed by the jigsaw-puzzle light of the stained glass, a crouching video cameraman backpedaling ahead.